Praise for Christine d'Abo

30 Days

"Well-developed and engaging characters, major and minor, lead to conflicts that feel both realistic and fresh, and difficult subjects are handled with empathy and gentle humor. Romance fans will delight in this sweet and spicy expedition."
—*Publishers Weekly* STARRED REVIEW

"Perfect for folks seeking a well-written, hot read with substance."
—*Library Journal*, STARRED REVIEW

"Christine D'Abo crafts a rare treat in 30 Days, a book that's equal parts sexy and heartwarming, fun and deeply emotional. Bravo!"
—*New York Times* bestselling author J. Kenner

30 Nights

"D'Abo turns up the heat and promises a fast-moving and fun story capable of making one swoon with delight and sigh with pleasure. Readers will get a kick out of Glenna and Eric's out-of-this-world chemistry, but will be even more entertained watching them try and hold back their true feelings for each other."
—*RT Book Reviews*, 4 Stars

"Steamy…Delightfully stimulating and kinky…Well worth reading."
—*Publishers Weekly*

Also by Christine d'Abo

30 Days
30 Nights
Submissive Seductions

Sugar Sweet

Christine d'Abo

LYRICAL PRESS
Kensington Publishing Corp.
www.kensingtonbooks.com

LYRICAL PRESS BOOKS are published by

Kensington Publishing Corp.
119 West 40th Street
New York, NY 10018

All Kensington titles, imprints, and distributed lines are available at special quantity discounts for bulk purchases for sales promotion, premiums, fund-raising, educational, or institutional use.

Special book excerpts or customized printings can also be created to fit specific needs. For details, write or phone the office of the Kensington Sales Manager: Kensington Publishing Corp., 119 West 40th Street, New York, NY 10018. Attn. Sales Department. Phone: 1-800-221-2647.

Lyrical Press and Lyrical Press logo Reg. U.S. Pat. & TM Off.

First Electronic Edition: July 2018
eISBN-13: 978-1-5161-0613-4
eISBN-10: 1-5161-0613-X

First Print Edition: July 2018
ISBN-13: 978-1-5161-0-665-3
ISBN-10: 1-5161-0665-2

Printed in the United States of America

For Mark.

Through the ups and downs we've faced, I love knowing you're always by my side.

Acknowledgments

Some books are beautiful gems that come to an author fully formed. They sparkle and shine as the words flow from the author's brain onto the page. This is not one of those books.

This book came amidst some personal turmoil, career angst, with a side-order of writer's block thrown in to keep things interesting. I'm convinced it wouldn't have been finished at all without the help of some key people.

A huge thank you to Jenny Holiday. If it weren't for our daily writing sprints, IM chats, and your unwavering support, I don't think I would have ever reached The End. You're a gift to the writing community. To my agent Courtney Miller-Callihan, I don't know how you put up with me, but I'm grateful for all that you do on a daily basis. Thank you for the phone calls and your patience while I talked out the problematic ending. And finally, thank you to my editor, Esi Sogah. Your kindness, keen eye and ability to see the heart of an editing problem are second-to-none. I'm honored to have the opportunity to work with you.

Chapter 1

Marissa sat on the edge of her bed in her underwear, pants down around her ankles and her apron still tied around her waist. Her phone was warm in her hands, the screen too bright in her dim basement apartment as another call came in.

This was number four—no five. Yeah, the fifth call in an hour. That had to be a new record. Yesterday she'd only had five calls all day, which meant another collection agency must have uncovered her new number today. There was a small part of her that wondered if Andrew himself was passing her information along to them. Not that she'd given her ex her new cell number, but he'd proven to be super resourceful in his bitterness, and Marissa wouldn't put it past him.

This was her continued punishment for breaking up with him.

Though technically, he'd broken up with her first.

The screen on her phone went black, and the indicator flashed red letting her know that there was another message waiting. She set her phone into her lap, kicked off her work pants, taking a moment to rub her sore calves. She'd been working double shifts whenever she could, in a vain attempt to keep on top of these debts. Even if she'd known they were coming, the chances of her being able to financially handle them all were small at best. She'd maxed out on student loans, and because she'd co-signed for Andrew's startup business two years ago, the bank wasn't keen on giving her another one, even if it would help her consolidate debts.

So double shifts between trips to the library to do research papers would be her life for the foreseeable future. She looked down at the blinking light. Morbid curiosity would get the better of her soon and she'd listen to whatever the demands were. She'd have to find a way to pay everything.

If she didn't, her dreams of starting her own business would never come to pass.

Andrew might have screwed up her past and present, but she'd be dammed if she'd cede him her future as well.

Setting her phone on the bed, Marissa found the energy to get changed. She needed to head into the library to meet up with Naomi. They had a group assignment due in three days and Marissa hadn't even started on her part of the project. The musty smell clung to her T-shirt as she slipped it on. Shit, she'd just washed these and had used those stupid scent booster beads. Nothing seemed to work. The air in her apartment was dank and left a residue over everything. She'd mentioned it to Shelia shortly after moving in, and a dehumidifier had appeared the next day. Maybe the damn thing was broken.

She turned to go check it, when the message light caught her eye again, taunting her. There was no reason to check, because she knew what was there waiting for her, even if she didn't know the exact words. It was simply another company that needed to be added to the list. She started out of the room, made it three steps before spinning around and snatching her phone. With a roll of her eyes, she pressed the button for her voice mail.

Beep. "This is not a sales call. This is a message for Marissa Roy. Please contact Raylon Group at 647-555-7354 to receive important information on how to repay your debt. It's imperative for you to get in touch with us or else your credit rating will be impacted. Again, the number is 647-555-7354."

She ended the call, and set her phone down on top of the dehumidifier. The motor wasn't running, nor was the bucket in the back full. She gave it a little bang on the top, before hitting it a second time, harder. The motor kicked in, snapping and chugging away as it pulled the moisture from the air.

Well, that was at least one thing she could fix.

She picked up the phone and slid it into her pocket when it rang again. Instead of her generic ringtone, this time it was the one she'd assigned to her mom. Shit. Marissa had been purposely forgetting to call her for weeks now, knowing her mom would do whatever she could to try and help her out of this. And while she loved her mom more than anything, she wasn't going to drag her into this mess.

Taking a breath, Marissa smiled and hoped it would come through in her voice. "Hey there. I haven't talked to you in ages."

"Hey baby." Her mom's voice came through crisp and clear, but for a moment was nearly drowned out by something loud in the background. "I missed you."

"What are you doing?"

"The church has a bake sale on the weekend and I said I'd make my cupcakes again."

Marissa's stomach growled at the thought of the buttercream frosting she knew would be paired with it. "Please save me some."

"That would mean you'd have to come visit me." She chuckled and what Marissa now recognized as the sound of beaters going, turned off. "How are your classes going?" There was no mistaking the pride in her voice. She'd never gone to college herself, and had been super excited when Marissa got into her business program.

"Good. I mean, I've only been at it a few weeks, but so far I'm enjoying them."

"I'm so happy to hear that. I don't know where you got your brains, because it certainly wasn't from me."

Marissa knew better than to say anything about her father. "Well, let's hope it stays like this until midterms. Naomi told me about a scholarship that's specifically for women in the business program. If I keep my marks up, there's a chance I'll qualify."

"That's amazing." Her mother's voice cracked, before she cleared it. "I'm so proud of you, baby."

"Thanks." Marissa sat down on her one and only chair.

"So, are you going to tell me what's wrong, or am I going to have to pry it out of you?"

Marissa's stomach soured. "Why would you think there's anything wrong?

"You think I can't tell when there's something going on with you? You're not sparkling and you always sparkle." Her mom laughed again. "Plus, you haven't talked to me in three weeks, which means you're avoiding telling me something. So, spill it."

No. She loved her mom, but there was no way she'd pull her into this. But Marissa also lacked the ability to lie to her, which meant she was going to have to get creative. "I've been good. Just…a lot of things have been coming at me. School and work. And…a lot of outside pressures. It's just been hard…financially. And I've picked up a bunch of extra shifts at the restaurant, but there've been some…unexpected bills."

"Sweetie, why didn't you tell me you needed some money." Her mom sighed. "God, I thought you'd gotten yourself into trouble with a boy or something. How much do you need? Did you want me to top up your meal plan? I just got paid myself, so you hit me at the right time."

Guilt was a horrible palate cleanser for telling lies. "Ah, yeah, that would be amazing." It wouldn't be enough to even remotely put a dent in what she owed, but at least she wouldn't have to worry about getting groceries for a while.

"I can log into the site and do that today. Though it sounds like there's something else you need."

Oh, you know, a couple hundred thousand or so. "No, that will be good."

"I can put a bit extra on the card. Give you some beer money. I know you're working hard, baby. Things will get easier for you soon. I promise."

"Thanks Mom."

Hanging up the phone, Marissa fought back a wave of tears. What a frigging coward she was, not even able to tell her mom what the hell was going on. But she knew, her mom would try and take over, she'd take on Marissa's bills until her own finances were depleted. Then, they'd both be screwed and Marissa would be even worse off for having dragged her into this. She had to find a way out that didn't involve family.

A knock on her door had her lifting her head. It was probably her landlady Shelia looking for the rent. Marissa would mention the dehumidifier was on the blink; maybe she had another one upstairs in the piles of *things* everywhere. Marissa was about three steps from the door, when whoever it was knocked on her door again, far harder than before.

"I know you're in there!" The very male voice sounded more than a little angry.

Marissa took a step back, looking to make sure she'd secured her deadbolt when she'd come in earlier. "Who's there?"

"You owe us money. Open up so we can talk."

Shit, could they do this? Weren't there laws or something preventing this sort of harassment? Maybe? *Probably not.* "I don't think so."

"I'm here for our money. Write me a cheque and I'll leave."

Marissa's mind raced and her body shook. "Your company has my phone number, I'm sure. Have them call me with the details and I'll follow up."

"Open the door!"

"Nope. Call me. Or send me an email if you want." A hard thud shook the door. "Did you just kick my door?"

"Over fifty grand. I want the money now."

Marissa's hands shook as she pulled out her cell. "I'm calling the police."

"You're a fucking lowlife, ripping off legitimate businesses. Pay what you owe, bitch." There was another loud bang, followed by heavy footsteps as whoever it was marched back upstairs and outside.

She couldn't move for a solid five minutes, her gaze locked on the old door as she strained to hear if the man was still hiding outside. There was no way she was going to leave now, especially if the man could potentially be waiting for her on the street. Shit, she was going to have to cancel on Naomi.

Fifty thousand dollars? *No freaking way.* If he was telling the truth, then that was in addition to the other loans that creditors were now chasing her for. She didn't remember signing her name on a loan that large. The most she'd done was five thousand dollars for Andrew to buy the stock he'd needed for his café. None of this made any sense.

And yet, she'd come to learn that Andrew wasn't the man she'd assumed he was. He had this manipulative side of him that she'd never seen—or had ignored the warning signs—and now she had to assume he'd been capable of anything. Including somehow getting her name added to a loan she'd never seen.

Tears spilled down her cheeks as the gravity of the situation pressed down on her. Even if she quit school, she wouldn't have the money to pay off what she now owed. And without the education she'd worked so hard for over the past few years, she wasn't going to accomplish her goal of opening her *own* business.

Her mind raced through the options, and while there were a few, it was one that her friend Naomi had presented her with that kept coming back to the top of the list.

But there was no way she could do that. Putting her trust in another man—a stranger at that—wasn't how she could get out of this situation. If anything, it might make things far more complicated.

And yet...

Wiping her tears, she went to her small kitchen table and opened her laptop. It took a while for her ancient computer to come alive from power saving mode, but when it did, the email from Naomi was still open from when she'd left it yesterday.

I know things have gotten hard for you. I was at this boot camp thing back in the spring talking about sugar daddy sites. Dude, it's legit and some of the girls at the thing said it was a Godsend. I've had good luck myself. You're hot and I'm sure you wouldn't have any problems finding someone. Here's the link. www.millionairesugardaddy.com. Aim high, right LOL! We can chat at school about it.

Love Naomi.

Marissa's finger hovered over the mouse button. The mere thought of looking for a sugar daddy should be repulsive, demeaning. Her mother would be furious if she knew Marissa was even considering the option. But if what Naomi had said was true, most of the time these guys weren't even interested in sex. It was more about companionship than anything else. Given how hard she'd been working and how little time she'd had for anything social, it wasn't a horrible idea to spend time with someone. And if she got some financial help out of the deal, then how bad could it be.

She moved the mouse over the link.

God, this was probably a terrible mistake. Maybe if she went back to the bank and talked to them again, they might be willing to consolidate the loans. Or she could declare bankruptcy and totally ruin her own chances of opening up her own business once she got out of school. They were only dreams, right?

What harm could there be in looking?

She clicked the link.

* * * *

Vince wanted to punch something, *anything* that wasn't his father. The older Mr. Taylor was currently talking to a woman who was easily younger than Vince by several years, and finishing off his third scotch this hour. The girl so far seemed to be holding her own, but Vince was ready to swoop in and extract her if she gave any indication that Geoff had crossed a line.

"The old man at it again?" Nate handed Vince a drink of his own, as he stepped beside him.

Vince nodded his acknowledgement as he took a drink. Several women stared briefly as they walked past, only to bend their heads giggling once they were by. He knew he and his best friend-cum-PR rep, made quite the striking pair standing there in their tuxes. Nate's dark skin was in stark contrast to his own pale tone, making them look as opposite as could be. But they were of equal height which drew more than a little attention whenever they entered a room. If the gossip sites were to be believed, two of the best bachelor catches in Toronto.

Nate shook his head as Geoff reached over and curled a piece of the woman's hair around his finger. "I don't know how he does it?"

"Don't admire him. He's slime." Once upon a time, Vince *had* admired his father and his ability to get the girl while closing a killer business deal. He'd done his best to emulate Geoff's freewheeling ways, until that had landed him into a pile of trouble. "He's trying to sleep with someone young enough to be his daughter."

"Yeah, I see that." Nate swallowed his drink and handed it to a passing waiter. "What do you want to do?"

Vince hated having to play protector, hated needing to intervene for a man who should fucking know better. But ever since his mom had left them, Vince had no choice but to do everything he could to keep his father from self destructing. "He's had too much to drink and needs to go home."

"Do you want to divide and conquer then?"

They'd come tonight at Geoff's insistence. The after party for the film launch opened them up to schmoozing with financial backers, actors, and the sort of crowd Geoff gravitated toward. Vince had intended to stay for a round or two, then bow out and head home for a run. But once his dad got drinking, Vince couldn't trust him not to make a mess of things.

When Geoff reached over and put his hand on the girl's ass, Vince stiffened. "Yup."

"I'll get the girl out of there and you deal with your dad." Nate nodded and was already moving before Vince could find a place for his drink.

"Nate! Wait." Vince carefully sidestepped a couple before striding quickly across the bar to his father.

"Mr. Taylor, Vince needed to speak with you." Nate winked at the young woman. "Hello, beautiful. I've been dying to dance all night. Interested? Or maybe we can have a drink?"

The look of relief on her face was so obvious it was painful. "Yeah, that sounds good."

Before his father could protest, Vince put a hand on his shoulder and led him in the opposite direction, toward the bar. "I think it's time to get you home."

"Little bastard. I was about to make my move." But Geoff didn't fight it when Vince started to move him toward the back of the bar.

With his arm around his dad, Vince waited until a group passed them before leaning close to his ear. "You know better than to corner a woman like that. Your therapist—"

"Is a fucking asshole. He doesn't know anything. I wasn't pressuring her to do something."

"It didn't look like that from where I was standing." Vince released his dad and took a step away. He was going to punch him if he didn't get him home soon. "I'm going to call the car."

Geoff waved him away. "Not yet. I haven't seen Simon. He was supposed to be up for the film festival. I need to see him."

Vince's chest tightened. His father and Simon Berry had been at odds for over a decade now. Their strange back and forth had caused Vince more grief both personally and professionally than anything else in his life. "I'm sure he's around somewhere. You can always email him later."

"I don't think you understand." Geoff leaned in, the strong scent of alcohol washing over Vince. "He's going to buy GreenPro."

Motherfucker. "We've talked about this. I don't want to sell the company. At the very least, we need to hold on to it for another year. The market might be ready by then."

It was an excuse, and a flimsy one at that. GreenPro was the last company that he co-owned with his father. For years, Vince had wanted to take charge and develop the green energy organization into something big. Its model made it such that every city in North America could be a potential market, which was far bigger than anything they'd ever worked on before. But his father…there was no way he'd let Vince take the reins and run with this. No, he wanted to sell, to get every penny he could from GreenPro, and take away the dream that Vince had of leaving his mark on the green sector. Or doing something professionally that would leave an actual mark on society.

Back and forth they'd gone, cock-blocking one another, trapped in an eternal stalemate. Both of them needed to approve the sale, or any changes with the company, and neither was willing to give an inch.

His father's narrowed gaze was a dagger pointed directly at Vince's head. "Simon knows what he wants to do with it. Better than you."

"I doubt that." Not that any of that mattered, because the last he'd heard, Simon wanted nothing to do with Geoff. "I'm surprised he's even talking to you."

Their quarrel had been precipitated by his father sleeping with Simon's now ex-wife. The fallout had Vince painted with the same carousing brush as his dad, which had helped with his television appearances, but harmed his business dealings. Simon's wrath had been more directed at his ex-wife than Geoff, which had never sat right with Vince. She wasn't the only one who'd been in that bed.

"I'm a changed man." His smug smile sent alarm bells off in Vince.

"I'm scared to ask. How?"

"I have a new woman in my life. She's young, smart and will lull Simon into a false sense of security. And if I pay her enough, she might even get him into a compromising situation that I can use to my advantage."

Vince grabbed his father by the arm and dragged him to the hallway that led to the coat check. Only once he knew they were alone did he let him go, turn around and get in his face. "What the hell did you do?"

"Nothing." He grinned. "Yet."

Five. Four. Three… "Elaborate, before I punch you and it ends up in the news."

"I've signed up for a site. To get girls."

"An escort site?" Vince took a breath. This was far worse than he'd anticipated.

"Sugar daddy." Geoff took out his phone and flicked open an email. "See, she's sweet and innocent. Simon would know an escort a mile away. But this? She needs money and I need some arm candy. She'll do whatever I ask, and she gets paid in return. Best business deal I ever made."

"Are you fucking kidding me?" Vince took the phone from him and stared down at the profile. Marissa Roy, age twenty-four. "She's a college student."

"Most of them are. They need help paying for school. I have a friend who put me onto this."

"I'm not letting you do this." There was no way in hell he would let his father anywhere near this girl. His father was a shark and would have no problem taking advantage of her.

"Too late. She's agreed to meet me on the yacht Friday night."

"Cancel."

"No. I've already agreed to the date. She's agreed to come and I'm expected to pay her for her time." Geoff leaned back against the wall and crossed his arms. "Scared I'm going to hurt her?"

"More like traumatize." He knew nothing about Marissa Roy, but even if she were the most capable woman in the world, he doubted she'd be prepared for his father. "Cancel."

"No." Geoff's grin was toothy as he cocked his head. "Unless you agree to deal with Simon. To let me work my deal to sell that fucking albatross of a company."

Why did it always come down to this between them? "I'm not letting you run the deal. And I won't let you see the girl."

"You run the deal then. But you'll need the girl."

"Why?"

"Simon thinks we're neutered if we're in a relationship. He'll think we'll be soft and then we can go in for the kill." The look on his father's face was pure malice. "I'll enjoy proving him wrong."

Vince knew he had no choice but to run with this. If his father was determined to try to sell GreenPro to Simon, Vince didn't have enough ownership in the company to override him. If one of them didn't give in, they'd continued to be caught in a perpetual circle of bitterness. That wasn't the type of relationship he'd wanted with his father. He'd tried to help support him after his mom had left them and done everything he could to pull his dad out of the depths of his despair. Even asking him to go in on the initial GreenPro deal had been his way to bridge their widening gap. It had instead turned out to drive a near permanent wedge between them.

Vince knew the only way he'd be able to move on with his life was to cut his father out completely. That meant regardless of how he felt about GreenPro, he'd need to give in to his father and sell it. But there was no way he'd let his father be the one in charge, or to use an unsuspecting woman in his plot. Marissa Roy needed to be kept as far away from his father as possible. "Send me her information. I'll meet her Friday." He'd pay her and then send her on her way. She didn't need to be dragged into this mess.

He'd half expected his father to protest, but the alcohol must have kicked in. A sloppy smile spread across his face. "About time you listened to me. I'm going to get my things and head out. The night is still young and you're cramping my style."

"I'll let the limo know you're coming out." Vince texted the driver, instructing him to take his father back to his condo. By the time they got through traffic, he'd be in shape to go to bed and nothing more.

Walking back out to the party, Vince caught sight of Nate dancing with three women, one of whom was the costar of the movie they'd seen earlier that night. Nate caught his eye and nodded toward the women and gave him a wink. He'd have to worry about his father, GreenPro, and Marissa Roy later. Walking to the group, he smiled. "Hello ladies. Time to have some fun."

Chapter 2

The sun had slipped beneath the horizon moments before Marissa stepped out onto the sidewalk. She readjusted the chain on her clutch, giving up when she realized it wasn't going to lie right on her shoulder, and instead, shoved it into the clutch itself. Stupid thing. Why she'd let herself get talked into buying it, she'd never know. Sure, yes, it was practical—she was going to need a place for her phone and ID and stuff—but now she'd end up playing with it all night.

She'd taken the price tag off the bag, seeing as she couldn't have returned it because she'd picked it up on sale. The dress though, she'd been extra careful with that tag. This baby, while looking absolutely amazing on her, needed to go right back to the store first thing in the morning. Naomi had been the one to convince her to try that particular trick. Marissa hated the thought of doing something so dishonest, but nothing she owned could hold a candle to the type of clothing she had no doubt someone rich would expect her to wear.

There was hardly any room left on her credit card, and as much as she might want to have the ultimate little black dress tucked away in her closet for special occasions, she could buy a hell of a lot of groceries for three hundred dollars. So, despite how shitty it made her feel, she went along with the plan to return the dress in the morning.

The sky was streaked pink and orange, giving the warm October night an ethereal glow. Marissa closed her eyes for a moment and tried to relax, to take everything that was about to happen in and not worry for a few minutes. It was strange, feeling the energy coming from her Toronto neighborhood; it was as though the night had come alive, prodding her forward toward her task. And she had to think of it as a task, something to be checked off her To Do list, because otherwise the thought of going on a date with a potential sugar daddy was nearly too much for her to handle.

A crash from the backyard of the house next door had her jump and turn. She glanced around, half expecting one of her creditors to come racing out from behind a tree where they'd been lying in wait for her. *Give us your money!!!* Her heart pounded and her hands shook as she peered a bit harder into the shadows, just in case. Maybe, if things went well tonight, she might get a little bit of money so she could fend some of these assholes off for a while. Maybe.

Shit, this is so fucking weird.

Naomi promised that everyone she knew who'd done this had nothing but awesome things come from their adventures. She'd told her about one girl she knew who'd gotten a free trip to England out of her arrangement. The girl had a separate room and everything. No reason to think that Marissa's kick at the can would have anything horrible happen. She wasn't asking for an international vacation, just a little pocket cash and money to pay her debts. That wasn't asking for too much.

Right?

And if sex was on the table as a requirement, then she could manage that as well. It was the twenty-first century and if she wanted to bone some older guy for money, then that was her business and everyone else could fuck right off.

She could do this.

She *would* do this.

Reaching into her clutch, she took out her phone and read the message once more. *Limo will pick you up at nine. Dress to impress. Geoff Taylor.*

The brief back and forth she'd had with Geoff had been weird. He was in his late fifties, divorced, and was some sort of business guy. He didn't go into many details in their email exchange and she wasn't about to ask him directly. Google brought up over five hundred Geoff Taylors in Toronto, so it wasn't exactly easy to narrow him down that way. He'd said he was looking for *arm candy* to go with him for a business dinner, and all she had to do was sit there and carry on a half decent conversation. Talking was her forte and it would be fun to sit and chat with a bunch of business types. Hell, she might even pick up a few tips for when it came to starting her own company.

A breeze kicked up, stealing the residual warmth that radiated from the concrete beneath her feet. If this limo didn't show up soon, she was going to die from exposure. Shivering, she rubbed her hands over her bare arms trying to encourage blood flow. She had to shift her clutch from hand to hand, doing her best to avoid the sequins from picking the material.

It was another five minutes before the sound of a car turning onto her street drew her attention. A stretch limo crept toward her, somehow managing to navigate the narrow Toronto throughway peppered with illegally parked cars. Holy shit, this was really happening. Not even buying the dress and getting ready had made tonight seem real.

She was going on a date with a millionaire. She, Marissa Roy—college student and damaged goods—was going out with an older, financially well-off man. Well, it wasn't exactly a *date*, more of a meet and greet. That's what the website called it at any rate.

Her heart pounded so hard she was terrified the driver would hear it when he climbed out of the front seat and jogged around to the door to let her in. "Miss Roy?"

"Yes. Thank you."

His smile appeared automatically, the reflex of a professional. "The bar is fully stocked. Champagne included. Mr. Taylor wanted you to be comfortable."

Having champagne in the back of a limo while on her way to meet her potential sugar daddy? Oh yeah, that was *totally* going to set her at ease.

Sliding into the back of the car she couldn't stop from staring at the interior. She'd been in a limo only once before. Andrew and his buddies had paid for one to take them to prom their last year of high school. It was nowhere near as nice as this one; Mr. Taylor's limo lacked color-changing neon lights and the smell of cheap air freshener and high school hormones. Totally a bonus in her books.

The driver slid back into his seat and looked at her in the rear view mirror. "Are you comfortable? Would you like the heat up? A drink?"

"I'm fine." Now that she was out of the breeze, the idea of breaking into a sweat was a real possibility. "How long will it take us to get there?" He hadn't mentioned the name of the restaurant where they'd be going. In his text he'd simply offered to wine and dine her so they could get to know one another.

"In this traffic? Thirty minutes. You can turn the music on if you'd like. The controls are to your right. If you need me, just hit the intercom button." Then he gave her one last smile and slid up the privacy window.

And that was apparently that.

Okay, that wasn't so bad. She sat in silence as the limo started down the road toward her destination. She lasted about thirty seconds before turning on the music to scan through the XM Radio stations. Nope. She turned it back off and looked out the window. Naomi would be laughing her fool head off if she knew how freaked out she was right now. *You're going to hook up with a rich guy who was old enough to be your dad. What the fuck are you freaking for?*

Mostly because she was probably going to be hooking up with a rich guy who was old enough to be her dad. Someone who she'd only exchanged a few emails with. Jesus, it was hard to fathom.

Okay, she had to get mentally prepared for this. She couldn't stop fingering the rough corner of her clutch. *I can do this. It's perfectly fine for me to do this.*

The drive went smoothly, surprising given the time of night and the traffic that normally filled the streets. She was more than a little surprised when she realized that they turned off of Lake Shore Boulevard toward Lake Ontario. She pressed the intercom button. "Hello?"

"Yes, Miss Roy?"

"I was just wondering where we are headed? I don't know of any restaurants down here."

"To the marina. Mr. Taylor is waiting on his yacht for you."

"Oh." That wasn't what she was expecting. "Thank you."

She was about to go on a yacht. With a millionaire. Who she hoped would be her sugar daddy.

God, her life was fucking mental right now.

The limo drove her to the outer harbor marina where she could see a large yacht docked a short distance away from the bobbing array of sail boats. She could see two people standing at the base of a dock as they pulled alongside. Shit, should she get out on her own or wait for the driver to open the door? She should wait, right? That's what rich people did. The driver lacked her hesitation and before she knew what was happening her door was opened and he helped her to her feet.

An attractive woman who looked to be in her mid-thirties came forward smiling. "Miss Roy, welcome."

"Thank you." *Don't fidget. Smile. Relax. She only looks like she'd eat you for breakfast.*

"I'm Caroline Macy." The woman smiled, her gaze drifting over Marissa's exposed arms. "Let's get you someplace warm."

"Thanks. It's a bit cool by the water." Fucking freezing was more accurate. *Keep your mouth shut.*

"Mr. Taylor is waiting for you. I'll show you the way."

Yeah, she really wasn't going to get used to this at all.

They fell into step, giving Marissa an opportunity to look the other woman over. She was beautiful, polished in a way that came with experience and money. "You work for Mr. Taylor?"

"I'm his assistant." And apparently not much of a conversationalist, because she didn't elaborate. Nor did she seem to have any patience for Marissa. Maybe Marissa wasn't the only one who wasn't sure about this arrangement.

By the time they'd reached the ramp to the yacht, Marissa was certain she was well on her way to developing hypothermia. Despite freezing, her hands had somehow managed to grow damp. She didn't dare dry them on her dress for fear of marking the satin. Great, the first thing she'd do would be to shake his hand and he'd be grossed out.

Caroline stopped short of the ramp. "Mr. Taylor is waiting for you. Dinner and drinks will be served and you will return in two hours. The car will wait to bring you back home."

Marissa couldn't quite put her finger on it, but there was something off in Caroline's tone. "You don't like me, do you?"

"I don't particularly care about you one way or the other." Caroline's mouth was drawn into a thin line, but Marissa could practically hear the wheels in her mind spinning.

That was a load of shit if she'd ever heard it. "Okay. You don't like the idea of what he's doing? Being my...whatever." While she could think *sugar daddy* in her head, saying the words to anyone other than Naomi felt wrong. Probably an indication that this might not be the right thing for her.

The distant look on Caroline's face flickered briefly. "I wasn't supposed to say anything, but tonight's plans have changed a bit."

"What's changed? I'm not okay with something changing." Her heart raced and for a moment Marissa thought her feet would automatically carry her back to the limo.

"Your date is going to be with the other, Mr. Taylor." Caroline looked past her and up, which immediately drew Marissa's attention. Standing at the top of the ramp was a face she was absolutely familiar with and he was not a fifty-something year old man.

The man standing there, waiting for her to join him was Vince Taylor, co-host of the television show, *Bull Rush*. Marissa had watched *Bull Rush* for years now, making notes on the sales pitches of the men and women who were hoping to pry venture capital dollars from the hosts' hands. Vince was notoriously brutal in his estimations, and rarely gave out money. But the participants who won him over ended up being the most successful in the show's alumni.

And here she was, about to go on a date with him.

Shit.

Caroline cleared her throat. "Tonight does come with some simple rules. You can keep your phone on you, but no pictures are to be taken. If anything should turn up in the tabloids resulting from this outing, any… arrangements you might come to will be null and void. Do you understand?" Caroline might look like a princess on the outside, but beneath the surface was a pit bull protecting her master.

"Yeah, sure."

Caroline nodded, giving her one final long look, before turning away. "Don't keep Mr. Taylor waiting. He doesn't like that."

That brief moment of dismissal was enough to fuel Marissa's desire to do this. Ignoring her self doubts, fears, and Caroline's attitude, she straightened her shoulders and carefully made her way up the ramp. A third of the way, she found enough courage to look up at the man standing ahead of her.

The pounding in her chest came back with a vengeance the closer she got to him.

Vince Taylor.

The images of him on television and in the magazines didn't do him justice. Even from this distance he appeared much larger than the six feet, three inches she knew him to be. His black curls were just long enough to be caught by the breeze and moved in waves around his head. As she reached the top of the ramp, his blue eyes locked onto her and passed a glance down her body. Vince had always appeared clean shaven on *Bull Rush*. Tonight, stubble covered his strong jaw and cheeks, a stark contrast to the polished look his tux gave him. Shit, the fabric fit him perfectly in a way she'd never seen on a man. His jacket lay just so across his broad shoulders, the sleeves falling perfectly down at his wrists. She wanted to look lower, to see if there was any hint that the rumors about his endowment were true.

Oh, you sooo need to get laid, girl.

It wasn't hard to picture falling into bed with him. He was exactly the type of man she'd fantasized about in the past. Though being faced with someone who could melt panties simply with his presence was, quite frankly, intimidating as hell.

Marissa finally reached the top of the ramp. Her clutch the only barrier between them, she didn't have a clue what do to next.

When all else fails, be polite. "Hello." She smiled and prayed she didn't come across as a doof.

"Miss Roy."

Okay, let's do this. She held out her hand, hoping her clutch had absorbed some of the moisture from her palm. "Hello Mr. Taylor. It's very nice to meet you. Though I have to say I'm a bit…surprised that I'm meeting you and not Geoff. Was this a ruse?"

He hesitated, his eyebrow rising slightly before he reached out. Rather than reciprocating her handshake, he lifted the back of her hand and leaned forward to place a soft kiss to her skin.

Jesus.

The shiver that raced through her was no doubt noticeable to him. Thankfully, he ignored it. "Welcome aboard. Perhaps we should get a drink, and then I can explain about this evening."

Okay, so something was clearly up and she was going to have to make a decision whether or not she was willing to take a chance and get on the boat, or if she should cut her losses and leave before things got weird.

"Yes please. A drink would be wonderful." Not only would it help to steel her nerves, but it would give her time to figure out what was going on.

His smile sent a shiver through her. "I can have the staff make you something sweet, if you'd like. A cocktail?"

Her nipples tightened, though she wasn't sure if it was from the cold or the heat in his gaze. "I'd prefer a dry wine."

Marissa feared that she was already going to get more sugar than she could handle this evening.

Chapter 3

She'd never been on a yacht before. Hell, the closest she'd ever been was the ferry over to Toronto Islands, which yeah, so not in the same category. The sound of the engine kicking on and the shimmy of the floor beneath her feet as they pulled away from shore was unnerving. For the next few hours, she was trapped on board with a man who the few details she knew came from his show and the tabloids—neither of which were necessarily reliable as a character witnesses.

At least she wouldn't starve.

The table inside the spacious cabin had been set with white linen and a single candle flickered as the centerpiece. The simple elegance didn't match the opulence of the rest of the room; leather seats, mahogany paneling, plush carpeting that made walking in her heels challenging. Not that she was about to take them off. Vince was so much taller than her naturally, she needed every inch she could fake to feel on even footing with him.

"Red, white or champagne?" He wasn't facing her, but his voice managed to fill the room.

"White, please." She wasn't really much of a wine person, but it seemed wrong to not accept a glass. Hopefully it wasn't some ultra-rich thing that she'd fall in love with and never be able to afford to get again.

The distance between them gave Marissa time to catch her breath. There were many things she'd anticipated feeling—nervous, awkward, and creeped out—but she hadn't anticipated aroused. Okay, yes, she was a normal healthy twenty-four-year-old woman who had no issues with sex. She'd been more than active since her late teens, and sex had been one of the few things she and Andrew had been good at, right up until the end.

The thought of having sex with Vince was so strange she couldn't wrap her head around it. Even hidden beneath his clothing, she could tell that he was fit, strong. He probably spent hours working out between trips to…wherever the hell millionaire businessmen went. Andrew wasn't out of shape, but he hadn't seen the inside of a gym after high school. There weren't muscles for her to squeeze or firm arms to wrap around her. The cut of Vince's tailored dress pants left little to the imagination, especially regarding his ass.

Tight. Perfect. The sort of ass she would want to bite. Which, okay a bit weird.

Being naked with Vince would be enlightening in many ways.

The pop of a cork being pulled drew her attention. With precise motions, two glasses were filled expertly and her host turned back to face her. "Here you go."

Marissa walked carefully across the cabin to join him, not wanting to lose her balance. "Thanks."

"You'll get your sea legs quickly. We're not going far from shore."

As he handed her a glass, their fingers brushed, eliciting another full body shiver. She was so screwed if this little bit of contact did this to her. This was supposed to be a business arrangement, not a private date night on *The Bachelor.* "Do you mind if we sit?"

He nodded, his face remaining impassive. "Of course. More comfortable location for us to have our talk."

Marissa turned and took a step, only to falter at the feel of his hand pressed gently to the small of her back. *Deep breath. In and out. Relax. Don't orgasm.* She increased her stride just enough to break the contact. "I have to admit, I'm a bit overwhelmed by everything. I wasn't expecting to be on a yacht ever in my life, let alone tonight for supper with a man I've never met before. But you're not even *that* man…so yeah. You mentioned an explanation. I think I'd like to have that now."

"You'll have it." He pulled out her seat for her, waiting until she was comfortable before moving around to the opposite side. "Given everything that had been communicated to you, the least I could offer was the night out you'd been promised."

Marissa stopped herself from reaching up to play with the loose strand of hair that brushed her cheek. "Well, I appreciate that. I have to say I'd been looking forward to this all week." Not entirely the truth, but close enough to count. She took a deep drink of her wine and sighed. Damn, that was good. She'd have to get the name of it before she left.

"Geoff Taylor is my father." Vince's expression hadn't changed, but there was something in his eyes, a look of anger that wasn't there previously. "I found out what he was intending to do and I wanted to put a stop to it."

He lifted his wine glass to his lips and took a sip without looking away. It was the same intensity he often leveled at the entrepreneurs on his show. She used to laugh when she saw someone squirm under his gaze, but now that she was being subjected to it, she was ready to contact each and every person and apologize.

"I can imagine it's…awkward to find out your dad has reached out to… ah, someone like me." Marissa managed not to squirm. *Go me!*

"I was more concerned for your well-being than his reputation."

"Oh." She swallowed down a too-large sip of wine, her eyes watering as she tried not to cough. "Thanks."

"As I said, we have time, so why not enjoy ourselves." The smile he gave her didn't reach his eyes, which was a real shame, because he had amazing eyes. "Tell me about yourself."

She'd seen that look before; every time she'd look the mirror since Andrew had broken her heart before shattering her life. It was the face of a person who'd given up on others. Who'd been betrayed beyond the point of no return. Not exactly what she expected from a man like Vince. It was hard to imagine what could have happened to him.

Marissa fingered the rim of her glass, uncertain of where to start. "What would you like to know?"

"I read your profile and the emails you shared with my father. You said you're attending college." His gaze dipped from hers, roaming down to her cleavage for a moment before snapping back up. *Interesting.* Perhaps he wasn't as immune as she'd assumed. "You're older than the typical freshman, which I found curious."

"I'm taking a business degree. I'd actually started it five years ago, but stopped when my boyfriend at the time opened a business of his own. He asked if I could help him out and I said yes."

"Why go back now?"

Oh you know, my ex thought I was cheating on him and took all the money from the business before leaving me holding the financial bag. "The timing was right. I needed to start over and finishing my education, doing something for me, felt like the right thing to do."

He nodded. "Except you needed money. Your boyfriend can't help you out?"

There were two ways she could go about this. First, she could dance around the topic, say what little she needed to, so he'd agree to their arrangement. Or she could lay all her cards on the table and hope for the best.

She was a terrible liar.

"I'm going to be honest. Andrew—that's my ex—well he left me." She took another sip of wine to fortify herself. "I was happy with my life up until six months ago. I…things didn't end well between us. I'm on my own and have some unexpected debts that I need to clear. I'm in school full time, I'm working double shifts at my job when I can and I've taken out as many loans as the bank will give me. But Andrew is making things difficult and I need to find a creative way to get out of this mess. So, here I am."

Vince's frown scrunched his face in such a way that somehow enhanced his good looks. "What unexpected debts?"

"Just…some bills I hadn't accounted for." As much as she wanted to put everything out in the open, she still wasn't exactly certain she could trust Vince. And her reasons were hers; they shouldn't matter when it came right down to it.

"I see." Before he could say anything else a waiter came out with two plates of salad.

She smiled up at the man as he laid her napkin across her lap. "Thank you. I'm sorry, I didn't get your name."

The waiter's eyes widened before he flicked his gaze to Vince. "Ryan, Miss." He didn't give her time to ask anything else and scurried away.

She watched him go. "Okay…" When she turned her gaze back to Vince, he was frowning. "What?"

Vince picked up his wine glass and leaned back to stare. "You're not the type of woman I was expecting."

"I'm not sure if that's a good or bad thing." She picked up a forkful of salad and shoved it into her mouth to stop from talking. The way her brain was currently spinning, nothing good would come out.

Clearly, he was a serious man. Marissa couldn't imagine the sort of life a famous millionaire businessman led. No doubt it wasn't as exciting as the movies made it out to be. Or maybe he faced as much pressure as the rest of the public. Was it enough to have millions, or was he trying to get to the next level, become a billionaire? Did it keep him up at night? Did he feel lonely? What kind of lover would a man like that be?

"What thoughts are racing through your head?" His smirk disappeared behind his glass. "The look on your face was fascinating."

Her face flushed and she squirmed in her seat. "I was wondering what kind of person you were. I don't know much about you."

"Not a tabloid reader?"

"Sure, but I'm not an idiot. I know most of that stuff is garbage."

"You'd be surprised how many people don't share your point of view." He cocked his head to the side. "Ever watch the show?"

Her face immediately heated. "Ah, I might have caught an episode or two."

"Regular watcher, aren't you?"

"My DVR was full of them, but Andrew took that went he went."

"Bastard."

"I know right! Who takes a DVR with someone else's shows on it?" Yes, she was still bitter, and she probably always would be.

Ryan silently drifted back into the room and removed their plates. Vince hadn't touched his salad, nor did he acknowledge the waiter when he removed it. It was strange, but it pissed her off, his lack of recognition of the man who was helping to make this evening a pleasant one. When Ryan came back again, this time with a steak dinner, she made sure to smile up at him again. "Wow, this looks amazing. Please pass on my thanks to the chef."

That earned her a small smile. "I will, Miss."

"Why do you do that?" Vince didn't bother to wait until Ryan had left.

Ah, there was the authoritative figure she remembered seeing on television. "Do what? Be polite?"

"Leave us." Vince was clearly speaking to Ryan, but he didn't look at him. The waiter cast a quick glance at Marissa before rushing away once again.

"I think he's scared of you." Not that she'd admit it, but she was a bit intimidated too. "Not a great way to run a staff." Or to win over a woman. Not that he was trying to do that. Obviously.

"You run a large staff yourself?" He cocked his eyebrow before picking up his knife and fork. "You haven't answered my question."

"Why am I polite? Because I believe in treating others with respect. You don't know them, what their lives are like. Giving them a smile when they need to see one might be the difference between them having a good day and them having a breakdown. It costs me nothing and it might mean the world to them."

"Did your mother teach you that?"

A surprised laugh escaped her. "She didn't have to. It's called being a good person."

His gaze narrowed. "Are you implying I'm not good?"

"I'm implying that I agreed to this evening to spend time with your father. You're here in his place without my knowledge, so excuse me if I'm not going to let myself get bullied for being polite to the people around me."

Silence descended over them as they ate, giving Marissa time to catch her breath. This was a far more intense meeting than she'd anticipated. She'd wrongly assumed that the persona Vince wore on the show was fake, that he would be charming in person.

Maybe that was a thing about him that the tabloids and celebrity gossip shows wouldn't know. Perhaps millionaire business man Vince Taylor was a horrible conversationalist. She stopped eating to watch him. At first glance he appeared relaxed, a man enjoying a good cut of meat. But the closer she looked, there was something else simmering just below the surface. She didn't have a clue what it might be and there was only one way to find out.

"Tell me something about yourself." The question came from her almost as quickly as it passed through her head. He froze, looking up at her. She set her knife and fork down and rested her hands in her lap. "Something that I wouldn't know from reading about you or seeing you on TV."

He resumed chewing. "I'm an asshole."

She snorted. "No, they have that down. In great detail. Something else. What's your favorite color?"

"Don't have one."

"Liar. Everyone has a favorite. Blue? Black?" She smiled at him when he set down his utensils. "Grey?"

"Green."

"Nice. I'm a blue person myself. I find it calming." She looked directly into his eyes, trying to find a semblance of peace in his stormy blue irises. The wine must be going straight to her head, because what she saw in him was anything but peaceful.

He crossed his arms. "If we're going to play twenty questions, then it's my turn."

You poked the bear, idiot. "That's fair."

"How many men have you had sex with?"

It was strange how a simple question ignited a fire inside her. Annoyance and arousal fought for prominence. "That's a very personal question."

"You're here because you want me to be your sugar daddy. It's reasonable."

If she thought she was blushing earlier, she had no doubt her face was currently beet red. "I'm here because I wanted your *father* to be my sugar daddy." And didn't that sound horrific to her own ears. "I'm here with *you* because you wanted to protect me." She made sure to infuse plenty of sarcasm in her air quotes.

He snorted. "My father reached out to you because he needed to come across as respectable for a business deal. He's not exactly known for being able to keep a woman on his arm for long."

"Neither are you." *Shut up, idiot.*

"I've taken over the deal and likewise, the need to appear respectable in the eyes of a man who holds no fondness for my family. While I have women I could reach out to, it strikes me that perhaps my father had the right idea. For once."

Shifting in her seat, she tried to force her brain to catch up to what was unfolding. "I'm sorry, you want to be my sugar daddy? And you want to know how many men I've slept with?"

"Possibly. And yes."

There were two ways she could play this; answer his question and see how things played out, or shut him down and walk away from one of the hottest men she'd ever laid eyes on. Considering she was on a boat in the middle of the lake, with a man she didn't know, it was probably best to play things safe. "One. I did some…things with a few other guys. But actual intercourse? Just one."

"Thank you." Vince smiled, and this time it reached his eyes. "Your ex?"

"Yes."

He nodded slowly, his gaze locked on hers. "Am I making you uncomfortable?"

"A little. This whole night wasn't exactly what I was anticipating."

"You're not what I was expecting either." He leaned forward, his voice dropping to a near purr. "Did you enjoy it? Fucking him?"

Rage or at least annoyance should be racing through her, not this unnatural desire to hear him say *fuck* again. "Not that it's any of your damn business, but yes, we were good together."

"What did he do that you liked? What did he like? Tell me."

"You want to know about—" She shook her head and looked down at her hands. "I don't talk about my sex life. Not even to celebrities."

"Not even with someone willing to pay you?" Vince reached into his jacket and pulled out a stack of bills. "That's a thousand dollars."

Shit. That was a lot of money. Sure, it might have been a drop in the bucket for him, but to her that was a good chunk of one of her debts, or rent, or hell, the books she really needed for this semester's business ethics class. *Oh the irony.*

He slid it toward the center of the table. "Don't you want it?"

"I do." And she did, desperately. Yet, there was that part of her, the same part that hadn't wanted her to sign up for the website in the first place, screaming that this was a line in the sand. Selling her time—or even her body—was one thing. Selling her confidences, even from a man who'd tried to destroy her life, well, that was apparently her breaking point. "But I can't."

Vince crossed his arms again. "Why? You said yourself your ex was an asshole who wronged you. Why the loyalty?"

Good question. "Surprisingly, it's not about him. I have to live with myself and my actions. Despite how badly he screwed me over, how much I would love to get even with him, I'm not about to go into the details of my past relationship with a stranger. I don't kiss and tell. As I said, it's none of your business."

He didn't look away, didn't relax. Silence stretched on from seconds to minutes. An unspoken war raging between wants and ideals battled inside her. Even when Ryan came back and removed their plates, replacing it with a delectable chocolate lava cake, Vince remained stony. Apparently, he wasn't the sort of man you could say no to. Well, better to know that now before things got too far. *Best enjoy things while I can.* Picking up her spoon, she broke into the lava cake and watched the rivers of chocolate spill across the cake. Wanting to giggle at the sight, she finished her wine with a single swallow.

Yep, definitely getting drunk.

Vince cleared his throat, wrenching her attention away from dessert. "As I said, for once I believe my father had the right idea. Dinners, social functions, maybe one weekend away. I will pay for your time, will provide an allowance for clothing and any accessories you might require. When my deal is done, then we can part company."

The sound of his voice made her jump, sending a spoonful of chocolate to the napkin on her lap. *Thank you, Ryan.* "What?"

The tension that had enveloped him lessened. "I needed to be certain you weren't going to sell me out. Tabloids pay well for even a little information. A photograph of us in bed? You wouldn't need to worry about any debts you might have."

"You were testing me?" Okay, that pissed her off. Who did he think he was?

Apparently, a jaded rich guy.

"Don't sound surprised. You're the one who just told me you like to put yourself in other's shoes. My reputation is my brand. The last thing I need is it getting out to my investors that I'm paying a woman for her time and company. But having you available would make certain aspects of this easier for me."

She was nothing more to him than a tool that needed to be acquired for a job. The right widget that would help him secure the big deal. Fine, she could at least appreciate that. It was really no different than what she was doing with him. She needed money and this was an easy way to get it. Even if that meant going against everything that she believed was important, some of her primary values.

Like the concept of not having to sell herself off to the highest bidder. *Shit, what the hell have I gotten myself into?*

He continued, apparently oblivious to her mental struggles. "Dates. Clothing. Spending money. From you I need your attendance and what you showed me here tonight. Be friendly and smile." Vince leaned forward, his forearms bracketing his untouched dessert. "One other thing. There won't be sex of any kind between us."

Chapter 4

Vince wanted to laugh at the look of shock on her face. He'd been nearly as shocked himself when he'd mentally decided to make the offer. His intent tonight had been to simply treat the young woman to a nice meal, good wine, and pay her for her time. He no more wanted a sugar baby—or whatever the hell they were called—than he wanted to get back together with his ex-girlfriend Thea. But the moment he came out to see what was taking Caroline so bloody long, and laid eyes on Marissa, the very carefully constructed plan he'd worked on evaporated from his mind.

It turned his stomach to think what his father would have done with her if he'd been here in his place.

Marissa stared at him for a good long minute before she gave her head an adorable little shake, sending her blond curls dancing across her head. "I'm sorry, what?"

"No sex. It's a relatively simple concept."

Her awkwardness was as cute, as it was priceless. He didn't crack a smile, nor did he give any indication that he was aware of her feelings. He had no doubt she'd be appalled at his ability to keep things compartmentalized, a necessary skill he'd learned the hard way. If people thought you had a soft underbelly, they tended to attack there first.

Not that her feelings toward him mattered. Nope, as far as she was concerned, he was the asshole mercenary business man from *Bull Rush*, who was only out to make a buck.

That meant no laughing at her cuteness.

It was hard admitting to himself that hiring someone to pose as his girlfriend made sense. His last two relationships both ended the same way—in the headlines, with his name dragged through the mud, so he had no desire to actually find someone to date. But his father had made it clear that Simon didn't believe that Geoff had changed, which meant he wouldn't trust Vince either. And seeing as Simon was the only one Geoff was willing to sell GreenPro to, thus finally getting out of Vince's professional life for good, then Vince was willing to do whatever it took to make this deal.

Including hiring a sugar baby to play house.

This would be so much easier if she wasn't so fucking beautiful.

The blush that had started high on her cheeks had now crept down her throat, getting dangerously close to her cleavage. She had spectacular breasts, full and round, perfect for squeezing. The black dress had been a good choice for her. It had been challenging to keep from plying her with compliments, to keep from seducing her with light caresses and whispered conversation. He'd done that before with other women; he was really fucking good at it.

Keeping Marissa at arm's length was for her benefit as well as his. This was about business for both of them. He had no illusions that she'd walk away from their arrangement as soon as she had her debts paid off. He didn't have time for a needlessly emotional departure, or her thinking that because they'd screwed he wanted more from her. A relationship, or even marriage.

No fucking way.

He wasn't a monster, despite some of the claims that had been bandied about in the media. Too many wealthy assholes in the world leaving things worse than how they'd found them. Society had painted him with that brush, and despite how much he wanted to protest the label, it was pointless. So, he wore it like an expensive suit, and kept his true self to himself. That also meant keeping it from his date. She was clearly smart and he had no doubt she'd agree to his terms once they were presented to her.

Marissa shoved another piece of chocolate cake into her mouth. She'd missed a bit at the corner of her mouth, drawing his attention to her full pink lips. His cock threatened to come to life when the tip of her tongue darted out to wipe away the treat, before she cleared her throat. "Really? No sex?"

"You sound surprised." It was something he'd assumed would be easy enough for him to abide by. All he had to do was keep it in his pants. And unless she had some hidden agenda, he couldn't imagine that it would be difficult for her to agree as well.

Marissa cocked her head and narrowed her gaze. "I am. I'd just assumed...I mean you're paying for..." She shook her head, sending the loose tendrils around her head bouncing. "I guess with us meeting because of a sugar daddy site, I figured sex was a given. I mean, you didn't find me through…" She sighed. "I'd been bracing myself all week for the sex thing. I was ready for the sex thing."

"If it's going to be a problem for you, then we don't have to take things any farther."

"It's not that. It was simply unexpected." Finishing her meal, Marissa stood, taking her wine with her. "I'm relieved, if I'm being honest. It makes things easier. In a way."

He couldn't image how vulnerable she must feel being in this situation. "More professional." Getting up, he trailed along behind her.

He'd noticed her having difficulty earlier, and had broken his self-imposed no-touching rule to help her to the table. The phantom feel of her warmth still clung to his skin where he'd connected with her back. She was full of life, still excited about the things to come for her. He might only be thirty-five, but he'd lived more than most. So had most of the women of his acquaintance.

The yacht shuddered as the engine powered down. Marissa stumbled again and grabbed the edge of the table for support.

"Why don't you take those heels off?"

Her eyes sparkled and her body relaxed. "You don't mind?"

He shook his head. What the hell was he supposed to say? *No, keep tottering around until you face-plant. I'll be sure to laugh.* "Not at all."

"Thanks. These shoes are new and I haven't mastered walking on a boat yet, let alone on carpet."

"Yacht."

She looked up at him owl-eyed. "Pardon?"

"It's a yacht, not a boat."

One moment she was a timid girl, the next she was laughing at him with her eyes. An impressive feat that made him want to take a closer look at her. "Sorry, I didn't mean to offend you. I'm even less experienced walking on a *yacht*. You're the first millionaire I've met." She sounded less than impressed.

"Multi-millionaire," he corrected. "Practically a billionaire."

She rolled her eyes.

He mentally slapped himself. *Way to prove the world right, asshole.*

Vince knew money was only one aspect of him that some people were attracted to. Power was the other. Being with him opened doors that otherwise would remain shut. Being in his circle of influence would provide her with opportunities that she wouldn't otherwise have. "I'm glad you find my status non-threatening. Over the next few months you'll be speaking with several people of means. They might not be as forgiving if you tell them you like their *boat*."

She removed her second shoe and smiled up at him three inches shorter than she was a moment ago. "I'll be sure to re-watch *Pretty Woman* to brush up on my rich-person speak."

Marissa was no Julia Roberts. Her hair was long, blond, and pulled into one of those messy bun things women her age seemed to favor. Her hazel eyes suited her complexion, as though someone had manufactured her to be a natural beauty, rather than her being blessed by winning the genetic lottery. Her pale skin was flawless except for the light dusting of freckles across her nose. He could imagine connecting the dots to see if they held a hidden picture that reflected her inner spirit.

Shit, he couldn't see her that way. He needed to treat Marissa the same way he did Caroline or one of his other staff. Shoving aside his uncustomary sentimentality, he moved sure-footed and took her glass. "More white?"

"Sure, though I have to warn you that I'm a bit of a lightweight. I haven't had that one before. I'm not a huge wine drinker. Well, I don't mind it, but the good stuff is usually expensive."

He shouldn't, but the urge to tease, to prod her ever so slightly was too strong to resist. "What do you consider expensive?"

"Well, normally if I'm buying any I keep to around ten dollars or under. Sometimes though I'll splurge and get a fifteen or twenty-dollar bottle."

They really did come from different worlds. He made sure to fill her glass a little higher, knowing she wouldn't be able to afford the six hundred dollar *Pape Clement Blanc* on her own. She had moved to the window. The view of Toronto from the cabin was beautiful. Lights from the CN Tower danced in the sky, accentuated by the shift of spotlights and flash of cars moving down Lake Shore. Jesus, she was stunning. Exactly the sort of woman everyone expected him to have on his arm. The type of woman he would have expected to marry once upon a time.

Oh hell no.

"Rules." He waited for her to turn around before crossing the cabin to join her. These rules were as much for her benefit as his. The last thing he ever wanted to do was act like his father. He held out her glass, taking a sip of his own as she did. "I think it's in both our best interests to establish them."

"Sure. Rule away." There was that sparkle in her eyes again. She turned to look back out over the city, though he could watch her face in reflected back at him from the window.

"I'm to give you forty-eight hours' notice before an event. There will occasionally be unexpected gatherings, but my schedule is normally booked well in advance, so I have notice." He looked down at her bare shoulder and noticed a tag peeking out from the confines of the dress. He hooked the thread and tugged the mark out. "I'll provide you money for clothing. Starting with this one." With a quick snap, the tag was freed.

Shock was an expression that she wore as well as the dress. "I...thank you."

"Of course, you can't go public with our arrangement. Yes, there's a chance that we'll be seen together, which is fine. But if people learn that I'm paying you for your company, it will cause me grief." That was the understatement of the century.

When Thea had blown up their relationship, they'd barely made it off the red carpet for the Juno Awards. The screaming match and her accusations of cheating had been caught by dozens of people and were up on YouTube before he'd even taken his seat inside. He'd been perceived as the villain, no doubt due to his role as the asshole in the show. He didn't want to give the public another reason to harass him.

"The money on the table is yours for your time this evening. I'll have Caroline provide you with a contact where you can get additional clothing and jewelry for our times together."

She nodded and swallowed down more wine as she caught his gaze in the window. "Any requests? Seeing as you're paying."

The question should have sounded crass, would have had it been asked by any of his other female acquaintances. Somehow when it came from Marissa, it was more teasing than testing. He was paying for her to play a part and intended her to fall into the role flawlessly. The last thing he needed was for any of his peers to suspect he was paying for her company. "I prefer my women to dress in dark or neutral colors. I don't want to draw unnecessary attention."

"Noted. Anything else? Designers I should avoid? Jewelry I shouldn't splurge on?"

Now she *was* testing him. "I would hope that you'd take this seriously. If this is nothing but a game to you—"

"I was wondering the same thing about you."

Vince frowned. "What do you mean?"

"If this was a game." Marissa turned and drank down a more than healthy portion of wine. "I mean, you tricked me into thinking you were someone else—"

"It really was my father."

"—and then you throw all these *rules* at me. I just wanted to try and find a way to help myself with a problem, not create more issues." She set her glass down and turned her back to him.

Okay, this wasn't at all what he was expecting. "Are you okay?"

"Not really." She shook her head and her shoulders dropped. "Can you have the captain or whoever drives the boat to take us back? I'm ready to leave." She strode over, picked up her shoes and took three hundred dollar bills off the pile of cash. "You took the tag off so I have to keep it now."

There were two things Vince wasn't used to dealing with: rejection and dismissal. Marissa had managed to hit him with both with a single sentence. She looked over the railing that led to the galley. "Ryan? Hello?"

"What are you doing?"

"Leaving. This isn't going to work."

"Why not?"

Marissa straightened, smoothing her hands down her dress before facing him. "This is a terrible idea. I thought I was okay selling myself off. I mean, it's just sex right…except you don't want sex. I was actually mentally ready for sex, but no sex is just confusing. And yeah, Naomi said there might be dinners and movies and stuff, but then *you're* here. And your dad is apparently so horrible that I needed to be protected from him. And…I thought I could do this but I don't think I can."

Vince opened his mouth to answer, shoot off a dismissal, something. Nothing came out.

If she noticed his hesitation, she didn't acknowledge it. "The only reason I was going to do this was because I can't see another way out of my current mess without having my entire financial future come crashing down around me. I'll be damned if I'm going to let Andrew's temper tantrum ruin my life, but I'm not about to make matters more complicated than they already are. I'll find another way to work this out. I just…yeah. I'm sorry."

How could he have thought she was an innocent or weak? There was a core of steel to Marissa that transcended her years. Her internal fire glowed in her eyes that infused every inch of her. Only a pathetic man would dare harm a woman like this, try to grind her down so he could influence her. Do anything to destroy her dreams.

Without looking, he set his glass down and crossed over to the intercom. "Captain, could you take us back to the marina?" He turned it off without waiting for a response. Before she could say anything else, he reached over and retrieved the remaining stack of cash. "Regardless of how tonight went I intended this for you. Never let anyone take advantage of your time and not provide compensation. You are your brand. Demand others treat it and you with respect."

She stared at him for several heartbeats before slowly reaching up and taking the money. "Thank you."

"You're right. I bullied my way into a situation without fully considering the consequences. My intent was to save you from my father. In the end, you had to save yourself from me. I'm sorry for that."

"You didn't actually do anything." The blush crept across her cheeks again. "You weren't that bad."

"I was an asshole. As usual." No wonder Simon didn't trust his family and the media looked for whatever they could on him. His tendencies to try and control everything in every situation got him into trouble on more than one occasion. At least Marissa had called him on it; many others wouldn't. "But now that I know you, I would like to help. At the very least, maybe I could offer you some ideas on how to get out of your predicament. Whatever it happens to be."

The yacht shuddered as it began to change course to take them back to land. Marissa looked behind her at the changing skyline before sighing. "Maybe."

"How about a fresh proposal? One between you and I and nothing to do with that site or my father."

Marissa bit down on her bottom lip. "What are you suggesting?"

His chest tightened and his blood rushed a bit harder and faster through him. Shit, he was nervous. He couldn't remember the last time he'd dealt with someone who could walk away with little more than a *fuck you, buddy*. Didn't know the last time he was this excited. "Maybe we go out to dinner. It doesn't have to be anything fancy, but it will be a chance to get to know one another properly. As friendly acquaintances." She smiled and something loosened in his chest. "At least this time you'll know that it's me who you're meeting you and not someone else."

"That seems reasonable." She pushed a lock of her blond hair behind her ear and smiled.

"If things go poorly, or even if one of us changes our minds, we cut our losses and walk away." Vince laced his hands behind his back and waited for her response.

For the life of him, Vince couldn't read her expression, get a sense of what she was thinking. But he knew, could tell on an atomic level, that he needed her to say yes. That feeling alone made another date worth pursuing.

Marissa finally let out a little sigh, held out her hand, giving him a smile that didn't quite reach her eyes. "I agree to your terms."

When she slipped her hand into his and squeezed, his body responded with anything but indifference. Vince was overwhelmed by the smell of her, the softness of her skin against his, the fucking light that danced in her gaze. She was young and fresh, and he wanted to drag her into his world where he would get her dirty. The dark, bitter part of him wanted to use her, wanted to fuck her just to hear what noises she'd make in bed.

No. The last thing he needed was to lose control and go down that path.

Marissa, oblivious to the war raging inside him, tightened her grip. "Deal," he said with a smile, his voice was little more than a whisper.

He'd won. For now.

Chapter 5

Marissa had the limo drop her off down the street from her apartment. While having to walk the half-block was going to be murder on her feet, it was better than having to deal with the barrage of questions that would inevitably come from her landlord, Shelia. She lasted until she reached the bottom of the walkway before she kicked off her shoes. The throbbing of her feet did little to help relax her, but at least she wouldn't accidently topple.

The bungalow appeared as normal as the others on the street. The shingles were new and Shelia was a surprisingly excellent gardener. The cuteness of the place is what had lulled her into a false sense of security the first time she'd arrived to look at the basement apartment. But opening the doors and seeing what was inside broke her heart. Unfortunately for her, it was the most reasonable apartment she could find given her limited funds, and despite the condition of her home, Shelia was a kind and wonderful woman.

Marissa walked up the stairs that lead to the side door, and took a steadying breath. Most days, Shelia had the door to the main house closed and locked, making everything seem like a normal arrangement. The stairs that led to Marissa's apartment were cluttered with shoes and the occasional bag, but for the most part gave no indication of anything abnormal. But sometimes, especially when Shelia was having a bad day, she'd leave the door to the house open. There was no escaping a conversation on those days.

Tonight, the door was open, the sound of a gameshow echoed out to her. Shit.

Marissa stepped into the foyer, dirt that had been previously tracked in now stuck to her bare feet. One step and a creak filled the air. It was loud enough to announce her presence as she stepped in and shut the door behind her. Maybe this time she could escape to her place without Shelia noticing—

"That you, Marissa?"

Nope. "Yes."

"I hope you had a good evening. Have time to chat?"

Marissa was under no obligation to socialize with her landlady—she was paying rent, not seeking refuge—but she'd learned from experience, it was better to give Shelia the few minutes of time she wanted, rather than ignore her. Shelia wasn't a bad person, not even in the slightest. But the condition of the living room gave Marissa a case of the creeps as much as it broke her heart.

She locked the side door knowing neither of them would be out again tonight, tucked her shoes under her arm, and carefully stepped over the piles of newspapers that had started to spread to the threshold. Mentally, she counted to three before plastering a smile on her face and crossing into the kitchen and through to the living room. "Hi there."

Shelia was exactly where she always seemed to be at night, sitting on her couch directly between stacks of books, takeout containers, and clothing. She was a bird of a woman, her black hair neatly pulled back into a low bun at the base of her neck and her skin pale. Her brown eyes were wide, and she blinked in a slow, deliberate manner that gave Marissa the impression she could see into her soul.

Every time Marissa saw her like this, she became unnerved. Shelia was crow-like, watching guard over her pile of treasures. Marissa tamped down on her impulse to turn and run, to grab her things and bolt so far away she'd never be found. Dear God, what kind of horrible human being did it make her that she wanted to flee? She took another step into the room, which was the farthest inside she'd ever dare go.

"Oh my." Shelia got up and effortlessly moved around the stacks of boxes and papers, to stand in front of her. Her smile lit her entire face, and for the briefest of moments, she looked genuinely happy. "You look stunning. I hope the young man appreciated what he had."

Shelia was clean, her clothing impeccable; a complete contrast to the landfill that comprised her home. Shelia reached out and ran her hand along her bare arm, reminding Marissa that she was a good, kind woman who did her best. Shelia had never been anything but kind and polite. She certainly didn't deserve Marissa's scorn.

Forcing down her negativity, Marissa smiled and prayed it looked genuine. "I hope so as well. He certainly appeared like he liked the dress." She really didn't know how thing were going to go between her and Vince. The entire evening felt as though she'd spent it in some weird third dimension.

"As it should be. Are you going to see him again?" Her brown eyes sparkled as she spoke, and her smile widened. "I know I don't know you well, but I hate seeing such a pretty thing as you all alone."

The smell of rotten food buried somewhere in the room made Marissa's stomach turn. God, she knew hoarding was a mental condition, but she couldn't figure out how someone like Shelia didn't seem to notice things like that. "With any luck things will work out."

"I'm sure they will."

"I'm surprised you're still up. It's nearly one in the morning."

The light in Shelia's eyes dimmed slightly. "I had some paperwork to do for work."

Marissa knew she had a job, something that paid well, but she didn't for the life of her know what it was. "That sucks. There's nothing worse than having to work this late at night."

Nodding, Shelia moved over to a pile of papers by her desk and turned her back on Marissa. "I also wanted to try and get some of this sorted tonight. I had a friend at work mention an article that they wanted to read, and I know I have it here somewhere."

If it was anyone else, Marissa would have offered to help look. "I'm sure you'll be able to find it."

"Eventually." Shelia smiled. "I won't keep you. I know you're itching to get downstairs and out of that dress."

She shouldn't feel relief at being offered such an easy escape, but she did. "Thank you. I'll talk to you later."

Careful to avoid hitting one of the stacks on the way out, Marissa went as quickly as she could through the mess to the stairs that led to her small home. She never bothered to take her apartment keys with her when she went out. Shelia had a copy in case of emergencies and she hadn't let her friends know where she lived, so no one would come looking for her here. Lifting the old boot that stood on one of the stairs, she scooped up her key, unlocked the door, and escaped inside.

The air was fresher down here, but not by much. The basement had that old musty smell that resulted from the distinct lack of sunshine and air. She'd brought her few remaining possessions from her old apartment and had managed to brighten up the place. Her Vinyl Pop collection of lady *Ghostbusters, Star Wars,* and the *Avengers* lined the mantel over the unused fireplace. Their bright colors stood in stark contrast to the dark faux-wood paneling. She'd rested her mounted posters against the wall where she'd wanted to hang them. It would feel more like home once she'd managed to get them up, even if it felt as though she were putting lipstick on a pig.

The main reason she'd agreed to the lease was the fact the bungalow was also a backsplit. Tossing her shoes by the door and her key on the small kitchen table, she marched over to the patio door and opened it up for the fresh air.

Marissa leaned against the frame and let the night air wash over her. The rush of traffic was practically nonexistent this time of night, letting her hear the chirping crickets somewhere in the distance. Their song helped ease some of the evening's tension from her.

What the hell was she doing?

More importantly, what the hell was she going to do with an arrogant television star and millionaire who wanted to use her as a companion?

Sorry, *multimillionaire*. Practically a billionaire.

She snorted in the dark.

This wasn't what she wanted from her life, to be used by another person for his own convenience. Yes, she would get money out of the arrangement, and thankfully there was no sex involved, but that was far beyond the point. She'd gone down this road with Andrew, had been used without being self-aware enough to clue in to the fact. After he'd left, trashing her life on the way out, she'd promised herself she'd never let that happen again. She was determined to fix this mess, and to do things on her own terms.

So why the hell was there a part of her that wanted nothing more than to crawl into Vince's lap and have him take care of her? He was cold, practical to a fault and with a simple look had managed to irritate her. Yes, he probably was putting on as much of an act as she was, but that didn't explain why despite how much he rubbed her the wrong way, she couldn't help but be curious about him.

The last thing she needed was to fall in love with a man who was far too much like Andrew for her liking. It was easy to look back on their relationship now, to see all the ways Andrew had been cocky and controlling. She'd also watched far too many episodes of *Bull Rush* to not be aware that Vince was every bit as controlling as Andrew.

And yet...

He'd given her a chance to back out. Given her a chance to try again, if that's what she'd wanted. He had nothing to lose from making the offer of dinner, and she had everything to gain.

If she wasn't misreading him and making a colossal mistake.

The weight of the world seemed to press down on her, her head falling forward. She'd been exhausted for weeks now, though it felt more like years. All she'd ever wanted was to be her own boss and have someone in her life who loved her unconditionally.

Given how much Vince had to lose himself, she suspected he wouldn't do anything to intentionally hurt her. As he said, his reputation was his brand, and she had the potential to damage it. But this couldn't be the only way to get herself out of this mess? Putting all her faith in a man was what had caused her problems to begin with. How was this any different?

No, she'd gotten into this mess on her own, and she'd damn well get herself out of it. There had to be some sort of debt consolidation she could explore, or a low interest bank loan. Hell, maybe she'd have to declare bankruptcy if she wanted this mess to go away. It was only seven years to recover her credit score. How bad could that really be?

Exhaustion hit her hard. As much as she wanted the air, she slid the patio door closed and dropped the security bar down. The last thing she needed was to have someone break into her place and try and steal something. *Oh, the irony.*

Stepping out of the dress, she hung it in plain sight as both a reminder and a warning. She'd agreed to a test date with Vince, but the more she thought about it, the more she knew it was a terrible idea. She'd go with him, enjoy the meal and then break things off. She'd have to tell Naomi at school that the sugar daddy thing didn't work out for her. *That* would be an interesting conversation.

Marissa quickly took her makeup off, before climbing between the sheets naked. The darkness wrapped around her, temporarily lulling her into a false sense of security and into sleep.

* * * *

"Bullshit it didn't work out for you." Naomi twisted in her seat to better glare at her. "Dude, I saw how many men flagged your profile. And there were some really hot ones there too. So, it's not that, which means it's you."

Marissa leaned her head back and let out the most dramatic sigh she could muster. This wasn't how she wanted this conversation to go. "Am I not supposed to have second thoughts about this?"

Naomi mimicked her position, turning her head just enough to be able to give her excellent side-eye. "I didn't."

"You didn't question the idea about offering yourself up to some random stranger, to doing anything they want for money? Not even once?" When Naomi shook her head, Marissa snorted. "Now I'm calling bullshit."

"Fine, maybe a bit before the first date. But it turned out to be so freaking awesome. He took me to the symphony and out to dinner. Then we went back to his place and—"

"I don't need to know the sex parts."

"And we talked. Dude lost his wife three years ago. They never had children and he was lonely." Naomi smiled and leaned in closer. "We talk a lot on symphony nights. They had season tickets and he didn't want to give them up, so that's why I'm there. I do give him the occasional blow job, but that's totally my idea."

Marissa groaned and covered her face. "Why am I such a prude?"

"Don't have a freaking clue. It's just sex. As long as you're the one setting the limits, who cares? You're both consenting adults."

"But one of those consenting adults has all the power in the relationship. I promised myself I wouldn't get into a position like that again."

The door to the classroom opened, cutting off the rest of Marissa's words, as their professor walked in. "Good morning. I have your test results."

Naomi groaned. "I fucking bombed that one."

"You always say that and you do fine." It had been their third test of the semester, and the first one she'd even felt remotely challenged with. She hadn't had quite enough time to prepare due to needing to pick up an extra shift, and the thought of her marks slipping even a little freaked her out.

Their professor dropped a stack of tests on the corner of her desk, before she flipped open her laptop and connected it to the projector. "You can pick them up on your way out. Today we're going to start our next unit on small business finance."

Marissa had to push away all thoughts of sugar daddies, money, and sex. This was one area of her business that had caused her the most problems. She'd be dammed if she let her attention wander. Flipping open her text book, she sat up and got to work.

Chapter 6

Marissa was exhausted by the time she got home. She'd had to race from her last class of the day to her job at the Pear Tree, where she waited tables until late. By the time she got onto the bus to head home, her feet screamed at her to get off them already, while her back ached in places she hadn't previously been aware existed on her body.

The movement of the bus nearly lulled her into a light sleep, when her phone beeped. It was a text from a number she didn't immediately recognize, though the message told her enough for her to know who the sender was.

Friday night, 8pm. The Catch. I'll send a car.

Vince certainly knew how to woo a girl. Marissa continued to stare at the words long past the point of necessity. She'd read about The Catch in a blog post online describing the most expensive and impressive places to eat in Toronto. Never once did she consider the possibility that she'd ever have the opportunity to eat there. It was a far cry from the Pear Tree and the free food she'd eat in the kitchen on her breaks.

God, she should say no and end things before they got started. She wasn't going to go through with this beyond the first date, so there was no point in leading him on. Though he had paid for her new dress and it wasn't like she was going to have many opportunities to wear it. Why not play dress-up again, take one night to relax and enjoy herself at someone else's expense? She'd let him wine and dine her, then tell him it wasn't going to work and thank him for the meal. Saturday, she'd go back to her normal life of waiting tables and studying.

What harm could it do?

She quickly thumbed in her response. *I'll see you then.*

Cinderella could go to the ball and come out the other side unscathed. She'd just have to be certain not to leave any glass slippers behind.

* * * *

Vince glanced down at his phone when it buzzed in his hand. Good, she'd agreed. It was strange not knowing what the outcome of his request would be. Even though she'd been the one who'd proposed the compromise, he hadn't been entirely certain that she was going to follow through. There'd been something about the look in her eyes that had screamed that she didn't trust him as far as she could throw him. Not that he blamed her in the least, given the nature of their relationship.

Caroline was flicking through emails on her phone, but he knew she was paying as much attention to him as he was to whatever she was reading. Placing his phone face down on the desk, he leaned back in his seat. "Do you still have your friend over at The Catch?"

She glanced up at him over the top of her glasses. "Yes. Why?"

"Think you could get me a reservation for two on Friday at eight?"

"That's short notice. I don't know if Danny can work his magic."

"I have no doubt he'll come through for you. Book the private room if it's available."

She rolled her eyes and went back to her emails. "Fine. Your ten pm call just got cancelled."

"Shit." He'd been trying to get Jace on the phone for weeks now. "Did he say why?"

Caroline sat up as she scanned the email. "He didn't say specifically, except to say that a previous call he's on is running late. Want me to reschedule?"

Vince had agreed to back a new casino development project months ago. The company had some sound ideas, and Vince wouldn't have put his money down if he'd thought for a minute the venture wouldn't have been a success. Leaning back in his chair, Vince closed his eyes and groaned. "Yes. I don't want to let this go too long. I have more than enough on my plate and this deal should be an easy win."

"I'll make a note." Caroline's thumbs flew over the phone's keyboard before she looked back up. "Your first call tomorrow morning is at nine with the Peter Thornton from New York for the GreenPro sale. Did you want me to get the boardroom for the call, or did you want to take it in the office?"

"I'll take that one in my office." His dad had threatened to come in for it, claiming he knew exactly how to twist Peter's arm to get him on board with Simon. "Don't put it on my calendar though. I don't want Dad to know the time."

Caroline's frown made her look far older than he knew she was. "It's not like he has access to that. He shouldn't at any rate."

"He'll find a way." It was crazy how inventive his father could get when he wanted to be involved with a deal. Never when Vince needed him though. God, never then.

Giving his head a shake, Vince stood up and stretched. "It's late and I'm done in. Let's call it a night." He came around the side of the desk, held out his hand and helped his assistant up. "Do you need a ride home?"

"I have the car." She crossed her arms and cocked her head to the side. "You never said who you were meeting for dinner Friday."

"I didn't."

"It's that girl, isn't it?" Once he'd told her about it, Caroline hadn't held back her displeasure about his taking over of his father's crazy sugar daddy plan one bit. And while she would do everything he asked her to do, they'd worked together too long for him to rub her nose into something that he knew she disapproved of.

Still, this was his best option to present himself as a respectable man, without putting his personal life in the line of fire, for a business deal that he didn't want to make in the first place. "Yes, I'm meeting Marissa."

"I thought you were going to pay her off and send her on her way?"

"I was. But while my father's methods are horrible, in this one instance his general idea was sound. Simon will be more amenable to listening to my offer if he thinks I've somehow gotten a woman to not hate me. Paying for that is far easier than finding someone."

Caroline looked away. "I doubt you'd have any issues finding someone to help you out."

"Not without them expecting something in return. At least this way we've negotiated everything up front. Easy and done." Well, not exactly. "As long as I can convince her not to leave. She was willing to go for one trial date to see how things went before she made her decision."

Caroline's eyebrows shot up. "To see how things…was she going to dump *you*? After the yacht?"

"Apparently, my asshole nature was on display."

She snorted. "That's a given. And she wasn't won over by your charm and wit? Maybe she's smarter than I gave her credit for."

Yeah, he really didn't want to get into this with her. "For the record, she only took three hundred from the money I had for her. And she only took that because I pulled the price tag off her dress."

"Of course, you forced her hand." Caroline punched his arm. "Didn't peg her as having a backbone. I guess I'm slipping in my people-reading abilities."

Vince turned her around and gave her a gentle push out the door. "That's because your boss works you too hard. Go home and rest. Sleep in tomorrow and I'll see you after lunch."

"You're leaving too, right?"

"In a minute. Just want to answer a few emails and then I'm out of here."

She shook her head. "Sure you will. Don't stay too late. You don't want to miss your call tomorrow. Goodnight."

"Night."

Vince waited for Caroline to leave before he turned to his computer and scanned his emails. He even went so far as to open one, half reading it before he closed it just as quickly. His eyes closed and he couldn't help but let his memories of the night on the yacht with Marissa wash over him.

She really was one of the most attractive women he'd seen in quite some time. Not glamourous, or pretty in that magazine Photoshopped way. Her beauty was disarming. He'd had to fight the urge during their entire conversation not to reach out and touch her. Not in any sexual manner, just this strange urge to feel that she was a real person.

He'd done his best not to openly stare at her, but that had been far more difficult than he'd originally assumed it would be. On a whim, he opened up the *millionairesugardaddies* website and went to her profile. Maybe if he'd done that before taking his father's place on the yacht, he might have been able to prepare himself for her.

Yeah, probably not.

He clicked through the few profile pictures she'd uploaded. While they clearly showed she was beautiful, if anything, they'd understated her features. The pictures hadn't captured that sparkle in her eyes every time she was silently judging him. Nor was there any way he could have prepared himself for the intoxicating scent that he caught a whiff of whenever she'd stood close. If it was a perfume, it wasn't one he was familiar with.

It had been tempting to press his nose to the side of her neck and simply breathe her in, to imprint that scent in his mind, to feel her body heat against him. Somehow, he'd managed to hold himself back. Still, it had him questioning everything about the date.

Why would someone like Marissa feel the need to ask for help through a site like *millionairesugardaddies*? Sure, it was easier than getting a loan, but there had to be more to it than that. He pulled out his phone and stared down at her last message. In a few days, he'd have her sitting across the table from him and he could ask her all the questions he wanted.

But did the answers really matter?

She had her reasons for starting an account as much as he did for agreeing to take her on. This was supposed to be just another business arrangement, and he should damn well keep that in mind. There was no reason to try and dig deeper than the surface. She had her life and he had his. She'd have been vetted by the site so he had to assume she passed the background checks they'd had in place. Still, he hated not knowing everything.

Caroline claimed it was one of his biggest weaknesses. He liked to think it was one of his strengths. Learning as much as he could about any investment opportunity ensured he didn't make a wrong choice and fuck things up. Marissa was an investment in his reputation. He'd be a fool not to learn everything he could about her.

Besides, Google was his friend.

It didn't take long for him to type in her name and find her social media accounts. He'd have to remind her that if they went forward with everything, that she would need to keep all accounts of their adventures off Facebook. Shit, she should have it set to private, regardless. Didn't she know about Facebook stalking?

He clicked through her pictures, looking at her smiling face and those of her friends. Most of the images were from high school, with some newer ones from her time at college thrown in. There was a large gap in time, which could simply mean she hadn't posted a lot over that time. Given how many images were here before and after, he assumed the missing time had to do with her ex.

It would have been nice to know his name, in case Vince needed to prepare for some backlash. Another note he'd have to ask her over dinner.

Vince shut down his computer and gathered his things. It was nearing midnight and by the time he got back to the house he'd be more than ready for his run. He'd started the habit years ago after his father's last run in with the media. He hadn't been able to go out into daylight without being mobbed by paparazzi, which had taken away his ability to run. So, he'd switched things up, running once he got home from the office and long after most photographers had given up their wait. It was far easier to slip out of the house and simply become another random person on the streets under the cover of dark.

Since then, he'd grown to love the solitude.

Toronto in the summer was beautiful, the glow from the city lights giving the streets and trees an ethereal glow. He rarely listened to music, instead enjoying the steady *thump, thump, thump* of his feet pounding against the concert sidewalk. Now that fall was upon them, the evening air cooled enough that he could wear his long-sleeved shirt with his shorts, his ball hat covering his head and masking curious glances. It was the only time he could simply be Vince, Toronto native, lover of pizza, and *Game of Thrones*, and not Vince Taylor, multimillionaire business investor with two fucked-up parents who had a very public divorce and subsequent public shaming.

Grabbing his things, he strode for the elevator. Yeah, he'd go for a run tonight. It would help clear his mind of Marissa, business ventures, and drive away the loneliness.

Chapter 7

Marissa felt far more comfortable in the black dress tonight. Maybe because she owned it now, after having taking the three hundred dollars she'd gotten from Vince and made a payment on her credit card. It wasn't glamorous, trying to be fiscally responsible, but it felt good to have some measure of control.

Even if that meant having to kick a multimillionaire to the curb.

And what the hell was wrong with her?

Marissa waited for the driver to open up her car door in front of The Catch. It was less weird getting into the limo this time around, even though she wasn't willing to let him pick her up at the house. This was the last time she'd be getting picked up at any rate. Though she'd half been expecting Vince to be in the car this time, and had been disappointed when the door was opened to reveal an empty backseat.

The moment she stepped onto the sidewalk, helped out of the limo by the driver, her gaze landed on Vince. He stood on the sidewalk, his dress shirt opened at the neck and framed by a perfectly fitted suit jacket. She'd been so stunned by the unexpected sight of him, she stumbled on the edge of the curb.

"Let me help." He seamlessly moved past the driver, capturing her hand in his and helping her out. "I'm sorry I wasn't able to be there to pick you up. I got caught on a call and couldn't leave sooner."

It had been a week since their last meeting. Marissa fought to keep her mouth shut as the sound of his rich baritone voice washed over her once more. "Thanks. And that's fine. I figured something like that had happened."

They'd spoken by text a few times since she'd said she would agree to come tonight. Nothing overly long or intense, mostly Vince asking her the occasional question and her thumbing a brief response. It had been strangely reassuring that he was at least curious about her, and not has cold as he'd come across on the boat.

Sorry, *yacht.*

Vince frowned down at her. "I don't think I want to know what went through your mind."

"Just a little mental self-correction." She dropped his hand and straightened up. "Well, Mr. Taylor, I have to say I'm impressed. I've heard so many amazing things about here, but I never in a million years thought I'd ever get to eat here myself."

"Please call me Vince when we're in public." He held out his arm for her to take, but kept his gaze averted. "I wouldn't want anyone to think we're anything but on a first name basis."

It was strange, he was still wearing that blank expression on his face, cold and unimpressed, but Marissa couldn't help but notice there was something else there. It was as though he was trying to stare at her from the corner of his eye. Filing that away in the back of her mind, she let him lead her into the restaurant.

It was hard not to stare at the décor as they were led toward the back of the restaurant. Everything was glass and chrome, with white accents. The patrons spoke in hushed tones, leaning in close as if they were scared to break the cone of silence covering the room. She'd been so preoccupied with her surroundings, she hadn't realized that they'd been led toward a private room in the back.

"Oh." She hesitated before stepping past the threshold.

There was a lit fireplace along the back wall that gave off just enough heat to take the chill from the air. The waiter walked behind a chair and pulled it out for Marissa to take. Vince waited until she was seated before he took his own chair. He watched the waiter like a hawk, as he placed her napkin on her lap and filled her glass with wine.

"Is this what we had the other night on the boat...err on the yacht?" She took a sip to confirm her suspicions, moaning her pleasure. "I do love this one."

"I remembered." He didn't exactly smile at her, but his expression softened somewhat. "I'm glad you enjoyed it."

"I do. And this place? It's amazing. I didn't even know they had a private room." She leaned around, trying to take in every piece, every detail. There was no way she'd be able to come back to the restaurant, let alone somehow get access to the private room. This one would have to be stored in the long-term memory banks for certain. "Thank you for bringing me here."

"You haven't even tasted the food yet." He picked up the menu, and his gaze traveled across the words. "They have a decent selection, though I'm not sure if you have any allergies or not."

"Nope. I'll eat anything." And for some strange reason, she winked at him. God, it had been ages since she'd flirted with anyone, let alone someone who she'd promised herself that she wouldn't see again.

Vince snorted, before turning his attention back to the menu. "Lobster looks good."

Never order the lobster. The words of a comedian she'd seen on Netflix came flooding back. She claimed they expected sex if you went with the most expensive thing on the menu. Then again, Vince had already claimed sex wasn't on the table to begin with.

She considered it for a moment longer before shaking her head. "There's no easy way to eat lobster without getting it all over you. But the tuna sounds amazing."

"How about we split the difference?" Vince flagged the waiter over from the doorway where he'd been waiting. "The truffle fries and the mussels for an appetizer. And the diamond platter for two for the main course."

"Certainly, sir." He took their menus and bowed slightly before leaving.

Marissa was certain her mouth was open. The diamond platter had oysters east & west, snow crab legs, shrimp, tuna, and poached lobster. It was well over two hundred dollars, and far more than she would have ever ordered for herself. "I guess it pays to date a millionaire."

"Multimillionaire." There wasn't any bite to his words and for the briefest of moments, his lips turned in a soft smile. "I don't come here very often, but it's one of the best dishes I've had."

Marissa found herself relaxing, leaning back in her chair as she played with the stem of her wine glass. "That's pretty high praise coming from you. I can't wait to try it."

Words then dried up in her brain, bringing the conversation to a halt. It's not like she knew much about Vince or his world to be able to dive into a particular topic. Considering she had no intentions of seeing him again after tonight, she didn't want to ask him a bunch of questions that would come across as too personal. So, what the hell did you ask a rich dude with a boat?

Well, there was always her old stand-by. "*Star Trek, Star Wars,* or both?"

Vince frowned. "Pardon?"

"Which is your favorite series? *Star Trek, Star Wars,* or are you one of those people who can't make up your mind and just go with whatever one is currently newer? Not that there's anything inherently wrong with that, except you should absolutely know which is your favorite and I'll think less of you if you don't."

"I see." Vince glanced at the fireplace and cleared his throat. "I'd have to say neither."

Interesting. Marissa leaned back in. "Really? *Battlestar Galactica* person? *Doctor Who*? Don't tell you don't watch any sci-fi because I'll have to leave the table before I get to eat and that will make me cry."

"Fine."

"Fine what?"

"I won't tell you that I haven't watched any sci-fi."

Marissa couldn't contain her gasp. "Wait, you need to clarify. You don't watch it because you don't like it, or you've never watched it because you're weird?"

This time he smiled full-on. "I've never been called weird before."

"How can you have gone your whole life and not at least watched some sci-fi? Sure, it's not for everyone. But normally they have at least tried it before passing judgement."

Marissa had fallen in love with *Star Trek* as a kid, watching re-runs of *The Next Generation* on television. Her mom had despised it, but that hadn't stopped her from saving all of her allowance and babysitting money so she could buy the DVDs. She based most of her friendships on whether or not they could tolerate her going on about the leadership skills of Captain Picard vs Captain Kirk. Or whether or not they liked the *Star Wars* prequels. Which, ew no.

"I don't have a lot of time for television or movies."

There was something about the way he said it, that didn't quite sit right with Marissa. All of her plans to walk away from this arrogant man, who had more money than people probably had business having, started to evaporate. Maybe she could offer a man like Vince something more than being arm candy for him at social events. Shit, he hadn't even seen *Star Wars*, which was simply not acceptable.

Taking another sip of her wine, she gave him her best smile. "Well, I'm going to have to change that."

And there was his frown. "Pardon?"

"If we're going to do this," she waved between them, "thing, then I need to know that we're going to have something a little bit more than simply showing up at events and smiling."

The small hint of his potential easy going underpinning, disappeared. "I was quite clear. There is to be nothing between us. No relationships, no sex. If that's going to be a problem for you, then I'll be the one to end things now."

Jesus, he was even more screwed up than she was. "I'm not talking about any of that. But let's be honest, if I'm going to come across as more than a rent-a-date for you, then we have to have some things that will make people assume we're having an actual relationship. Correct? Or am I just being a fool here?"

"You're correct." He leaned forward, his forearms pressed against the edge of the table. "You could tell me why you needed the services of that site rather than simply getting a loan."

Her fingers tightened around her wine glass. "Why do you want to know?"

"As you said, it will help us come across better." He cocked his head to the side and narrowed his gaze. "I'm curious." She was sitting in one of the best restaurants in Toronto about to eat a meal she'd never order for herself. It was probably the least she could do to be honest with him about her reasons. Even if they made her look like a complete idiot.

"I told you Andrew left me and took some of my things?"

Vince nodded.

"He also defaulted on several business loans that I'd co-signed for him. We'd already been broken up over a month when the first debt collectors started showing up. At first, I'd assumed it was a one-off and paid them what they were owed. Then the next month, I got another call. Then more. I couldn't keep up with them all."

Vince sat back as the waiter brought their appetizers, scowling. Marissa grabbed a truffle fry, dipped it into the aioli and shoved it in her mouth. "Oh my God, that's the best thing I've ever had."

Vince growled at her, and glared at the waiter, who quickly scurried away. "Did you have a lawyer look at the contracts? Can you sue him? Or at the very least set up a consolidation loan?"

Dread and frustration mixed oddly in her stomach, making her squirm. "It's my name on the contracts. I signed them willingly. Yes, I could consolidate the loans, to a point. But things keep coming out of the woodwork, and I don't know how long this will go on. I'm a student, with debts of my own and when I talked to the bank, they weren't really keen. The sugar daddy site…it was a bit of a Hail Mary pass to try and get ahead of things."

Marissa had to fight to keep her gaze on Vince's, tired of feeling weak and small, tired of constantly being on the losing end of life.

He slowly nodded, picked up his wine and took a sip. "Regarding your need to educate me in all things sci-fi, what are you proposing?"

It was her turn to look surprised. "Really? As simple as that?"

"It is. You were honest with me, about something that must be incredibly difficult for you to verbalize to others. I'd like to try and help."

Marissa swallowed against the unexpected tightening of her throat. "Thank you."

"So...your proposal?"

"Homework." She relaxed back against her seat before picking up a mussel. "Oh, this smells great too."

"While I appreciate the sentiment, I have no desire to do your business courses assignments."

"Shit, I hadn't even considered that." He'd be an amazing resource for some of her courses. "I was thinking more along the lines of me giving you television show assignments and you going home to watch them."

He blinked at her. "Seriously?"

"Dude, you haven't seen *Star Trek*. Though, really you can skip the original if you want and simply start with *Next Generation*. It's a bit blasphemous, but I don't want to push my luck either."

"You're doing a pretty good job of pushing." The lines around his eyes softened enough that she didn't fully believe him. "I don't have a lot of time to watch television."

"I don't either. Hell, I don't even have cable because I can't afford it. But you can always squeeze in a show or two on a flight, or when you're cooking. Shit, that's how I watched the first two seasons of *Bull Rush*."

Missing some of her favorite shows was one of the things that had stung when she realized she couldn't afford to pay for cable any longer. She'd get caught up at some point on DVDs or see if she could borrow access to someone's streaming service, but it was one more small piece of joy that had been snuffed out from her life.

And again, fuck you Andrew.

Vince plucked a fry from the plate and popped it into his mouth after frowning at it. "I can't watch the original. I had a friend show me one once and I lasted five minutes."

Marissa sat up straight, unable to fight the grin that exploded across her face. "It's an acquired taste."

"I think I'd prefer *Star Wars*. I have enough politics in my daily life."

"Smart. A movie is far easier to get through." Marissa's heart pounded at the thought of Vince curled up on a couch watching Luke Skywalker looking across the Tatooine desert at night. "I can loan you my collector edition Blu-rays." Her brain screeched to a halt. "Or not. I...don't know where they are right now."

She knew exactly where they were—Andrew's possession. Having ruined her financially had hurt, but it was the little betrayals that had dug deep. Like him walking away with her *Star Wars* movie collection, because he'd bought them for her as a gift and she "no longer deserved them."

Shifting in her seat, Marissa made sure to put her smile back in place. "Regardless, I'm sure you can find your own copies. But you need to try and watch it before we get together again." She cleared her throat. "If we get together again."

The waiter came back with their meals, which was a welcome distraction from her increasingly troubled thoughts. She'd been such an idiot when it came to everything she'd done with Andrew. And here she was, starting down another bad road with a man who wanted nothing to do with her beyond being a rent-a-date.

"I was under the impression," Vince picked up his glass and took a sip of his wine, "that you weren't interested in going on another date with me."

"I wasn't. I'm not." She groaned. "I don't know what I mean anymore. The last few months have been absolute hell and all I'm doing is second-guessing every decision I've ever made."

It was more than that. She'd loved Andrew since high school. Dating him had been exciting, and wonderful. He wasn't a horrible man, like the people her mom had tried to warn her off of. Not that Andrew had the best family, but until the end of their relationship, he'd kept her far away from them and hadn't done a bloody thing to make her think he was even remotely like them.

"Let me see if I'm understanding this." Vince leaned back in his chair, before tapping his fork on the edge of the plate. "If I agree to watch *Star Wars*, you'll agree to go to New York with me for my next business event."

Marissa sat up straighter. "Sure. Yes. I will agree to New York if you watch the movie."

"This means a lot of you, doesn't it?"

Shit, he was totally judging her for her geeky tendencies. "I know it's not very posh, and it's not like I'm going to talk about it or anything when we go out. I'll be all smiles and business conversations when we're out. I just need to know that...I have something in common with you."

"I understand." It was odd, but she could tell that he did. "Fine. I'll begin my journey to a galaxy far, far away and you'll go with Caroline to get some new clothing for our trip."

"Wait, I thought you didn't know anything about *Star Wars*."

Vince rolled his eyes in a very un-multimillionaire kind of way. "I haven't been living under a rock. Everyone knows that's how it starts."

"And do I have to go with Caroline?" Marissa could still picture her death glare as she'd left Marissa to her fate on the yacht. "She hates me."

"She has the expense account, so yes. She doesn't hate you. If anything, she's upset with me because I went against her better judgement and took over Dad's date without telling you up front."

"Ah, she just doesn't trust me then. I can live with that." Her stomach chose that moment to growl, bringing her attention back to the delicious feast that was laid before her. "Unless you have any objections, I'm totally going to have some of that lobster. Because it looks amazing and there's no shell."

She didn't wait for Vince, and quickly filled her plate with a sampling of everything. It had been years since she'd had anything this decadent to eat, not to mention that she hadn't had anything to eat since breakfast.

Vince followed suit, though nowhere near as enthusiastically. "Your ex took your movies, didn't he?"

Marissa paused, her fork halfway to her mouth. There was no point in lying or trying to mislead him. Andrew had screwed her over and she'd been partially to blame. "Yes. Every single one he'd ever bought for me."

"I see." And then he ate a shrimp.

She stared at him for several seconds more before finally eating her own bite of food. There'd been no sympathy like she'd received from her friends, or the expression of outrage her mom had railed at her. It wasn't exactly dismissal, but certainly nowhere near supportive.

Strangely, it felt good.

For months now, Marissa had been an emotional wreck. Every time Andrew's name came up in discussion, her emotions would be wrung dry and her body left a stressed-out mess. For the first time since this entire mess had begun, someone gave Andrew the correct amount of fucks—none.

It was liberating.

A smile crept across her face, and she left herself enough the taste of lobster. Maybe having someone like Vince in her life wasn't going to be a bad thing after all. "You can give Caroline my phone number. Tell her that I'll meet her wherever she wants."

Chapter 8

Vince stared at the phone as Peter Thornton spoke. Peter was oblivious to the drama that was currently unfolding in Vince's office. "So the party is where the real deal will most likely happen. As far as I know, Simon will be in attendance there, but plans to let his executive handle your pitch in the afternoon. Depending on how things go that night, he'll give them the go ahead or not."

Geoff had barged into Vince's office two minutes into the conversation. How he'd found out about it, Vince didn't have a clue. Caroline hadn't put it on his calendar and as far as he knew, no one else was even aware of the call. Currently, his father was leaning back in the large leather guest chair, smirking at Vince. "Hey, Peter. Geoff here."

There was a pause before Peter cleared his throat. "Hi. I didn't know you were in on this meeting."

"I was running a bit late, so Vince had to start without me." Geoff narrowed his gaze, but Vince didn't squirm. "What are we going to need to do to ensure Simon bites on this?"

This was completely fucked up. Vince couldn't understand why Geoff wanted to force his hand and push this deal into Simon's lap. Vince had wanted to have a part to play in the clean energy sector for years, and GreenPro had been his best shot. They didn't need to sell, and Vince could run with the company, and turn it into something great.

Leaning forward, Vince kept his gaze on the speaker phone. "Did you have a chance to look at the proposal I sent over?"

GreenPro had been a brilliant idea when it had first come about. The company wanted to take manure and turn it into renewable energy. The idea was to start with pet waste in cities and to expand it from there. It had the opportunity to be amazing, to expand into a global means to produce green energy. When Vince had first stumbled on it, he'd seen it as opportunity to have his business legacy be more than *Bull Rush*. He could change the direction of his company, put his considerable dollars behind an idea that could make the world a better place.

And now, he had to walk away from it so he could finally have his father out of his life.

"I did. From an investment opportunity, it hits everything Simon typically looks for." The unspoken *but* came through loud and clear. No matter how good things looked on paper, the chance of Simon signing on while Geoff was involved greatly reduced the odds. His father knew this. Why he was insisting on being involved made no sense to Vince.

Geoff stood and began to pace. "I know what he wants. You just pass it along and tell him this will be a onetime offer. I don't plan to play his little games on this deal. Make sure he knows that."

"Peter, how about I send you some additional information to look over, and we can touch base before New York. Say, Wednesday morning?"

The relief in Peter's voice was palpable. "Sounds good. I'll be in touch soon."

Vince ended the call, and spread his hands out flat on the desk. "Why did you do that?"

"What, let him know that we're not going to take any shit from Simon this time around?" Geoff threw his hands up. "Good fucking business sense. I knew you wouldn't say it, so I did."

"I wouldn't say it, because we don't need to antagonize him. Peter is doing his best to make sure this goes the way you want."

"The way *we* want."

"No, *I* want to keep GreenPro, to take it public and expand what they can do. You're the one who is insisting on this deal with Simon."

Geoff marched back to the desk and leaned on it, putting his face inches from Vince's. "What the hell do you know about running an energy company? You're a fucking television star. Simon might be a pretentious ass, but he's the best person to take GreenPro to the next level. And if memory serves, making sure this company succeeds is what you want."

Vince clenched his teeth. "You know it is."

"You're the one who's sanctimoniously preaching about being a good corporate citizen. Ensuring GreenPro is successful is a part of that." Geoff pushed away from the desk and smiled down at him. "You'll make this work and Simon will take GreenPro to the next level."

"Fine." Vince needed him gone before he lost control and punched him. "Just leave me to run things. You showing up unannounced makes things difficult." Understatement of the fucking century. "How the hell did you find out about the meeting?"

Geoff's smile was nothing short of predatory. "I have more than a few friends in the office. Did you know that some of your staff think you're an asshole and love nothing more than to help out your poor father who you treat unfairly?"

Vince stiffened. "So, you tricked them."

"Tricked? I believe that's a matter of perspective." Geoff shrugged before turning to leave, but stopped. "I meant to ask you how your meeting with that sweet little thing went?"

Marissa was on her way to meet Caroline to go on a shopping trip. He'd been thinking about her up until the moment his father had showed up. "Things didn't go exactly how I'd planned." Not a lie, but he didn't want to give his father any ideas about how much he'd enjoyed spending time with Marissa. "I'm not sure she'll come to New York."

"That's too bad. It would have been nice to have met her. Keep me posted." This time, he did leave.

Vince took a breath, held it for a moment before letting it, and all the tension he'd been holding, go. Why couldn't he have a normal relationship with his father? Considering it had been just the two of them since his mom had left, he'd always hoped things would get better between them. But Geoff had gone down a path that Vince couldn't follow. He pushed Vince away at every opportunity.

He'd been alone for so long, lacking in familiar connections, that Vince didn't even know what it was like to have someone to love unconditionally. He'd thought he'd found that with Thea. He'd never been more wrong.

At least with Marissa, there were no pretenses. She'd be there for him when he needed her, and he'd help bail her out. And if he got to treat her to a few nice dresses, some jewelry that she'd normally never be able to afford, then all the better.

He had no idea how long she and Caroline would be today. Caroline had told him the name of the store where she was taking Marissa, but it didn't mean much to him. As long as she looked the part for New York, then he didn't care where they went or how much they spent. He wanted Marissa to smile.

The fact that she'd been screwed over as much as she had, by someone who'd claimed to love her, he knew how much that hurt. Thea had done her part to stomp on his heart, and it had taken him a long time to heal enough to finally move on. If some nice clothing could ease the pain of what her ex had done to her, then Vince was happy to foot the bill.

Leaning back in his chair, he grabbed his phone and fired off a text to Caroline. *She can have whatever she wants. Sexy conservative, if that's a thing. Get something for yourself as well. Consider it a bonus for going above and beyond.*

Then for good measure, he texted Marissa as well. *Have fun shopping.*

He wanted to be there with her. Wanted to see her changing in and out of the dresses that would cling to her body, to see the light in her eyes shine as she morphed into the stunning woman he'd seen on the yacht, transformed from the regular college student who no doubt could give more than a few people a run for their money.

He also had some work of his own to do before they left for New York. He fired off one more text, this time to Nate. *Where's the best place to pick up Blu-rays of Star Wars?*

* * * *

Marissa stood shoulder to shoulder with Caroline as they walked into La Boutique Rose. She'd never even heard of this place, but she knew from the second she'd crossed the threshold that she wasn't even remotely their normal clientele. "I feel like a plebe."

Caroline snorted. "It's a bit over the top here, but I know what Vince likes. This place will be our best bet."

"Hello ladies." An older woman crossed over to them, a painted-on smile perfectly in place. Her gaze crossed from Marissa to Caroline, as she raised a single eyebrow. "How may I help you today?"

Caroline clearly wasn't new to dealing with stores or their employees who perhaps didn't believe they belonged. "We're shopping for an event." She handed over her platinum card. "Start a room for her please. Marissa."

If the woman was impressed, she didn't let on. "Of course. Please let me know if you don't see what you're looking for. We have additional dresses out back that would fit your size beautifully." And with a slight nod, she was gone.

"Yeah, she wouldn't have been so friendly to me on my own." Marissa hated that despite her confidence in most areas of her life, something as simple as a shopping trip would have pushed her deep into the well of self-doubt.

"They're never outright rude to people here, but you'll get that look if they're questioning your bank account." Caroline pointed toward the far back of the shop. "Evening dresses are this way."

Despite the fact Caroline couldn't be more than a few years older than her, Marissa felt as though she was a child trotting behind her mom. "You've shopped here before?"

"Once or twice. Normally when Vince is trying to apologize to me for being a colossal ass." Caroline reached into the rack and pulled out a midnight blue dinner dress. "Understated, yet head turning. What size are you?"

Marissa stared at the dress. It was glorious and no doubt crazy expensive. "I'm a twelve."

Caroline pulled out another one. "Vince said the dresses need to be a bit on the conservative side." She reached in and liberated a rich red dress that had a plunging neckline and would barely come to Marissa's knees. "But if we're shopping, let's make sure you get some fun things as well."

It was strange, one moment Marissa was convinced Caroline hated her and everything that she'd agreed to do with Vince, and the next she was like a sister-in-arms. If it was another test, this wasn't one Marissa was going to pass. She took both dresses from Caroline, draping them over her arm. "I'm not here to take advantage of him. I just needed some help and he offered."

Caroline didn't look at her, instead keeping her gaze on the clothing. "I know. I wasn't certain about you at first, but I do know Vince. He doesn't do anything without a good reason."

Shit, Marissa couldn't help but hear the note of sadness in her voice. "Are you in love with him? Because if I'm causing problems by being here, I'll totally back out."

Caroline was laughing before she'd finished talking. "In love with Vince? Oh my God no. He's great to work with, but we are so not compatible."

"Then what?"

It was weird seeing this confident woman, who clearly had her shit together falter ever so slightly. "I've seen him get screwed over more than once. He tries to come across as invincible, but deep down he's lonely. I promised myself years ago I'd make sure nothing else bad happened to him. Why don't you go try those on?" She smiled as she moved over to another rack. "We'll take pictures and tease Vince with them."

Clearly, she wasn't going to get anything else from Caroline. Marissa nodded and headed toward the back and the dressing room. It wasn't until she was safely hidden away from curious eyes that she looked at the prices.

"Holy shit." She slapped her hand over her mouth to keep any additional sounds from escaping.

The blue dress was over a thousand dollars.

The red dress was nearly two thousand.

This was…insane. And exciting. But mostly insane. That said, she was well past the point of dismissing the need to buy clothing if she was going to go forward and play this part. Standing there, looking at a dress that she could sell to pay off some of her debts, Marissa came to a decision. She was going to do this, go all in playing the part of Vince's sugar baby. In her mind, she shifted everything over from *oh shit, why am I doing this* to *hell yeah, I'm doing this.*

No more regrets or second guessing herself. This was a job, one of the best paying ones she'd ever had. Everything else aside, Marissa was an excellent employee.

She quickly got changed, putting on the red dress first. "Get your camera ready, Caroline. We're going to blow Vince's mind."

Chapter 9

Vince had been fighting his hard-on for days now. He should have known Caroline would have gotten back at him for sending her shopping with Marissa, but he hadn't realized Marissa would have been involved.

He still had the pictures of each dress she'd tried on securely on his phone. There'd been ten in total, each one sexier than the previous. Why he'd assumed Caroline would have been on his side for even a moment was beyond him. She'd been even less help when she'd gotten back, refusing to tell him which of the dresses Marissa had decided on.

"You'll have to wait until the weekend."

And waited he had.

It was his imagination that made that normally simple task all the more difficult. Images of Marissa in various shades and fabrics would pop up in his mind at the worst possible times. Board meetings, phone calls, hell, he couldn't escape them even during his nighttime runs. Each day closer to Friday he got, the greater the frequency Marissa would come to mind.

Now, he was sitting in the back of his limo on his way to pick her up at her house. "How much longer, Steven?"

His driver looked back at him in the rearview mirror. "Five minutes. She's usually waiting outside on the street when I get there."

"In the driveway?"

"No, on the actual sidewalk. I don't even have a fixed address for her. She only gave us a house range."

That was odd. "Thank you."

He could appreciate her not wanting to give her address out to a complete stranger, rich or not, at the beginning of their adventure. She should trust him by now, shouldn't she? Not that he couldn't figure it out if he really needed to, but he got the impression if he crossed that line, then she'd put an end to their relationship.

Another thing they'd have to discuss with her once they arrived in New York.

He tucked away his tablet, pulling his mind from work so Marissa would have his undivided attention. While he had no intention of their relationship being anything other than professional, the last thing he wanted was for her to feel uncomfortable or her presence not wanted.

It was most definitely wanted.

They turned the corner onto a narrow side street, and Vince immediately saw Marissa standing on the sidewalk, as Steven had predicted. She had one medium-sized suitcase beside her and she was wearing a dark green dress that wasn't one of the ones Caroline had sent him a picture of.

Without waiting for Steven, Vince got out of the limo and stood before her. "Hello Marissa."

She shivered, a slight blush coloring her cheeks. "Hello Vince."

"You look stunning." While the dress wouldn't raise any eyebrows, the material clung to her in the perfect way to accentuate her body. Steven swooped in and spirited away her suitcase, while Vince held out his hand for her to take. "You and Caroline clearly had fun."

"We did. She's quite the fascinating woman. I picked her brain about a few of my business courses, which was immensely helpful. I had a test today, and I'm fairly certain that I aced it." His surprise must have been noticeable, as she smiled up at him. "What, you didn't know she'd been working on her business degree?"

She slipped her hand into his as she spoke, and he immediately wrapped his fingers around her. "I did not." He shouldn't be surprised by Caroline's secretive nature, but he was hurt that she'd never mentioned it to him. Perhaps they weren't as good friends as he'd assumed.

"Yeah, she's doing this crazy multiple weekend MBA program. I don't know how she finds the time."

A group of young men were walking down the street toward them. They'd spotted Marissa, and began whistle. Shit, he didn't want anyone to see her. Didn't want to share even a glimpse of her with anyone unworthy. "Let's get going."

Marissa slide into the backseat of the limo and he shut the door before walking around to the other side, where Steven had opened the door for him. Only once they were safely hidden from the rest of the world, did Vince relax.

"Are you okay?" He looked over to Marissa who was frowning at him as she fiddled with her passport. "You look a little stressed."

"I don't get stressed." Tense. Frustrated. Horny. But never stressed. He gave Steven a look in the mirror that had him close the privacy barrier. "Can I get you a drink?"

"Yes please." Even though he knew she'd been in the limo twice now, she still appeared as excited as a kid at a party. "This is so much better than going to Pearson on the subway."

"We're not flying out of Pearson. I rented a private jet."

Marissa blinked at him. "Of course, you rented a jet. What the hell was I thinking?"

"You were thinking like someone who doesn't have more disposable income than they can spend. It won't take us long to get to the airport and be on our way."

Marissa shifted in her seat, the hem of her dress inching further up her thigh with each movement. "Well, this will be another thing I can cross off my bucket list. A jet and a trip to New York. An awesome weekend already, and we haven't even left."

Vince heard her words, but he was more focused on his erection that had roared to life. A little bit of skin, and he was as horny as a teenager. "I watched *Star Wars*."

If he thought she'd been thrilled before, his phrase ignited a storm of excitement he'd never witnessed unfold in another person. "Did you love it? What was your favorite part? There's just something amazing about the scene where he finds Uncle Owen and Aunt Beru burned, and the look on his face. I know exactly what he's thinking and feeling. My heart breaks every time."

Vince couldn't look away from the light shining in her eyes. Her entire face positively glowed as she spoke, sending his own heart racing. He swallowed hard. "I have to admit, I had to replay that scene. I didn't realize what I was seeing at first."

"I was seven when I saw it for the first time. Mom glossed over it as much as she could, but when I wouldn't leave it alone, she had to tell me that they were dead bodies." She leaned forward and took the glass of wine Vince had poured for her. "It was my first experience with a portrayal of death."

He could picture her, curious and excited watching this movie for the first time. "No wonder it left an impression."

She turned sideways to face him, and leaned her head against the seat back. "And you didn't answer my question. What was your favorite part?"

A few scenes came to mind, but given how important this movie clearly was to her, he gave it some thought. "After Obi Wan dies. When Luke has to get back to work to prevent the fighters from blowing them up."

Marissa frowned. "Why?"

"I could relate. He needed time to process everything that had happened to him in such a short period of time, but he couldn't. He had to keep going, keep fighting." It was strange being able to relate so perfectly to a fictional character, and yet, Vince knew intimately what that feel of necessity was like.

Marissa sipped her wine and smiled at him. "I knew you'd enjoy it."

In that moment, Vince felt something click into place in his brain. The way Marissa looked, the joy she had in sharing something that was special to her, melted something inside him that had been holding him back. Without thinking, he reached out and cupped the side of her cheek. "I'm going to kiss you now. You can tell me to stop if you want."

"I thought you said no sex?" But she didn't pull away from him. Instead, she sat up straighter.

"This isn't sex." Yes, he was willing to draw that really flimsy line in the sand. "It's a kiss."

Her gaze flitted to his mouth, before snapping back to his eyes. "Why?"

A thousand excuses passed through his mind in a blink, but none of them were the truth. They'd started this arrangement with honesty about what they both wanted, there was no sense in changing things now. "I don't know. I simply want to kiss you."

Marissa licked her lips her blush spread across her cheeks. "Okay then. But just one."

Vince's cock pulsed at the thought of touching her in any way remotely sexual. It had been months since he'd been with anyone. Thea had been his last, and given how things had ended between them, he'd been more than content to stay far away from any sexual relationship. But resisting Marissa had been like trying to hold back from the lull of a siren's song—bloody fucking impossible.

All he needed was one kiss, a gentle brush of skin on skin that would then sate his curiosity and help get these frustrating images from his mind. Once he knew what she tasted like, what her skin felt like under his mouth, only then could he *know* she was the same as every other woman. He could label her, create a little compartment in his mind for *Marissa*, and get on with his life.

He leaned in slowly, anticipating the first brush of skin on skin, nearly holding his breath for that contact. But if nothing else, he should have learned that Marissa wasn't like the other women of his experience. Without hesitation, she reached up, cupped his cheek with her free hand and kissed him hard.

Fuck.

The taste of wine exploded across his tongue, as she licked at the inside of his mouth. Her nails lightly scraped against his cheek, picking at his stubble as she slid her hand along his face. His shock at her taking the lead fell away, only to be replaced with his overwhelming desire to consume every inch of her.

Somewhere in the back of his mind, he was aware enough to reach for her wine glass and set it in the cup holder beside him. He managed this entire process without breaking their contact. With both her hands free, Marissa cupped his face and held him in place while she deepened their contact. Vince sighed, and let her take charge of the very thing he'd wanted to do with her since he'd first watched her step onto his yacht.

Her skin was soft and the scent of something floral drifted from her skin to wash over him. He wrapped his arms around her, practically pulling her onto his lap. God, this was such a deliciously horrible idea, but there was no way in hell he was about to stop kissing her. Not when her breasts were pressed against his chest and her thighs were draped across his legs. Especially, not when Marissa was making that cute little purr in the back of her throat.

Vince let her direct the kiss, loved that he didn't have to be the one in charge. Marissa knew what she wanted, and wasn't afraid to take it.

When she finally pulled back, her eyes were heavy and her lips were swollen. "Just the one kiss."

"Yes." His voice came out low and rough. He didn't sound like himself and his skin felt as though there was an electric current coursing beneath it. "Just the one."

"That's good." She licked her lips. "Because this isn't about sex. Neither one of us wanted that."

Right. The no sex policy had been his idea.

He didn't want another woman to capture his heart, only to manipulate him into a toxic relationship based on lies. Thea had used her body to get to his bank account—and he'd been fool enough to fall for it.

But Marissa was different. Wasn't she?

He ran a finger down her cheek, taking pleasure in the way she leaned against his touch. "I can't do another relationship. I need your help, and I'll help you in return. But that's all I can offer."

"Well, that and a single kiss." If Marissa was upset by his confession, she didn't show it. "That's fine. I'm not exactly ready to throw my hat back into the dating ring. Andrew really fucked me over and while I know you're not him, I need…space."

It was strange, their relationship. They came from completely different walks of life, and yet they'd both been burned in similar ways. "So, we work together. Business partners in a little venture that will allow us to both come out on top."

The smile Marissa gave him made her eyes sparkle. "Sealed with a kiss."

"Indeed. This weekend we'll have fun. You'll make me look good, and I'll help out with some of your bills." It then hit him. "We never did talk about your fee for coming with me."

"How about this?" She leaned half against him and the back of the seat. "You agree to pay off one of my debts and I'll make sure every single person at this party thinks you are the kindest, sweetest person they've ever met."

He had no doubt she'd be able to pull it off. "My goal is to ensure ETS Investments buys one of my companies. My father is insisting on us selling to this particular company, and this one alone."

Marissa nodded. "Okay then. I'll help you win them over and you'll pay off my bill." She held out her hand. "Deal?"

Rather than shake it, Vince lifted the back of her hand to his lips and kissed her. "Deal."

Marissa shivered. "Good. Then tell me everything I need to know about this group and we'll get started."

Chapter 10

Marissa had only been in New York for an hour now, but so far everything was well beyond her expectations. If she'd thought the traffic in Toronto had been bad, it was nothing compared to the drive from the airport into the city. The limo had picked them up, making the entire ordeal far easier to handle. Well, except for the fact she'd hadn't quite recovered from their previous limo ride. Her lips were still sensitive from their kiss, her body primed and ready for action.

Thank God, she was going to have her own bed, because she needed to get herself off in the worst way.

She'd never heard of The Greenwich Hotel, but Vince assured her that her stay would be a treat. That was the bloody understatement of the century. The lobby had been elegant and far more spa like than she'd assumed a hotel would be. But that was nothing compared to the moment Vince opened the door to the penthouse suite.

Marissa held her breath as they walked inside. "This is the most beautiful room I've ever been in." She walked fully into the room, touching the tables, chairs, even the walls as she went. "Oh God, there's an outdoor hot tub!"

"No two rooms are the same here." Vince draped his coat along the back of the chair. "I asked for the penthouse specifically for the outside terrace. Tomorrow while I'm at my meeting, you can enjoy the complementary spa treatment. I hear it's wonderful."

The city lights brightened the night sky, and the sounds from the city echoed up to her as she stepped out onto the terrace. This was a fantasy world compared to her tiny basement apartment. The smell of must and mold had been swapped for incense and wood. She continued to touch everything she saw, as though this dream would somehow become less real if she couldn't remain grounded. The brick ledges and stone paths led her around the secret garden, high above the city streets.

She could feel Vince's eyes on her as she made her way around to the stone hot tub. The water gurgled as it flowed, steam rising into the air with an effervescent hiss. "I'll definitely be trying this out later."

"They can get you a swim suit if you don't have one." Vince stood in the doorway, his arms crossed and his lips turned into a soft smile. "They have bathrobes waiting for you in your room."

Shit, she'd forgotten that part of the deal was her having her own room for this little adventure. "Which one is mine?"

"I figured I'd let you pick the one you'd be the most comfortable with. They've brought our bags up to the living room for now."

Seeing him standing there, light from the outside fireplace flickering across his skin, sent a shiver of sexual awareness through her. God, he was far too fucking handsome for his own good. For hers as well. It was going to be brutal to keep her hands to herself, to keep their arrangement completely about playing a part, and having nothing at all to do with sex.

It was getting more difficult to remember why having sex with him was such a bad thing to begin with.

Forcing her gaze away, she sat down on the edge of the hot tub and dangled her feet inside. "What time is your meeting tomorrow?"

"Not until eleven. We'll have time to eat and I'll be able to get you set for the day. We don't have our first event until three."

She'd have to make sure she had her game face ready. "Excellent. That will give me time to get ready."

Vince toed off his dress shoes, before walking over to join her. He stood still as he pulled his socks off and rolled up his dress pants to his knees. "It would be easier if we just got naked and went in."

Her nipples hardened. "I believe that goes against the rules, Mr. Taylor."

Vince snorted. "It does. I guess this will have to do." He sat down beside her, and slipped his feet into the water, careful not to get his pants wet. "That's far more relaxing than it should be."

"Oh please. You wear dress shoes all the time." She picked up the stiletto closest to her. "These things are brutal."

Vince took the shoe from her, examining it closely. "Honestly, I don't know how women don't break their necks in these things."

"I'm impressed with women who can run in them. I have a friend, Naomi, who I've seen race to catch a bus in heels. I swear she could run a six-minute mile wearing them."

There was something wonderful about hearing Vince chuckle. It was a sound she suspected he didn't make all that often, which was a shame. It was magical, warm in a way that felt like a hug. "You're far too serious."

His gaze shifted to a point in the sky. "That's something my life requires from me. Serious, smart. But I have to be enough of a playboy to make the media happy. The coverage helps keep my business relevant."

"And staying relevant is what helps pay the bills." It was so weird hearing some of what she'd learned in her business classes being spoken of so cynically. "I'm sorry that's how things have gone for you."

"I'm not." There was something in his tone that gave her the impression that wasn't exactly true. "I'm a rich, white male who is in complete control of his life. I have so much privilege I can't fathom what it means to struggle. What kind of man would I be to not be grateful for the life I've been given?"

Marissa stared at him hard. For the life of her, she didn't know if he was somehow trying to get her to feel sorry for him, or if he was genuinely aware of the blessings in his life. "You'd be an utter asshole."

"Exactly. That's something I try to avoid at all costs." He reached down and splashed some water with his fingers. "Though if you ask Caroline, I fail miserably at that."

"You do come across as a bit of a controlling jerk at times." She reached down and splashed some water as well. "But you're helping me out, so I can't exactly be too hard on you."

"I do try and help others. That's one of the reasons I want to see GreenPro in the right hands, it has the potential to do a lot of good. We need more sources of clean energy if we're going to make a dent in climate change."

"In order to do that, you need to sell it to these ETS Investment people?"

He frowned. "No, I'd much rather keep the business myself and see how far I can take it. But I'm not the majority owner, my father is. He wants to sell it to Simon's company, and I'm not exactly in a position to stop him. Like it or not, I need to ensure ETS buys GreenPro."

She'd never considered someone in Vince's position would feel as though they had no control. "And in order to do *that*, you need me to pretend to be your significant other so they think you're respectable."

"Let's say Dad's history with Simon is complicated at best. I've unfortunately been painted with the same brush as him, which makes these negotiations difficult. Having you…paying you to be here, it takes away some of my tarnish. If someone as down to earth as you will be with me, then perhaps I've been redeemed."

"As long as we both behave." Her words were meant to be teasing, but they sounded serious even to herself.

"Yes, both of us. It shouldn't be that hard to remain professional."

She knew that he wanted to keep things as calm and steady as he could. But while she didn't want to open up something that neither of them could control, there was no denying the connection they shared in the limo. "That might not be as easy as either of us anticipated."

Vince looked over at her, and for the first time since she'd first met him, he looked to be completely relaxed. "You're not exactly the type of person I thought you would be."

"You either. When we met on the yacht, I had...assumptions. Given how many problems I've had with men recently, I thought someone like you was the last type of man I'd ever want to be around, let alone kiss." Marissa ignored the way her face heated, praying her blush wouldn't be overly noticeable in the glow from the patio lights.

If Vince noticed, he didn't say anything. "I shouldn't have done that."

"I seem to remember being the one climbing onto your lap." God, there'd been no stopping her once she'd gotten the idea in her head. She'd needed to feel his lips on hers, wanted to know how hard his body would be beneath her. "I promise, I won't do anything else like that while we're here."

Come hell or high water, she'd keep it in her pants.

Vince nodded, before climbing to his feet. Water trickled down his legs, making little rivers in the coarse hair that covered his skin. "I need to check some emails."

Exhaustion washed over her. "I think I'll call it a night as well. Best go pick out my room."

She was about to push herself up, when Vince reached down and offered his hand. "Allow me."

Shit, the feel of his skin on hers, his strength as he helped her to her feet sent a shiver through her body. "Thanks."

They didn't immediately pull apart, and Marissa gave in to her desire to lean her body fully against his. God, this was such a horrible idea. Hadn't they just finished saying that neither of them wanted to take things beyond the kiss? Her past with Andrew was still causing her daily trauma, something that she needed to sort through before she could even think about having a relationship with someone, let alone develop feelings for someone who'd clearly stated that they weren't interested. That would be far worse than anything that had happened with Andrew; instead of being duped, she'd be walking into a disaster, eyes wide-open.

Marissa let Vince's hand fall away as she moved back to the penthouse. "If it's okay with you, I'll take the bedroom closest to the bathroom. I tend to get up through the night, and I wouldn't want to wake you."

"I can bring your bags in for you." He fell into step behind her. "Why don't you go check it out and I'll grab them."

"Thanks."

The marble floor was cool against the wet soles of her feet as she padded through the living room to the far bedroom. Marissa held her breath as she stepped inside, her gaze touching upon the beautiful natural stone and wood. Along the center of the back wall sat the large, queen-sized bed. The solid piece of wood that comprised the headboard must have come from one hell of a big tree. She couldn't imagine how the hell they'd been able to get it into the penthouse in the first place. The fireplace was already lit, the warmth from the flames filling the room and chasing away the chill from her damp legs.

The scrape and grind of her suitcase wheels snapped her attention back to the door. Vince didn't hesitate as he stepped inside and spun the case around. "Ah, this is an excellent spot. If the fire dies down and you get cold, there are extra blankets in the closet. The kitchen is fully stocked, as is the bar. Make sure you help yourself to whatever you want. And if there's something missing, let them know downstairs and they'll get it for you."

"Thanks." It was hard to look away from Vince; shadows from the fireplace dancing across his chest and face. She forced herself to turn her back to him. "I better get changed and turn in for the night."

Vince didn't respond immediately. She listened as he shuffled around for a moment, before clearing his throat. "I'm going to head out for a run. I won't be longer than an hour."

Shit, now she was going to have images of him all sweaty, pounding the streets of New York. "Okay. Have fun."

"I'll see you in the morning." And with a click of the door behind her, he was gone.

Marissa sat down on the edge of her bed with a sigh. God, her life...

Her cell phone in her purse rang. She scrambled off the bed, snatching it from her purse and answering it before looking at the call display. "Hello?"

"Hello Marissa."

Andrew.

Marissa swallowed, her gaze flicking to her closed bedroom door. "What the hell do you want?"

"Baby, I'm just calling to check in on you. Can't a friend stay in touch?"

"You're not my friend. You fucking screwed me over." Her voice echoed in the room. The last thing she wanted to do was have Vince come in and see her a mess. "How did you get this number?"

"Your mom is still a sweetie. I told her that I wanted to apologize to you and she was more than happy to give it to me."

She was going to have to have a long conversation with her mom once she got back to Toronto. "Don't bother putting me on speed dial. I'll be dumping it as soon as I get home."

"Oh. Where are you, baby bird?"

There was a time long ago, when she'd loved his pet name for her. Now, the sound of it turned her stomach. "None of your goddamned business."

"I just want to make sure you're okay."

"Then you shouldn't have fucked me over. Goodbye." Without waiting for another word, she ended the call. Then she turned her phone off.

Dear God.

Her entire body shook as she set her phone beside her on the bed. Andrew never did anything without a reason, nor did he simply reach out to see how she was doing. He didn't give a flying fuck how she was.

No, Andrew was clearly up to something.

She couldn't afford for him to know how badly she was doing, nor about her deal with Vince. While she doubted there was anything Andrew could do to him, Vince didn't deserve to have her shit-show of a life spill over onto him.

She'd have to keep her phone off and her mind focused for the rest of the weekend. She'd be there for Vince, help him however he needed her to so he could sell his company and then she'd get the hell out of his life.

For both their sakes, she had no choice.

Chapter 11

Vince knew something was wrong the moment Marissa crept out of her room that morning. The sparkle that had been in her eyes last night while they'd flirted in the hot tub was gone. The smile she gave him as she walked into the kitchen didn't reach her eyes. Wrapped up in the fluffy bathrobe, she looked like an orphan plucked from the streets from one of those feel-good movies.

It didn't suit her.

"I made an assumption that you like coffee. If I'm wrong, there's also a variety of teas."

She shoved her hands deep into her pockets as she walked around the side of the counter. "Coffee, please. And I'll take some cream if they have any."

"Of course." Vince topped her up and handed her the mug. He gave her another look, trying to figure out if she was simply not a morning person, or if something had happened when he wasn't looking. "Did you sleep well?"

"God, yes. Those sheets are the softest things I've ever felt. I'd take them home with me, but I don't think I could afford the bill." She took a sip of her coffee and moaned. "That's so not bargain coffee."

"I'm partial to Jamaican Blue Mountain coffee. I've stayed here before and I believe they've made a note about my preferences. It's always stocked when I stay over."

She looked at him for several seconds before giving her head a shake. "Must be nice."

It was weird how he'd never been as painfully aware of his own privilege as he was around her. Not that she ever did any one thing to make him uncomfortable, but rather her reactions to the things he took for granted cut like a paper cut. Not deep, but painful and annoyingly present.

Marissa slid onto the stool and took another long sip of her coffee. "How was your run? I didn't hear you leave. Or come back for that matter."

"Good. I needed to stretch my legs after all the sitting yesterday."

He'd also needed to put a damper on his libido after sitting with her in the hot tub. Running with a hard-on had been painful, but thankfully the exercise helped cool him off. It would have been far too easy for his own liking to have picked her up and kissed her until they fell into bed. Seeing as that broke all of his self-imposed rules, Vince had to get out.

Coming back, sweaty and tired he'd thought everything was fine. Until he climbed into the shower in the bathroom next to where she'd been sleeping. *Hello again, hard-on.*

"I'll probably try and get out for a walk today." She hugged the mug between her hands as she leaned her elbows on the counter. "There's so much I want to see."

His meeting with Peter was set for three hours from now. Vince had wanted to review some notes with him, to ensure he had a feel for everything Simon Berry would want to discuss. It was practical, given how little time they were going to have in New York, how badly he wanted ETS to buy GreenPro.

But standing there, staring at Marissa and seeing the excitement on her face, where moments earlier there'd been sadness, did things to his insides he didn't fully comprehend. "Where do you want to go?"

"I've always wanted to go to The Met. I've seen it in so many movies, and read about it in books. It looks amazing. God, and I want to see either the Statue of Liberty, or the Empire State Building. Or go to Times Square."

The more she spoke, the more palatable her excitement became. Vince didn't remember a time that he'd been that excited about sightseeing. Hell, he didn't remember the last time he went and did anything for pleasure in a city that wasn't Toronto. Sad state of affairs, but the truth. When you know you can come back to a place at any moment, it takes away some of the urgency to squeeze in as much as you can into every moment.

How many times had he been to New York? And of all those times, how many did he take time for himself to look around? None.

Marissa swallowed down the rest of her coffee. "I know you said something about a spa visit, but I don't want to miss out on seeing anything."

A tingle deep in his chest threatened to explode through him. Excitement wasn't supposed to feel this way, was it? He cleared his throat, hoping she didn't notice the impact she was having on him. "How about this? You go to the spa treatment while I change my meeting to a call. Once you're done, I should be finished as well and we can go see the city together."

She blinked at him, a smile exploding across her face. "Really? That wouldn't be a problem? I mean, we're here for your work stuff. I don't want to do anything that could jeopardize your sale."

He waved away her concern. "It's not a problem. I only need to touch base with my contact, and I can do that just as easily on the phone as I can in person. The real meeting will be tonight over dinner. That's when we'll need to be ready to go."

It was surprising how good he felt seeing Marissa's excitement. Gone was the dark cloud that had accompanied her from the bedroom and in its place, was a radiance that lit the room. "Oh. This is amazing. Okay. Ah, how about I get dressed. Then I'll figure out the spa thing."

God, he wanted to laugh at her silly grin, but he squashed his own giddiness down and replaced it with a smile. "Not much to figure out. I'll call down and they'll get ready for you. Go change and we'll get this day started."

He didn't have to prod her twice. In a heartbeat, she was on her feet and bounding back to her bedroom.

Vince stood in the kitchen, watching after where she'd disappeared. His body was warm from her excitement, his mood radically improved from the dour concern he'd been feeling over the details of this sale. He was going sightseeing with a woman he barely knew. And yet, it didn't matter. Marissa took pleasure in the unexpected things. In the short time she'd been in his life, she'd forced him to really look at the things he took for granted.

A trip in a limo became an erotic ride.

Putting his feet in a hot tub, a hedonist delight.

And now a sightseeing tour, an adventure he couldn't help but look forward to.

Things in his daily life were suddenly exotic, exciting; his perspective on his life skewed whenever he saw how she looked at things.

It wasn't exactly what he'd expected when he'd decided to go forward with the sugar daddy plan. For all his money and privilege, he'd assumed their relationship would be nothing beyond his ability to provide for her during their agreement. How closed minded was he to assume she had nothing she could bring to the table. Everyone had something to offer, no matter their social or economic status. His father had taught him that early on in his life. Clearly, it was a lesson Vince had forgotten.

He put his mug down and walked over to the phone. "Hello. Ms. Roy will be ready for her spa treatment within thirty minutes. Is that a problem?"

"Not at all, Mr. Taylor. Please send her down whenever she's ready and one of our girls will be waiting."

He hung up when Marissa came back out. She'd slipped into a sundress that hugged her frame perfectly. "I don't know if it's too cold out for this, but I figure I can change if I need to once I'm done."

"You'll be fine." He'd make sure they had the limo take them anywhere they wanted to go. "They'll be ready for you once you go down."

"Okay." She looked around, making a beeline for her purse. "I haven't gone to a spa since my eighteenth birthday. It was a gift—" She froze, the expression on her face falling. "It doesn't matter."

No doubt, it had been a gift from the ex. "Don't worry about your purse. Everything is covered. If they have any products that you want, they'll add it to the bill."

"I don't think I'll need anything."

"I insist. The last few times I stayed here I didn't take advantage of the spa. I need to get my money's worth this time."

Thea wouldn't have argued and would have made sure to get as much as she could. It would have simply been an expected part of her experience. With Marissa, he wasn't sure she'd ask for anything beyond the basics. He got that she didn't want to be beholden to him any more than necessary, but what was the point of having a sugar daddy if she didn't take advantage of him?

Marissa set her purse down with a shrug. "We'll see. I might not even like the stuff."

"I'll be here when you're done. Then we'll go out for lunch and see the sights."

Vince stood with his hands in his pockets as she came over and placed a kiss on his cheek. It was only a peck, but the brush of her lips against his skin was as erotic as the kiss they'd shared in the car last night. "Thank you."

He didn't move again until she'd left the penthouse. Only once the door was safely closed did he reach down and press hard against his erection. Shit, keeping things professional was proving harder than he'd anticipated. It was one thing to be sexually attracted to her, but it was something else to feel this emotional tug.

Marissa was too sweet a person to be anything but upfront with her. She'd been honest about what she'd wanted from him. She didn't deserve for him to change the rules, to steer her toward a sexual relationship when he'd been so adamant that wasn't what he'd wanted.

You need to keep it in your fucking pants, asshole.

As soon as the sale of GreenPro went through, Vince would pay off whatever debts Marissa had and set her free. Then, he could get on with his life and leave her to enjoy hers.

* * * *

Marissa's body still tingled from the cream the masseuse had rubbed all over her skin this morning. Despite what Vince had said, she didn't take any of the products that the spa had to offer for herself. Yes, it would be amazing to have them to use, but it would also be a reminder that she wouldn't be able to afford to have them again. Eventually, this fairytale would come to an end and she'd wake back up sleeping in her hovel.

She did, however, get a small package to take home to Naomi. It was because of her Marissa was in New York enjoying the experience of a lifetime, the least she could do was bring her back a thank-you present. She'd safely tucked the few creams that they'd wrapped up for her into her suitcase before Vince whisked her away in the limo.

"I know you might be hungry, but there's more to see at The Met than we'd be able to manage in a day. We can grab something quick, but you'll want as much time as possible inside."

Stepping inside the museum had been overwhelming. She'd believed Vince when he said they wouldn't have time to see everything, but there was enough in the great hall to keep her busy for ages.

He held out his arm for her, and she took it without a thought. "Left or right?"

She looked in either direction. "Which do you recommend?"

"I've only been here once before, years ago. Everything I would have known would be outdated." He pulled out the little map. "Egyptian or Greek?"

That was a no-brainer. "Egyptian."

He turned them toward the right. "This way."

Marissa was floored by everything. She'd walk over to a display, reading as much as she could, talking to anyone who seemed to know more than she did, all while Vince trailed along behind her. It was one of the most amazing experiences of her life and she had a near-perfect stranger to thank for it.

They'd barely made it to the armor section when Vince stepped up against her. "I hate to do this to you, but we need to head out. We'll need time to change before supper."

Right, their event for tonight. It was amazing how quickly she'd forgotten about the reason they were in New York to begin with. "Sure. Sorry."

He shook his head, his lips twitching in a half smile. "Why apologize? This is the best afternoon I've had in a long while."

"I doubt you following me around a museum is the best day you've had ever. I mean, you've been to resorts and other countries. I know you've been to movie premieres and have been on television." She slipped her arm around his and let him lead her to the entrance. "But I appreciate this. I'm going to have to find a way to get back here so I can see the rest."

There was something odd in the way he looked at her moments before they stepped out into the sunlight. If he was going to say something about their day, he held it back. "The car is this way."

Climbing back into the limo was beginning to feel less strange than the first few times she'd done it. It was even beginning to feel natural having Vince slide onto the seat beside her. "Tonight will be a formal event. I might have to leave you to speak to the spouses while I make my pitch to Simon. If that happens, I won't abandon you for long."

She snorted. "After everything that you've done for me today, don't worry about it. I'll be the best pretend girlfriend you've ever had. I'll have them eating out of my hand in no time."

At least, she hoped she would.

Vince pulled out his phone and scrolled through his emails. "As long as you have a good time, that's all that matters. I'd hate to see you upset again."

Her mind was racing a mile a minute, but screeched to a halt. "What do you mean?"

"You were upset this morning when you woke up. Yes, this weekend is about work, but there's no reason why you can't have a good time as well." He set his phone down and looked her right in the eyes. "The real world is far away in Toronto. Right now, for the next twenty-two hours is about having fun. Relaxing. Nothing can hurt you here while you're with me."

Marissa forgot how to breathe. "I…I'm not hurt."

Vince narrowed his gaze. "You mean I completely misread you this morning? You weren't upset?"

"I mean, I was. I'd gotten a call…look that doesn't matter." She licked her lips, unable to form a logical thought. "I don't need you to protect me."

"I'm not. You're here helping me out. I want you to know that I'm here to help you as well. Think of it as a bit of a strange friendship."

"Friends?"

He cocked an eyebrow and went back to reading his email. "There are worse things we could be."

There were also better things they could be—like lovers.

No, no no no, that so wasn't going to happen between them. She did not need the complication of a physical relationship with Vince being added to everything else going on in her life. Even if she wanted nothing more than to strip him naked and crawl all over his body. "Sure, we can go with being friends."

Vince smiled. "Good."

Marissa wasn't so sure about that, but she was certain she'd find out one way or the other.

Chapter 12

Marissa's heart raced as they entered the restaurant and stepped into God only knew what kind of situation. Vince had filled her in on the details of his business dealings with ETS Investments and how the CEO Simon Berry was far more conservative than she was probably used to. She didn't exactly consider herself as crazy liberal, more of a live and let live person. But she really didn't know any super conservative people, unless she counted Sarah Murphy from her mom's church. But even Sarah was more about her own actions than what other people did. No, Marissa was a pretty average girl when it came to her outlook on life.

Then again, Vince was her sugar daddy, so clearly she was more open minded about certain things than some other people would be.

Vince's large body beside her was a reassuring presence as they walked into a private area. She'd chosen the midnight blue dress Caroline had insisted she buy, knowing it looked good on her, but shouldn't raise any eyebrows. Well, except for Vince's when he saw her step out into the living room.

If looks could strip a person, she'd have been naked on his bed in half a second.

"Relax, Marissa." He gave her hand a little squeeze. "You look like you're going to break in two."

"I'm just scared I'm going to screw this up for you." The closer they'd gotten to the restaurant, the more she'd started to freak out. "I know how important this sale is."

Vince leaned in and placed a kiss on her temple. "You let me worry about the sale. Enjoy the food and drinks and be yourself. Everyone will love you."

It wasn't as though she was ever going to see any of these people again. She took a deep breath and put on her best smile. This was her job, the entire reason she'd come to New York in the first place. She could do this.

"Vince!" A man several inches shorter than Vince, but every bit as handsome, strode over to them. His brown eyes belied intelligence. "Dear God, where have you been hiding this beauty?"

Nothing changed on his face, but Marissa couldn't help but notice the slight tensing in Vince's arm. "Peter, good to see you. Marissa, this is Peter Thornton, a business associate of mine who's helping me coordinate the sale of GreenPro. Peter, this is my girlfriend, Marissa Roy."

"Well, you're a lucky man." Peter took Marissa's hand, and instead of shaking it, lifted it to his lips, kissing her softly. "Wonderful to meet you."

"Likewise." The blush warmed her face in record time and she grinned as he winked at her, releasing her hand. "Are you as excited about poop power as Vince is? Or do you simply see this as a great investment?"

Peter looked at her for half a moment before bursting out laughing. "Oh, I like her better than the last one." He began to scan the room. "Simon isn't here yet, but I expect he'll be along shortly."

"That's fine. It will give us a few minutes to get prepared. I'll catch up with you once I get Marissa settled." Vince grabbed her hand and led her away from Peter toward a waiter. "I need a drink."

"He seems like a nice guy. Are you two good friends? Also, *girlfriend?*"

"We've partnered on a number of deals over the years. Peter is actually a good friend of my agent. He helped me land the gig on *Bull Rush.*" He grabbed two glasses of wine from the tray, one red and one white. "Here. And I can't exactly call you my sugar baby, can I?"

Right. That was a bit of a problem. "Girlfriend it is."

"If anyone gives you a hard time, let me know." Vince's gaze had locked onto someone who'd just entered the room. "There's Simon."

"So, it's show time?"

"Yup." He swallowed down a far too healthy portion of his wine, before placing it on a passing waiter's tray. But before he took a step, his entire body tensed. "Fuck."

Turning to see where he was looking, she was surprised to see an older man standing there, someone who looked vaguely familiar. "Who's that?"

"My father." The way he said the word *father* made it sound more like a curse than an endearment. "He's not supposed to be here."

So this was the elder Taylor who Vince had found it necessary to save her from. "Didn't you say he's the reason you have to try and sell to Simon in the first place?"

"Yes." The tension rolled off Vince in waves. "But he's not exactly predictable. Not to mention, he and Simon don't exactly get along."

"Why?"

"Dad slept with Simon's ex-wife."

"Oh." Well, that was going to make things challenging. "His name's Geoff, right?"

"Yes."

She watched as Geoff moved around the room, flirting and smiling with every woman he saw. In a lot of ways, Vince appeared very much like his dad. They had the same smile, same charm. She gave him a good hard look and knew exactly what she had to do. "You leave your father to me and go make your sale with Simon."

"No." Vince turned and took her by the hands. "Whatever you're thinking, don't."

She'd agreed to come to New York to help him in any way possible. While she'd assumed that had meant playing nice with the people he introduced her to, now she saw the chance to really help. Vince looked angry, and even a bit nervous. Vince Taylor, playboy multimillionaire was worried that things wouldn't go his way. "Remember what you said earlier, we're a team. Our weird little friendship is stronger than whatever your father has planned. Introduce us and I'll keep him busy until you're done speaking with Simon." How hard could it be to smile and flirt with him? To keep him occupied long enough for Vince to do what he needed to?

"You don't know what he's like." Vince reached up and cupped her cheek. "There was a reason I chose to meet you that first date, rather than let him."

"I know. And you've warned me. But look around." She waited until he did as she asked. "There are tons of people here. And it's not like I need to distract him for long. Just enough so you can take Simon somewhere so the two of you can chat. Then you can come rescue me." After everything that had happened with Andrew, she had more than enough experience dealing with assholes that she could handle Geoff Taylor. "Trust me."

Vince looked startled for a moment, before finally nodding. "I'm not going to leave you for long."

"You'll leave me for as long as you need to secure the deal. Now, why don't you introduce me to your dad?" He started to move away from her, but Marissa held him back. "Actually, one moment, please."

"What?"

She reached up, straightened his tie and smoothed down the lapels of his jacket. "No sense in giving your dad a reason to give you a hard time."

His gaze was intense as she fiddled with his clothing, and it sent a shiver through her. Vince Taylor, multimillionaire and television personality, looked ready to devour her. Probably not the best look if he wanted to shake off his playboy reputation, but there wasn't much she could do about it now.

Marissa bit down on her lower lip, suddenly overwhelmed by the intensity of his gaze. "Shall we go say hi?"

Vince nodded, and took her hand in his. It was different than having her hand on his arm. Their fingers laced, their palms pressed together was far more intimate than even the passionate kiss they'd shared in the limo.

"Father." Even knowing Vince was angry that his father was in attendance, there was no way anyone would have been able to tell from the warm way he greeted his dad. "I'm surprised to see you here. I didn't think you were coming."

Geoff Taylor was as handsome close up as he was across the room. Vince had clearly gotten his good looks from his dad, though Geoff's blue eyes were so pale they almost appeared gray. When he turned his gaze fully on Marissa, she fought the urge to squirm and squeezed Vince's hand a bit tighter.

Geoff's gaze slide back to Vince. "My schedule opened up and I was able to be here after all. I let Simon know that I would be around tonight. No sense in giving the old man a heart attack."

"I'm sure Simon appreciated knowing." There was a coolness to Vince's tone that hadn't been there moments before. "I've already worked things out with Peter. We're discussed the benefits of the sale with their board, which went well. Simon will most likely accept their advice to buy the company. It appears that you're going to get exactly what you want."

Marissa hated not knowing what to do, but there was no way she was going to insert herself into this conversation. Because despite what was being said, she knew there was more they were communicating with what they *weren't* saying. The last thing she wanted to do was to make things worse for Vince.

But her moment of invisibility vanished when Geoff turned fully to face her and smiled. "You're being rude, son. Who's this gorgeous creature?"

Vince's muscles tightened, but she gave his hand a gentle squeeze before dropping it and offering her had to Geoff. "Hi there. I'm Marissa. Vince's girlfriend."

Geoff frowned briefly before letting out a laugh that drew the attention of the people around them. "Of course, you are." He lifted her hand and kissed the back of it, much the same way Peter had. Unlike Peter, the brush of Geoff's lips on her skin didn't exactly sit right with her. "Pleasure my dear. You look far different than your pictures."

She tried to keep her body relaxed, but it was proving difficult with Geoff's continued hold on her hand. "Better I hope."

There was something in his gaze as it traveled down her body that unsettled her. "I'm sorry we didn't have a chance to meet sooner, but it seems my son was intent on keeping you all to himself."

"Marissa is here to help, nothing more." Vince swayed closer to her so his shoulder brushed against hers.

"I'm sure that's the truth." Geoff clearly had his own ideas what it meant to have a sugar baby. "Well, at least I didn't raise a fool."

Off behind them an older man and a younger woman walked into the room. Several people close to the door started smiling and speaking a bit brighter. Others walked over and spoke with the man. Both Vince and Geoff turned and she knew immediately that this was Simon Berry.

Simon was an older man, slight in stature, with a full head of white hair. He smiled at them, but Marissa got the impression it was one of instinct rather than any actual pleasure. Geoff took a step toward Simon, but Vince put his hand out and stopped him. "What are you doing?"

"Going to speak to my friend. I didn't come all this way to sit on the sidelines."

"You weren't supposed to be here at all." For a brief moment, Marissa thought Vince might punch his dad. "You'd agreed to let me run this sale."

"And you will." Geoff took another step, but Vince didn't let him go. "You're going to cause a scene."

"I'm trying to prevent one."

While their little drama was unfolding, neither man noticed Simon see them and begin to approach. Marissa cleared her throat and not knowing what else to do, she stepped between the men and smiled. "Hello Mr. Berry. I'm Marissa Roy. Thank you so much for inviting us to your event tonight."

Unlike her introduction to Peter or Geoff, when Simon took her hand, it was for a simple shake. "A pleasure to meet you, Ms. Roy."

She wasn't some naïve kid, who'd never been involved with a business deal before. She'd accompanied Andrew on several of his little ventures when they'd been together. She'd insisted on that given she'd signed her name on several contracts. Being under the gaze of someone in a position of power wasn't anything new.

What she'd never experienced before, was to feel as though her brain were being dissected. "Nice to meet you as well."

He then let his laser gaze pass between Vince and his father. "I was surprised to hear you were coming, Geoff. Vince never mentioned it when I spoke with him last week."

"It was a last-minute decision. You know how those things go."

"I do." Simon turned to Vince. "I heard your presentation to the board went well."

Marissa watched as Vince's shoulders relaxed and his easy smile slipped into place. "It did. They brought up some excellent questions. A few that I actually need to get back to them with some answers."

"I have a few questions of my own." Simon looked at her a moment longer before turning his attention fully on Vince. "Perhaps we should manage our business first. Then we can enjoy the rest of the evening."

That was a dismissal if she'd ever heard one. "Geoff, did Vince tell you that he took me to The Met today?" She gave Vince's hand a squeeze before turning and placing her hand on Geoff's arm. "I've been to the ROM before, but this was crazy impressive." Carefully, she began to walk, hoping Geoff would come with her.

When he did, she caught Vince's gaze. He smiled and his relief was obvious. Simon then led him to a table in the far corner of the room.

"That was neatly done on your part." Geoff fell into step beside her. "I can see why my son is paying to have your around."

Marissa stopped moving, as numbness struck her in her chest. "He's not paying me." Well, not in cash. Not yet at least.

Geoff snorted. "I assume you paid for your own flight and clothing? Or is that dress from a previous sugar daddy? With your looks, I wouldn't be surprised if you had them lined up around the block."

Marissa dropped his arm and took a half step away. "I'm not like that."

"Why shouldn't you be?" He let his gaze travel down her body. "You're beautiful and clearly perceptive. A woman with your talents should take advantage of them."

This was the reason Vince had tried as hard as he had to keep Marissa away from his father. And for the first time since she'd signed up for the website, she felt uncomfortable. "If you could excuse me for a moment. I need to find the ladies' room."

The moment she stepped away, she really did feel the need to pee. It only took a few minutes to make her way down the hall to the private bathroom attached to the reception area. The air was cooler, some citrus scent filling the air. Marissa did her business, came out and washed her hands. Looking at herself in the mirror, she took a moment to fix her hair and check her makeup. Okay, so she'd agreed to run interference for Vince and she'd lasted all of five minutes. No doubt, Geoff had used her absence to find wherever Simon had taken him and interjected.

Shit. She was going to have to apologize to him once the night was over.

Two women came in chatting, but their voices dried up when they saw her standing there. She gave them a smile and a small nod. "Hello."

One snorted as she walked past, while the other glared. Okay, guess people don't talk in bathrooms here. With a final glance, she walked out.

Only to see Geoff standing close by. His smile gave him the appearance of being harmless, but Marissa knew better. "Hi again."

"I wanted to make sure that you were well, Ms. Roy." He pushed away from the wall and closed the gap between them. "You left me in such a hurry, I was concerned."

Don't freak. You're in a public place. There are two women in the next room and anyone could come by. "I'm fine now. I guess it was too much excitement and alcohol together."

"Well then, why don't I take you back to the party. To make sure you're okay."

He held out his arm as a man made his way down the hallway toward the Men's. Marissa hadn't felt this awkward, this intimidated since the last creditor pounded on her door. But she wasn't going to let herself get bullied into something she didn't want to do. Ignoring Geoff's arm, she turned and started down the hall.

He quickly fell into step with her. "I can see why Vince likes you."

"We have a good friendship. An unusual one, but solid."

"Vince hasn't dated anyone since Thea. And as cute as you are, you're clearly not in his league." He pressed his hand to the small of her back as they walked, sending a shudder through her. "I'll have to go back to that site and see if I can find someone else. I could stand to have a bit of eye candy of my own these days."

Marissa stepped away, and immediately started looking for Vince. She found him not far from where she'd left him, still talking to Simon. Though the moment her gaze landed on him, Vince looked up at her and frowned.

Geoff stepped closer to her once again, clearly oblivious to her silent plea to Vince. "Unless you want to see if the son is anywhere as good as his father? We can step out for a few moments. He'll never even know you're gone. I promise to make it worth your while."

She wasn't normally a person to get upset when some guy was being an asshole. If she were back at work or the college, Marissa would have slapped Geoff, or at the very least laid into him with a verbal lashing that would have made a sailor blush. But she was here to help Vince's reputation, not ruin it. When she saw Vince shift his body, as though he was going to come to her rescue, she gave her head a sharp shake.

Marissa looked back at him, laced her hands behind her back, and gave him a smile that had him take a step back. "Look Mr. Taylor—"

"Geoff, please."

"Geoff. You clearly have the wrong impression here. Vince and I have an understanding. One that is far more PG than you're probably expecting." She lowered her voice, and leaned in a bit closer. "And I can't imagine it would help your sale if someone were to get the wrong impression of who I was to him. We're friends. Ones who are helping each other out in a tough situation."

"Then he really is a fool." He reached up and ran a finger gently down her cheek. "When you get tired of him, you let me know." Geoff then turned and wandered off toward the bar to chat with a group of men who'd congregated there.

Marissa took several deep breaths, allowing her body a chance to relax. That had been way harder than she'd anticipated, and it blew her mind that she hadn't royally screwed it up. Her own father had been absent in her life, having left when she was still a baby. She'd often prayed when she was a little girl for him to come back into her life, and offer to sweep her off her feet and take her to a fairytale land where she could be a princess. Rich and happy in her life.

She couldn't imagine having a man like Geoff as her dad, making her feel as though she needed to keep tabs on him, the way Vince did. The money and power he clearly had, made him a predator, only out for what was best for him. No wonder Vince was closed off and bitter. If she'd been raised by Geoff, money or not, it would have changed everything about her.

Looking around the room, she couldn't help but feel out of her element. These people knew nothing about the struggles of having to do whatever it took to pay the bills, or worry about paying off her student loan once she finished her studies. Even without Andrew screwing her over, this sort of life would always be out of her grasp. Was she jealous? Maybe. A little. To live this sort of life, to never have to worry about getting what you need, it was a seductive prospect.

No wonder Vince was reluctant to date. How the hell would he know if someone was in love with him, or with the idea of the life he could offer.

She finished her drink, and reached down to press a hand to her growling stomach. Looking around, she made a beeline for a waitress holding a tray of something that appeared to be shrimp. She'd just popped one into her mouth when one of the two women from the bathroom came up to her, cocking her head as she sipped her own beverage. "Geoff's a letch."

Marissa had consumed enough wine that her internal filter was slower than normal. "That's an understatement. My skin crawled when Vince introduced us, but that was far worse." Probably not the thing to say about her *boyfriend's* father, but there was no hiding her discomfort.

"I like you." The woman laughed as she held out her hand. "I'm Steph. My husband is on the board for Mount Sinai Hospital."

"Marissa. I'm Vince Taylor's girlfriend."

"Yes, I got that." She smiled in that secretive way certain women can manage. "We were about to take bets on how badly Vince would beat Geoff up, but you defused that situation nicely. Well done."

"Thanks." Marissa twisted the little napkin that she'd been given with the shrimp. "Do you know Vince well?"

"We run in similar circles. He doesn't come to New York often, but whenever he does we sometimes manage to have supper."

Marissa let her gaze travel over to where Vince was still talking to Simon. "He's quite the man."

"He is. Mind you, I've heard more about him from his ex than I ever have from him. She loved to chat about his…abilities in the bedroom. Apparently, he can do things with his tongue that most women would kill to experience. Not that I'd need to tell you that."

Her blush heated her face. "I'm not one to kiss and tell."

"Another way you're different from Thea. We never knew if half the things she said about him were true, or if she was simply bragging. She was a bitch either way."

It wasn't rational that she should get pissed off over what some woman Marissa had never met had done in the past. Marissa didn't know a thing about the woman who'd apparently ruined Vince for relationships. It's not like she was even dating Vince. Not for real.

And yet…

Steph clearly knew both Vince and Thea, and based on the look on her face, she was *dying* to say something. What could it hurt to give her the opportunity?

Marissa narrowed her gaze. "Thea was horrible. What she did to him…"

And there was the spark! Steph moved closer, bending her head lower. "I know. She'd pretty much told everyone she was pregnant and it was his. And the way she liked to drape herself over him, it was easy to imagine. I couldn't believe it was a scam."

Oh. Shit.

Steph kept going. "And then when she lost her shit on him after he called her out, I mean, they were on the frigging red carpet. Who does that?"

Marissa let the rage fill her, knowing it was the only way to chase away the shock. "He's got a reputation, but he's not like that at all. He's been nothing but kind and supportive to me."

No wonder Vince wasn't interested in having a relationship.

If Steph cared about Marissa's opinion, she didn't show it. "That's good." She straightened up so her breasts jutted out farther than before. "Hello Vince. It's been an age since I saw you last."

He walked up behind Marissa, and pressed his chest to her back. "Steph. How's Saul?"

"Good." She motioned behind her. "Over near the hors d'oeuvres, no doubt. I'm sure he'd like to say hello."

"Maybe another time. Sweetheart, unless you want to stay a bit longer, I'd like to head out."

"Oh, but they're just coming around now with some more of the shrimp."

"Now. Please."

There was no mistaking the tension in his voice; he was pissed. "Of course."

With his hand on the small of her back, Vince guided her toward the door. "If I don't leave, I'll kill him."

Marissa had never been much for the whole possessive caveman routine, but it was kind of funny seeing Vince like this. Shit, maybe she really had drunk too much. "Yeah, I don't think we want you convicted. Let's go."

Whether it was from Vince's behavior, the revelations Steph had exposed, or simply her alcohol-tinted state of mind, Marissa's body because ultra-aware of him. She managed to hold off doing anything while Vince called for the limo to come around. She held back as the driver opened the door for her to climb in. Even when Vince took his seat next to her, she didn't even look at him. It wasn't until the driver slid into his seat and the car took off, did she turn to face him.

"I know you're pissed. I was too. And I know we agreed to the no sex thing. But fuck that."

His eyes widened. "What?"

She reached for his fly. "Unless you have a super problem with me giving you a blow job right now, that's exactly what I'm going to do."

She waited for a moment, looking him straight in the eyes in case he wasn't ready for this. But when he said nothing, she grinned and lowered her head.

Chapter 13

The breath in his chest caught when Marissa slipped her hand into his pants and wrapped her long fingers around his rock-hard cock. In every relationship he'd had prior to this exact moment, he'd normally been the one doing the seduction. Even Thea, while no wilting flower in bed, let him take the lead whenever it came to sex. He was the one in charge, the one directing the relationship.

But sitting in the back of the limo, he watched Marissa work his pants open, and take his cock out.

"Lift your hips up a bit. I don't want to catch you on the zipper." She chuckled, that deep throaty laugh of hers that did amazing things to his libido. "That would put an end to our fun really fast."

He did as she said, his bare ass now on the cool leather of the seat. "I don't know how long we'll have. Traffic is heavy this time of night, but the driver might go a different route."

She waved his concerns away. "I'm not overly concerned."

"I don't have a condom." The thought of sex happening tonight hadn't even entered his mind. He'd been focused on Simon and GreenPro and holy shit, her tongue was warm.

"Are you clean?" She flicked the tip of her tongue across the top of his cock once again. "Because I'll kill you if you infect me with something."

"Yes. I'm clean."

"I mean, still would need a condom for sex because babies and shit. But if you swear you're clean, then I'll give you the best blow job of your life. The best orgasm." Another flick of her tongue, followed by her nails teasing his balls.

"You're that confident in your abilities, eh?" She pressed her tongue to the nerve bundle on his cockhead and gave him a teasing flick. "Fuck, yes, I'm clean. Was tested after I broke up with Thea." Given how she'd lied to him, he couldn't trust anything she'd ever said. Thankfully, the test had come back negative. "You?"

"I'm not relevant at the moment. But yes. Clean. Andrew was my only partner and yeah. I've been tested since then because he was a lying prick."

"Good." Because if there'd been a problem, he wasn't exactly certain he would have stopped her in this moment. "Have at me."

There was something about the look on her face, a teasing spark that told him he was going to be in for one hell of a ride. She kept her gaze on his until her mouth slowly covered the head of his shaft. She might have still been looking at him, but Vince wouldn't have known. His eyes slammed shut when she swirled her tongue across the nerve bundle. She moaned as she lowered her mouth further down his cock, increasing the suction as she went.

Vince lifted his hand to rest it to the back of her head, but stopped somewhere in the air before landing where he wanted. That was because Marissa had stretched out on the seat, so she could lower her face to his balls. She gently sucked one into her mouth while stroking his cock with her hand.

"Fuck." He pressed his head back hard against the seat. "You're good."

She hummed again, this time licking a trail up between his balls, back to the head. "I love blow jobs."

God, she was night and day different from Thea. She'd hated going down on him, which hadn't really bothered him at the time. Thea more than made up for it with other things. But he'd always considered blow jobs intimate in a way that others probably didn't. A trust factor he had to always keep in mind.

Marissa lifted her head to look at him, even as she continued stroking him. "You're drifting."

"Huh?"

"You're cock goes a bit softer when your mind wanders. Which means I'm not doing a great job." She shifted her body as she reached down with her other hand and teased the sensitive skin beneath his balls. "Is there something else you like that I'm not doing?"

"Nope, you're good." Probably not the best to be mentally comparing Marissa and Thea. "I'll behave."

"You better." She let her finger dance across his asshole. "I'd hate to punish you."

He couldn't help but laugh. "Maybe another time. When we're not in a limo."

"Interesting." She moved her hand back up and returned to sucking his cock.

It was his turn to groan as she did a *thing* with her tongue, a swirl-flick that sent a bolt of pleasure straight through his body. His balls tightened, even without her nails scratching across them. God, it had been too long since he'd been with a woman, too long since he'd let his guard down enough to enjoy the intimacy that came with sex. Every time he'd even thought about it, Thea's face would float to mind.

But not now. Not with Marissa's wicked mouth teasing. Not with the perverse sounds of her sucking, slurping, her wet saliva trapped between his shaft and her hand. The smell of his arousal and sweat, scenting the air around them.

The limo slowed to a jerky stop, sending Marissa down his cock, nearly to the base. His eyes flew open and she groaned as she pulled back.

"You okay?" He cupped her cheek, tracing a path on her skin with his thumb.

"Fine. Was a bit unexpected." If she had any issues with continuing, she didn't show it.

The limo jerked forward again, but this time Marissa was ready for it, pulling back at the last moment. "This isn't going to work."

She shifted her body once more, this time getting to the floor between his legs. She pushed his dress pants all the way down, leaving him completely exposed from the waist down. Vince watched, taking in every move she made, the micro-expressions on her face as she slid her hand along the top of his thigh, teasing the fine hairs. He was fascinated by the flush that covered her face as she resumed her ministrations.

Shit, she really was good at this.

Vince couldn't keep his focus on her for long, as his rising pleasure threatened to overtake him. His balls tightened as she tugged and teased them, and he knew it wouldn't be much longer to see through her promise of giving him the best orgasm of his life. He wanted to drag this out as long as possible, to memorize as much of the experience as he could. Forcing his eyes to stay open, he reached down and cupped the side of her head. His fingers brushed the soft hair at her temple.

"You're so beautiful like this. On your knees with my cock in your mouth." He let his fingers drift down and trace her open, cock-filled mouth. Marissa's eyes widened, her pupils were huge, staring up at him in the dark of the limo.

She moaned, pulled up until only the tip of her tongue touched his cock. For a brief moment, he worried that he'd said the wrong thing, made her feel uncomfortable. But the sparkle was back in her gaze, and she lowered her head and closed her eyes.

If he thought she was good before, he'd been a fool. She'd been toying with him.

Now she was serious.

Suction the like of which he'd never felt before surrounded him. Marissa reached between his legs and teased his asshole and surrounding skin with her nails. Vince sucked in air, greedy for any oxygen he could manage as she devoured him. God, he wasn't going to last. Not when she could swallow him down like that.

His hands gripped the edge of the seat as he fought to keep his hips still. Giving up on that, he fucked up into her mouth, no longer able to hold back. "Gonna fucking come."

The words barely left him when the first spurts of his hot cum shot from him. Marissa groaned, swallowed it down, sucking every last ounce from him. He tried his best to bite back his cries, failing to contain them all. His body shook as his orgasm raced through him, firing off nerves in a cascade of pleasure. He gasped for air, even as sweat beaded across his skin, dampening his shirt.

With a wet pop, Marissa pulled off him, reclaimed her wine glass and drank it down.

Vince's heart pounded hard enough, he had no doubt she was clearly able to hear it. "Your turn."

He gave her to the mental count of three to let his words skin in, before he yanked up his pants. She blinked at him, her lips shining from the wine and his cum. "What?"

He pulled her up onto the seat beside him, and switched positions so he was now on the floor between her legs. He said nothing, instead watched the ripple of emotions cross her face as he reached beneath her dress and pulled her panties down. The black, lacy thong was tiny enough he wasn't sure it actually covered much of anything. As he slipped it free from her feet, he shoved it into his jacket pocket. "My prize."

"I want those back. It matches my bra." She was breathing heavy now, her eyes locked onto his. "I'm not even kidding."

"I'll buy you another set." There was no way she was ever getting those back. "I'm not even kidding."

Grabbing her by the hips, he pulled her forward so her ass hung over the edge of the seat. Her pussy was exposed now, the pink of her lips, the dampness that clung to her pubic hair threatened to send another wave of pleasure through him. "I'm going to eat you. I'm going to lick you until you're screaming. I want you to come so hard you're pulling my hair out."

"Fuck." She pressed her head back against the seat. "Fuck."

"Not yet. But I'm going to make you come." Using one hand to spread her labia, he lowered his nose to her mound and breathed in the scent of her. "Amazing."

Marissa tried to squirm away from him, but he held her still with a hand pressed to her stomach. "Easy there."

"You talk too much." Her hand fell to his head and she nudged him lower.

"That's a new one." But he took her hint and without any further preamble, sucked her clit into his mouth.

Marissa's moans filled the limo as she bucked her hips up. Yes, this was what he wanted. To feel this primal ownership, this driving need to want to make a woman squirm beneath his touch. His cock twitched back to life as he licked circles around her clit, flicking it with his tongue much the same way she'd done to him moments earlier.

The taste of her was rich, her juices flowing enough to already cover his chin. God, she was so horny, ready, he could only imagine what it would feel like to thrust his cock into her body. While there was no way they could do that now, he still needed to know. He thrust his finger into her pussy, turning it to press against the top of her slick passage and her G-spot.

Marissa sucked in a breath. "God."

Her juices trickled down his finger as he pumped into her, matching the beat of his tongue. Her pubic hair tickled his nose as he pressed his face firmly against her. It wasn't an annoyance, more a reminder of how different Marissa was from Thea, who'd hated her body hair and removed as much of it as she could.

Vince couldn't care either way.

Marissa's thighs shook around his face, the flutter of muscles beneath her skin as he lapped at her. Her hand came to rest on the top of his head, her fingers twitching whenever he'd hit a spot she clearly liked. The faster he licked, the harder her hips bucked, the firmer he fucked her with his finger. After a moment, he added a second one, stretching her pussy.

He wanted to fuck her. Wanted to own her in a way he'd never felt with any other woman. It was wrong. Primal. So screwed up he couldn't imagine saying the words out loud for fear of sending her running away. But it didn't change this desire to want to take her back to the penthouse, throw her into the bed and not let her up until they couldn't move.

Groaning, he needed her to come. Needed to taste her, hear and feel her climax on his mouth. He reached up and found her taut nipple through her dress and squeezed. Marissa gasped, and pressed his head down hard against her pussy.

Yes, that's what he wanted. He sucked her hard as he continued to tease her nipple, until her entire body shook. He listened for the sharp intake of air, felt her body still briefly, before she bucked her hips up hard against his face.

"Fuck!" She screamed with her mouth closed as she came.

Vince didn't stop, continued to lap at her as his mouth filled, and his nose became plugged with her cum. He didn't stop until he began to see spots from lack of oxygen and forced himself to suck in a breath of his own. Only once her hips collapsed back onto the seat, did he slow the flicks of his tongue and finally pull away.

Marissa was panting, her face flushed and the loose tendrils of her hair now stuck to her damp skin. Her half-naked body was the most erotic thing he'd ever seen in his life. She was beautiful.

Mine.

Oh, that was a dangerous thought. Marissa wasn't his. She was here to do a job, one that he'd set the rules for. She was here to earn a wage, to pay off her debts, and then move on with her life. She wasn't a prostitute, wasn't his girlfriend. Hell, he wasn't even certain if she liked him beyond what he could do for her.

No, that wasn't true. There wasn't any guile to her. Marissa was open and honest, and did everything in that manner.

Mine.

Shit, he wasn't going to do that. Not to either of them.

When she finally opened her eyes, he made sure to give her his best grin. "How'd I do?"

Her giggle filled the limo. "You're okay. Can I get my panties back now?"

He climbed back into the seat beside her. "Nope."

"Dude, I really do need them."

He probably shouldn't be that guy, should listen to her request and return what was rightfully hers. He *probably* should. Instead he picked up his wine glass. "Maybe later."

It wasn't as though she didn't know where he'd stashed them. Hell, he wouldn't have stopped her if she'd tried to take them back.

Marissa leaned over and looked at his jacket pocket. "Dare I ask what you're going to do with them?"

"I don't know yet."

She gave him an eye roll. "You're weird."

Vince chuckled, surprised by how good it felt to tease someone, to simply be silly and have fun for the sake of goofing off. "How about I promise to give them back to you once we get back to the penthouse. I like knowing you're naked under that dress."

Her face flushed once again as she squirmed in her seat. "Fine. But I'm holding you to that. This is my favorite set of sexy lingerie."

He had the sneaking suspicion this might be one of her only sets of sexy lingerie. "Deal?" Holding out his hand and waited for her to take it.

She shook her head and his hand simultaneously. "Deal."

As soon as her skin touched his, he watched her shiver. He wasn't the only one impacted by their shifting relationship. Which meant if he were to propose an amendment to their deal, there was a chance she'd take him up on it. A chance they could enjoy one another fully while she helped him with his little public relations challenge.

A chance Vince was willing to take.

Chapter 14

It was a bizarre feeling walking from the limo to the hotel with no panties on. Marissa's pussy was still damp from their little sexual explosion, and the wind was blowing hard enough to send shivers through her core.

She'd never admit it to Vince, but she'd been turned on when he'd slipped her panties into his pocket. It was an act of possession, one she'd never expected from him. A part of her had been annoyed that he wouldn't give them back when she'd asked, though she was under the impression if she'd really pushed for them, he would have relented.

The larger part of her had enjoyed the thrill of going commando. It was so weird that something as simple as leaving off a piece of clothing made her feel that liberated.

God, her life must really suck balls if that's all it took to shake her libido free.

Vince let her walk ahead of him through the lobby to the elevator. He wasn't touching her, but she swore she could feel the weight of his gaze on her skin. No doubt him knowing that she was bare beneath her dress, that he was the reason for it, was as much of a turn-on for him as it was for her.

They were absolutely going to have sex once they got upstairs.

Given the nature of their relationship, Marissa couldn't help but wonder if this changed anything for her. Before the limo, sex hadn't been an option, so she hadn't felt she'd crossed any lines. Vince hadn't forced the issue, and she hoped that if she said no, if she rebuked his advance, then he would have backed off. But he was the one with the money. He was the one who had the ability to pay off her debts. Did this change anything, or was she being a fool?

"Now I get what you meant." Vince's voice surprised her in the small elevator.

"Pardon?"

"You're thinking loudly." His lips did that half-smile thing of his. "What's wrong?"

"Nothing is wrong." She waited for the doors to slide open and for him to step out. She didn't move, forcing him to put his hand out to stop the doors from sliding shut. "I mean, we are about to go have sex, right? I'm not imagining that?"

He cocked his head to the side. "That's completely up to you."

The elevator dinged at her, but she stayed put. "I think I want to have sex."

"Then we have sex." The elevator dinged again. "Please come out."

She did as he asked, but didn't move away from the elevator. "Does that change things? Like if we have sex, will you expect it? Does it become part of our arrangement? I mean, if it does then I'm sure I'll find a way to deal, but I need to know before we take this next step."

Vince stepped up to her and framed her face with his hands. "This isn't part of the deal. This has to be something that you want, and not some obligation. I never set out to make this about sex. I needed someone who could help me deflect some of the issues I was having with my reputation. That's it. If you never want to do it again, then we don't."

By the time he was done with his little speech, Marissa's heart was pounding so hard, she felt it in her throat. "Tell me you have condoms."

"The room comes stocked with them."

She didn't wait for him to say anything else, grabbed his hand and pulled him toward his bedroom. The room wasn't that much different from hers; a large bed filled most of it, while a desk and fire place were also there. The scent that filled the air struck her as somehow more masculine, though she was fairly certain it was in fact no different than what was in hers.

Strange how the mind worked.

Only once she was all the way into his bedroom, did she drop his hand and turn to face him. "So, here's how this is going to work. I'm going to strip naked, while you go and find those condoms you mentioned. Once you have what we need, then you're going to come back and we're going to screw until we yell so loud they hear us in the lobby. Deal?"

Vince's eyes were pretty much the teleprompter for his internal dialogue. With each word she spoke, she could see his desire, his arousal, his complete agreement with everything she'd said. It didn't surprise her then, when he spoke, that his voice was rough from his arousal. "Don't move."

She cocked her head to the side, knowing exactly how she must look to him. "Butt naked?"

"Not an inch." He turned and bolted for the bathroom.

God, this was actually a hell of a lot of fun. With Andrew, sex had been good, satisfying. But there'd never been this nearly electric spark that arced between them. Whenever they'd finished, their conversations would immediately switch to something else, something boring. They rarely took time to relish in what they'd just done. Marissa had always assumed that was simply how it was between couples, especially those who'd been together for a number of years.

But this? Her body shivered from the anticipation of what she knew was about to come. Vince possessed a laser focus that Andrew never could manage. When Vince looked at her, she swore her very thoughts were visible to him. That somehow, he was able to see deep into her brain and know exactly what she wanted.

It was the single most thrilling thing she'd ever experienced.

Vince strode back through the door with a bottle of lube and a string of condoms. He'd removed his tie, lost his jacket somewhere along the way, and had undone the buttons of his sleeves. If she'd been wearing panties, they would have been dampened from her arousal.

Shit, she wasn't normally a woman to want to have sex more than once in a night. Not that there was necessarily anything wrong with being a one and done kind of girl, but the thought of going again, to feel Vince's body on her, in her while she orgasmed, nearly pushed her over the edge.

"Good. You didn't move." His eyes were wide, and he looked nearly wild. "I wasn't sure you'd listen."

"I almost didn't. If we are doing this as equals, and not as sugar daddy and woman who's taking his money, then I get to be the one in charge. I get to tell you what I like and what I don't like. If I want to be on top, or shove something up your ass, then I'm the one who gets to suggest it. And if you want to do something that I don't like, then I have full veto power." There, that was a firm and clear statement of what she wanted. It was like she really was in charge.

Vince swallowed hard. "You want to shove something up my ass?"

Marissa couldn't stop the burst of laughter. "Well, I don't have a burning desire or anything. But you seemed intrigued by the idea back in the limo."

He looked away and chuckled. "You're so different from any other woman I've ever been with."

"That's because when you're not rich, you have to be creative." She stepped closer and tugged down one of the straps of her dress. "Now, I believe we were going to get naked and fuck."

Yes, there was the growl she'd heard him make back at the restaurant. "Let me."

"Nope."

Another growl. "Marissa."

"Vince...sit on the bed."

It took him a moment, but she was pleased when he eventually complied with her request. She turned to face him, her back now to the warmth of the fireplace. "I'm not a dancer, so I won't embarrass myself with an attempt at a striptease. Instead, I'll just do this."

She kept her gaze locked on his as she reached behind her and tugged down the zipper that held the dress in place. The fabric loosened immediately, as gravity pulled it down, nearly exposing her breasts to him. She held it in place, letting the straps fall uselessly to her mid arm as she swayed slowly.

Vince watched her every move with rapt attention. It was strange to see where he focused his attention; her arms, her neck, her legs as she kicked her shoes off. When he moved his gaze to her breasts, she let the dress slip a bit further down, showing off a generous amount of skin. He clenched his hands, balling up a part of the duvet cover as he did. "You're a tease."

"I am." And yet, she really wasn't. This was never the sort of thing she'd have done with Andrew. There was something about Vince that brought the wild side out in her. She turned around so her back was now to him. "That fire is so nice."

She let the dress slip down to her waist, so her breasts could now enjoy the full warmth from the fire. The silk clung to her ass, resting as though it were on a ledge. Marissa reached up and cupped the weight of her own breasts, squeezing them and enjoying the tingle that filled her.

"I'm so fucking hard right now." She heard him shift on the bed. "I can't believe how much you're turning me on."

"This is what happens when you have fun, when you let yourself go. It's something I have to remember for when I go back to Toronto." She looked over her shoulder at him and smiled.

He'd reached down and had opened the front of his pants, his cock pushing out from beneath the band on his briefs. The head of his cock glistened in the firelight, a beacon enticing her to come and taste.

She turned, letting the dress fall to the floor and revealing her full naked body to him. "Right now, I'm done with being patient."

Vince watched her move closer to him, leaning back on his arms when she reached the side of the bed. "You're stunning."

"And you're overdressed." He lifted his hips as she tugged his pants off, followed by his briefs. His cock jutted up, hard and leaking.

It was hard for Marissa to ignore it, but she wanted him as naked as she was. Her hands shook as she undid his buttons, messing up more than a few. Clearly, he was as impatient as she was for them to have sex, because he set to work on the buttons on the lower part, meeting her in the middle.

She'd felt his abs, the muscles in his arms and chest over the course of their time together. Feeling it and see the perfection that comprised his body were two completely different things. She stood straight as he pulled the shirt free of his arms, and finally leaving them naked.

Equals.

The surge of boldness she'd experienced moments earlier had petered out, leaving her at a bit of a loss for what to do. Normally with sex, she'd start with a blow job, and move on from there. But they'd done that, both having come not long ago. Thankfully, Vince wasn't as confused as to what to do next.

He reached up and bracketed her waist with his hands. His thumbs traced lazy patterns across her skin, making her wiggle away from the sensitive spots. "Join me?"

Yeah, that sounded like a perfect idea.

She let him guide her to the bed, and together they shifted and stretched out until they were both filling the middle of the mattress. Without her shoes, he was so much taller than she was. Her toes brushed against his calves, teasing the coarse hair that covered his skin. Her breasts were pressed against his chest, her nipples tingling from the contact.

Vince shifted lower so their faces were close together. She could smell the mix of her cum on his face and the wine they'd shared. Reaching out, she ran a hand across his cheek, relishing the feel of his stubble against her.

This was different. It was nice. But she really wanted to fuck him now.

Marissa wrapped her leg around his waist, and rolled them so she was now sitting on top. "Where'd you throw that condom?"

He lifted up the packet without looking. "You going to make sure I'm ready for action?"

She gifted him with an eye roll, before ripping one of the foil packets open and shifting lower so she could roll it down his cock. "You're good with your mouth. I'm curious to see how good you are with this."

"Is that meant to be a taunt? If it is, we seriously need to work on your game." He gasped as she squeezed his cock and gently pressed her thumb to the middle of his balls. "Yes, ma'am."

That little acquiescence sent a shiver through her. "You're lucky I'm really horny, or else I might request we do a little roleplay."

Vince licked his lips. "I'm no one's submissive."

"Maybe not." She shrugged before lining his cock up with her pussy and slowly sinking down. "But I get the feeling you might like someone taking over every now and again."

Whatever else she might have teased him with, those words vanished as she settled into place on his shaft. Vince returned his hands to her waist, holding her firmly in place. He didn't do anything until she opened her eyes and looked down at him. Only then, did he buck his hips up, forcing himself deeper inside her.

Her clit was swollen and her pussy wet, making the pleasure even more intense as she matched his thrusts. They easily fell into a rhythm, their bodies pulling away, only to come back together with a glorious burst of pleasure each time. Her breasts swayed and bounced with each contact, her nipples tingling. Without thinking, she reached up and pinched them, relishing the bolt of pleasure that seemed to connect to her clit.

Vince's grip tightened on her, lifting her up higher on each upswing, so she could slam back down on him harder. "Pinch them again."

She moaned, letting her head fall back, no longer able to keep gravity from winning. She rolled her nipples between her fingers, tugging and teasing the sensitive tips in the way that no man ever seemed to get. Each time she pinched, her pussy pulsed around his cock, squeezing his shaft now soaked from her juices. Higher and higher her body climbed until she knew there was no way she'd be able to stop from coming.

Before she tipped over that edge, Marissa forced her eyes open and looked down at Vince. Sweat covered his skin, glistening from the light of the fireplace. His muscles rippled beneath his skin, as he thrust up harder and faster into her.

But it was the look in his eye, the possessive darkness squarely aimed at her that pushed her over the edge. One second she was looking at him, the next she sucked in a breath and screamed.

The pleasure hit her in powerful waves, over and over. There was no recession, no chance for her to catch her breath or relax her muscles. Her body curled forward as she squeezed her nipples to the point where she no longer felt them. Vince didn't stop, didn't relent until the second she sucked in a breath, collapsing slightly.

She didn't have time to stop him, or even realize what he was doing. In a blink, he'd rolled them so she was now on her back and he was able to pound into her. She clung to him, let the tide of her orgasm surge again as he pressed his face to her neck as he fucked her hard. There was no way she'd be able to come again, but the feeling of his muscles working hard, before tensing, nearly pushed her over the edge.

Vince roared loud against her neck, his body losing the rhythm as he came. One, two, three more thrusts and he finally came to a stop.

Marissa had been fucked nearly senseless. Her body ached from her release, from the too-powerful pleasure. She placed a kiss to his cheek and unable to keep her eyes open any longer, let sleep claim her.

Chapter 15

Vince had a problem. It was about five feet, nine inches in length and had blond hair. Marissa Roy was not at all what he'd been expecting when he'd set out on his little sugar baby adventure. She was too young, too inexperienced to truly fit into his world, and yet everyone who looked at her saw the same spark he did. She lit up the room whenever she walked into it, drawing attention to herself and somehow making everyone around her feel special. It was unintentional, completely natural, and utterly distracting.

After his father's unfortunate presence and his own abrupt departure from the party last night, Vince had needed another chance to speak with Simon. Vince had been immediately aware of Geoff's pawing of Marissa the moment it had begun, and Simon had gone so far as to call him on his lack of focus. Not that Simon had any love for his father, but if Vince had wanted to show that he was better than Geoff, then getting into some sort of fight with him wasn't the way to go. It was best for all involved for Vince to get Marissa and get out of there before his dad tried anything else.

Vince had hastily arranged to meet Simon at Peacock Alley at the Waldorf for breakfast this morning. He knew it was a favorite location of Simon's, and if nothing else, he needed to pull out all the stops to ensure Simon would seriously consider his pitch and not go against what his own board was suggesting. All he had to do was ensure his father didn't show up to ruin everything, and everything would be fine.

Too bad Marissa had come out of the bedroom wearing a pair of slacks and a shirt that were far too enticing for her own good.

"Why are you wearing that?" He couldn't take his gaze from the swell of her breasts or the teasing amount of cleavage that peeked out from the folds of fabric.

She looked down at her outfit and frowned. "What's wrong with it? I thought it was a nice match."

Crossing the room, he stopped a few inches from her, his cock already hard. "You're too fucking beautiful." He reached up and slid his hand down the side of her breast, enjoying the way she shivered. "All I want to do is cancel breakfast, strip you down and stay in bed for the rest of the day."

Her face was flushed and her eyes wide as she ran her tongue along her bottom lip. "That wouldn't bode well for your sale."

"Hence, the problem with your outfit."

It was a horrible idea to move his hand so he now cupped her breast, his thumb teasing her taut nipple through the fabric. He was supposed to be better than this, not be a slave to his dick, to be able to push those thoughts aside and focus on what was important. He was supposed to be better than his father.

Vince let her go, and took a deep breath. "We should probably get ready to leave."

Marissa's mouth had slipped open as she continued to stare up at him. "What time do we need to be there?"

"Ten."

She stepped closer and began to pull apart his tie. "We have time."

"We shouldn't do this." He reciprocated and made quick work of the buttons on her shirt, being extra careful not to pull them off. "This wasn't supposed to be about sex."

"Will you shut up?" She yanked his tie off, and was even faster than he was with his shirt. "Because I'm getting tired of that excuse. We're both consenting. And I'm really horny now."

Well, it was fine if she was on board. "Yes, ma'am."

Tossing her shirt to the floor, he didn't bother to remove her bra, picked her up and carried her over to the kitchen counter. The pants were going to be a problem, but working together, they were able to quickly remove them and her panties. Dressed in only her bra, Vince took a moment to savor the sight before him. He picked up her feet, and placed them on the counter, so her pussy was fully exposed to him in all its glistening glory.

"I need a snack before breakfast." Scooting her back, he bent forward and licked a long swipe up the length of her.

Marissa groaned, her body shaking beneath him. "You're really good at that."

"Lean back."

She did, using her arms as a prop so she could still look down at him. Vince held eye contact with her as he stuck out his tongue and flicked it across her clit. It was glorious to watch her suck in a breath, and bite down on her lip. Another flick of his tongue and her eyes closed. God, he'd forgotten how much he loved doing this for a woman he liked. For someone who he had a connection with, even if it wasn't anything more than friendship. The awkward angle was going to make it difficult for him to keep at this for long, so he reached over and slid one of the stools over so he could have a seat.

"Guess I'll have my brunch buffet a bit early."

Marissa laughed, the sound of which brought warmth to his chest. Now comfortably seated, he wrapped his arms around her legs, tossing one of them over his shoulder, leaned in and sucked hard on her clit. Her laughter turned into another moan, which only encouraged him on. Slipping a finger into her pussy, he fucked her with it, setting a fast pace in time with his mouth.

This was fucking heaven. The smell and sounds of her washed over him as he coaxed her pleasure from her. Her juices coated his face, the pressure of her foot pressing down against his back, and his cock throbbed from the orgasm he knew was going to hit her soon.

Marissa began to buck her hips in time to his tongue. She stretched back on the island counter, her head dangling over the edge. Her legs began to quiver, her thighs twitching on either side of his face. Yeah, she was so close now, he knew it wouldn't take much. Pulling his hand from her pussy, he reached up and pushed his fingers beneath the edge of her bra. It was a stretch, but he was just able to capture her nipple between his fingers. He squeezed the peak as hard as he could in the same rhythm of his tongue again, knowing how much she liked that.

It was all she needed. "Shit!" Marissa sat up, her hands flying to the back of his head, pushing his mouth down hard as she cried out. He lapped at her as she came, swallowing down everything she gave him, even as his body cried out for oxygen.

He rode out her release until she finally freed his head, leaning back once again. Vince stood, sending the stool flying backwards to land on its side. He'd shoved a condom in his pocket earlier—because while he hadn't planned on sex, it was apparently always on the table when it came to her—which he fished out before undoing the opening of his pants. Vince shoved his pants and briefs, before awkwardly slipping the condom on.

Marissa had scooted her ass closer to the edge of the counter and braced her feet on the edge. "Fuck me hard."

Vince had to close his eyes and take a breath as he lined up. God, she could push him close to the edge with a single sentence. It was only after he got himself under control again, did he open his eyes and thrust into her. "This is going to be a short ride."

God, her smile was like a bullet through to his spine. "Good."

Grabbing her by the knees, Vince mercilessly pounded into her. Her pussy was still hot and quivering from her orgasm, and the feeling of it clenching around his cock was nearly too much for him. It was difficult to keep his eyes open, but he didn't want to look away from the sight of her splayed out on the counter, her bra half pushed up and her body flushed. This was how he'd likely remember her in the middle of the night when he was alone in his room. He'd fuck his hand thinking of this moment, how open and free she was, how amazing she felt around him.

Vince groaned as his balls tightened, signaling that he wasn't going to last much longer. He adjusted his grip, and thrust into her until pleasure exploded through his body.

"Fuck!" The cries didn't stop, grew louder with each thrust until every last drop of energy was bled from him. Finally, the waves of his orgasm wavered, taking the last of his ability to stay upright. He fell forward, his face pressed to her breasts, as he struggled to regain his equilibrium.

For several long moments, the only sound that filled the room was their uneven breaths. Vince couldn't hold his hips up any longer and his softening cock slipped from her body. "That was awesome."

Marissa laughed, just as the telephone rang.

Holding the condom in one hand, he forced himself to move and answer it. "Yes?"

"Mr. Taylor, your limo is here. Would you like me to ask the driver to wait?"

"We'll be right down."

Marissa was already moving before he'd hung up.

* * * *

They'd barely made it through Sunday morning traffic, but managed to arrive for breakfast with a few moments to spare. Simon and his wife Natalie were already waiting, but had only just been seated.

Vince held out his hand and Simon shook it. "Sorry to keep you waiting. We got held up in traffic."

Marissa's smile widened, even as she blushed. It was a beautiful sight to behold. "Vince told me about the brunch here. I'm very much looking forward to trying it."

Natalie patted the chair beside her. "Marissa, why don't you join me and we can let the men talk about their deals."

Ah, Simon must have worked things out with his wife ahead of time. He leaned in a placed a kiss on Marissa's cheek. "Play nice."

With her on his left, Vince sat and turned to his right to speak with Simon. "I'm sure you have some questions. Why don't we get them out of the way over a coffee, then we can enjoy the rest of our meal."

"Your father would always insist on eating first." Simon poured cream into his coffee. "Claimed he never wanted to miss the meal if the deal went south."

"I'm not as pessimistic as my father."

"No, I can see that." Simon took a sip before gracing Vince with one of his practiced smiles. "Why not split the difference? We eat as we talk."

Vince wasn't fool enough to try and force Simon's hand over something as simple as a meal. He knew he was being tested, and wasn't about to fail. He gave Marissa a quick glance as he stood. "Lead on."

It was easy to make business small talk with Simon, even if his mind wasn't completely on it. Despite having washed his face thoroughly, he could still smell Marissa every time he took a breath. It was making it increasingly difficult to keep his focus on playing nice with Simon instead of sneaking glances at her. He could see from that Marissa and Natalie currently had their heads bent forward in conversation. With no way to hear what they were saying, he could only imagine it was something naughty, based on the identical smirks on their lips and the flush on Natalie's cheeks.

He gave Marissa a questioning look when they returned to the table, but she ignored him. "You should get something to eat."

"That's an excellent idea." Marissa stood and waited for Natalie to join her before heading over to the buffet.

"I'm surprised you haven't sold GreenPro to anyone else before now." Simon speared a piece of smoked salmon, holding it an inch from his mouth. "It's an interesting business model."

Vince forced his attention back to the older man, hoping his obsession wasn't obvious. "My father and I made the initial investment years ago, back when the technology wasn't even available. The idea was sound and I knew eventually the need for green energy sources would catch up. I have a lot invested in this project and I need to know whoever takes it over will see it through to its full potential."

Simon frowned briefly before stuffing the salmon into his mouth. "I assume you're willing to walk away without regrets once the sale is complete. The last thing I'd want would be to constantly receive unsolicited advice on the direction of my acquisition. More importantly, I want to be sure that your father won't have anything to do with this. I want your word as a businessman that he will be gone."

For a heartbeat, Vince wanted to say he couldn't. He didn't want to walk away from GreenPro's potential. He didn't want to hand it over to anyone, let alone someone who he couldn't guarantee wouldn't cannibalize the bits and pieces from the company to suit his own needs. But selling the company was the only way he could sever ties with his father, leaving Vince with no other option.

"Please, Simon. How long have you known me?" He gave himself a moment to collect his thoughts and took a sip of his coffee. "Once I know the sale is right, I take my investment and go on my merry way. You won't have to worry about some nosy Canadian causing you grief. Father is as anxious to sell GreenPro as I am."

"Pleased to hear that." But he didn't exactly look convinced.

Vince leaned forward. "To ensure everything is above board, we can write it into the contract. I don't want you to have any reservations about this deal. I'm well aware of your history with Geoff, and I promise that I'll ensure he stays as far away from you as possible."

"I was...surprised to see him at dinner last night. He hasn't shown his face around me in a number of years." Simon's gaze snapped to his wife as she chuckled. "What's tickled your funny bone, dear?"

Vince had been on the receiving end of Simon's snappish tone many times in the past. It had a way of unnerving a person. Despite having been married for over a decade, Natalie wasn't immune to it either. "Marissa was telling me about a conference she'd attended."

The light blush on Marissa's cheeks deepened to a bright red. "Yes, I was. It was a few years ago and I was seriously lacking any sort of experience. I managed to get myself into quite a bind."

Vince had gotten quite adept at reading her expressions over the past few days. There was a lot more to that statement than she was saying. Simon narrowed his gaze, but neither Natalie nor Marissa said anything else.

Shit.

Setting his coffee down, Vince got to his feet. "Marissa, would you like to see the chocolate fountain? I guarantee you haven't had a better experience than this."

"I'd love to." She gave Natalie a smile and a wink. "Remind me to tell you about the session I attended after that one." And without another word, she placed her hand on his arm and let him lead her to the chocolate.

"Dare I ask what the two of you were actually discussing?"

She didn't look over at him, her gaze locked onto the sweet treat they were approaching. "Honestly, I was talking about a conference."

"You don't seem the type to go to many of those. Was this for school?"

She took a plate and filled it with strawberries and pineapple slices. "No, it was FanExpo. I was telling her about the time I dressed as an anime character and what happened when I ran into someone who was cosplaying as my love interest. Andrew nearly decked the guy when he came up and threw me over his shoulder, spanking my ass as he took off with me into the crowd."

Vince's stomach turned and for a moment he couldn't move, couldn't speak. "You told her *what*?"

Marissa must have practiced the innocent look she was now giving him in the mirror. "What? She's nowhere near as conservative as Simon is. We got chatting about last night and what Geoff had done. Then about your reaction and I couldn't help tell her about FanExpo." She then turned and started dipping her fruit into the chocolate. "I love these things. Though this smells better than the cheap stuff that I usually have to use. Mom had a mini fountain that we'd use on movie nights."

Vince chanced a look over where Simon was currently grilling Natalie. From the look on his wife's face, she wasn't thrilled about it either. "Shit."

"What?" Marissa followed where he was looking. "Oh no."

"I doubt she'll say anything to make you look bad, but I can't imagine he'll be in a good mood." God, this was the last thing he needed.

When he turned back around, Marissa's eyes had widened and were shining with unshed tears. "I didn't think my stupid little story would cause any problems. It's not even all that funny."

He didn't want her to feel bad about how much of an asshole Simon was. "Don't worry about it. You were being yourself, which is all I can ask of you. Simon and I were just talking about Dad and that always brings up the reason why Natalie is Simon's second wife." Vince knew he'd have to be on high alert once they got back to the table.

"Did you want any of the fruit?"

Looking back at Marissa, the tension that had threatened to rear up inside him dissipated. She *hadn't* done anything wrong. No matter how much his father wanted to sell GreenPro to Simon's organization, or Vince wanted to be done being under his father's thumb, he realized that it wasn't worth selling his soul to accomplish those things.

Dear God, what was happening to him?

Setting his plate down, he took Marissa's from hers. "That's not nearly enough to enjoy the full experience. This is some of the best chocolate you'll have."

Vince knew she'd been living up to her end of the bargain, she'd played the part of his girlfriend perfectly—too much so, if their adventures in bed were any indication—the least he could do was fall into place as the dutiful boyfriend.

And did that make him sound like he was a teenager again.

It was worth it, to see the hurt clear from Marissa's eyes, even as her gaze lingered on the other couple for a moment. "Thanks. I think I will."

She turned and added more fruit and chocolate, ignoring the looks of others around them. Vince wanted to growl, to bark at anyone who was looking at her in any way that resembled a rebuke. She was sweet and kind, and he'd be damned if anyone faulted her for that.

They were about to head back when she popped a strawberry into her mouth. "That's amazing."

"I knew you'd like it."

"I feel bad for her." She licked the chocolate from her fingers.

"Natalie? She can hold her own."

"No doubt, but it's exhausting having to be constantly on guard around someone like that. Toward the end of our relationship, Andrew was always questioning what I was doing, where I was going, and what I was saying when he wasn't around. It went well beyond him not trusting me any longer. The paranoia hurt a lot."

Vince couldn't press her for any more information as they were back within hearing range. Instead, he put on his best smile as he pulled out the chair for Marissa. "She's got quite the sweet tooth. I don't know if I'll be able to drag her out of here."

Natalie smiled at them both, but the light that had been in her eyes earlier had been snuffed out. "I'm on a diet, otherwise I would have joined you."

"You're a stronger woman than I am. Though I'm sure you can have some of the fruit if you want. Whenever my mom's on Weight Watchers, she gets excited about fruit being free points, or something." Marissa held out her plate and smiled brighter when Natalie plucked a strawberry from the plate.

Simon got to his feet quickly. "Unfortunately, we have to cut our breakfast short."

"We do?" Natalie frowned, her gaze shifting from Marissa to her husband. "But we haven't finished eating."

Vince internally cringed at the look Simon gave his wife. Natalie stood, retrieving her purse as she went. "It was lovely to meet you, Marissa. Vince, I hope you'll bring her for a visit the next time you're in the city."

"I'll be sure to give you a call." Vince didn't know whether to be pissed off that Simon was walking away from the deal and he'd still be stuck with his dad as a partner, or relieved that he'd get to hold on to GreenPro a bit longer. "Simon, I hope you won't mind if I give you a call next week so we can discuss the details further? Or if anyone on the board has any additional questions."

"I'm not sure if I'm free. Call my assistant and she'll let you know."

Vince knew his business mask was securely in place, but it threatened to crack when Marissa set her plate down and gave Natalie a quick hug. "It was wonderful to meet you. I'm sorry you have to leave." She then turned and held out her hand to Simon. "It was great to meet you again, Mr. Berry. I hope you'll be able to speak more to Vince about GreenPro. It's such a marketable idea, I just know it will take off."

Simon looked down at her hand, back to her eyes, before glancing at Vince. "Have a safe flight home. I need to pay the bill." He then turned and walked away.

Natalie's mouth fell open. "I'm so sorry. He gets like that sometimes."

If Marissa was upset, she didn't show it. "Don't worry about it. And here's my email address. Drop me a note and I'll tell you the rest of that story." She scrawled her email address on a scrap of paper from her purse. "Take care."

Rage had exploded within him, but he managed to hold everything inside until Simon and Natalie were out of earshot. "That asshole."

Marissa sat back down and began to pick away at her fruit. "I get the impression that he'd be a jerk to people even if he wasn't insanely wealthy."

"The fact that he's like that is the reason he's insanely wealthy." Vince continued to glare at the now vanished couple, before reclaiming his seat. "I don't think he's going to go for the sale."

Having pierced a pineapple spear with her fork, Marissa began drawing circles in the chocolate on her plate. "I'm sorry."

"For what?"

"For ruining the deal. You wanted me with you to ensure you presented the best possible image to him, and instead of doing that I was the cause for the deal falling through."

Vince squeezed his hot coffee mug in his hand, needed the short burst of pain to help calm him down. "You didn't. Simon was looking for an excuse to raise a stink. If it wasn't you, it would have been me. I've been fighting an uphill battle on this the whole way. He hates Dad and I'm sure before this is over, things are going to be said about what happened back then."

He reached over and placed his now warm palm on her hand to give it a squeeze. When she turned her hand over, and laced her fingers with his he couldn't help but smile. His attention had been so focused on the contact between them, he hadn't been prepared for the camera flash.

Spots danced in his eyes, as chaos erupted around them. A man who looked to be in his mid-forties stood in front of them, shoving a phone in her face. "Are you Vince's girlfriend? What's your name?"

The waiter and maître d' rushed over to pull the offending photographer away. Vince got to his feet, following several steps before the maître d' came back. "I'm so sorry, Mr. Taylor. We didn't notice he was taking pictures from where he'd been sitting. It wasn't until he came to your table that we noticed. Did you want us to contact the authorities?"

"There's not much you can do about that." He didn't think that the man was paparazzi. More likely someone who recognized him and saw an opportunity to make a quick buck.

"Rest assured, he'll be permanently banned from the establishment." He looked over at Marissa, and smiled. "Of course, your meals will be covered. Consider it an apology."

While he hated the intrusion, that was always the risk of being recognized in public. He nodded and shook the man's hand. "Accepted." It was only when he sat back down, his emotions slowly coming to settle, did he look over at Marissa. Her face had drained of color, her eyes wide. "Are you okay?"

"I'd like to go home."

While getting accosted periodically by photographers wasn't anything new to him, he'd forgotten that it wasn't exactly something that she would have experienced before. "Sure. I'll call the limo to take us back to the hotel. Or we can go back to The Met for a while. There's lots more we can see."

She gently set her fork down, folded her napkin, and gripped the edge of the table. "I mean to Toronto."

Vince frowned, shifting in his seat to look at her better. "We're scheduled to depart tonight. I can see if they can change the flight plan, but that can cause problems."

She got to her feet, her gaze flicking around the room. "Fine. But I have to get out of here."

He should have suspected she'd have been upset by something of this nature. "Let's go."

But when he moved to put his arm around her, she deftly stepped to the side avoiding the contact. "Thank you for breakfast. I won't forget this."

Strangely, that didn't sound like a good thing.

Chapter 16

Marissa had felt sick to her stomach from the time they'd left the restaurant, to the moment they finally stepped into the charter plane. It was shocking how painful it had been having the bubble of her fantasy weekend burst. One moment she'd been eating breakfast at the Waldorf freaking Astoria; the next she'd gone into a panic knowing a picture of her and Vince could end up in the tabloids.

It was weird how *knowing* something like this could happen to her, and *actually* going through the experience were two completely different things. Sure, it was to be expected that someone would snap a picture of them—she'd read too many tabloids over the years not to realize that—and yet, there was somehow a part of her that had assumed it would never happen.

The problem wasn't the picture itself, but who might see it. What the hell would her mom think about her being with a millionaire in New York? Shit, what would her *creditors* think? If anyone thought for a moment that she had access to unlimited wealth, they'd never stop harassing her. And when they realized that she didn't have any money to pay them back, she could only imagine that some of the less than scrupulous ones would start harassing Vince. That alone would be reason enough for him to kick her to the curb.

And while the thought of him no longer being in her life bothered her, it was really the only logical conclusion to all of this. The wrong people would see her, want money, and he'd feel obligated to pay, no doubt assuming she wouldn't have been in that position if not for him. She really should have had a plan to keep from having her face in the media.

Vince had kept his distance since the photo incident as well. He'd been surprisingly calm about the entire matter, which was weird to her. How could it not bother him to have someone jump up and snap a picture of you without your permission? Yes, everyone had a camera on them, and yes, she'd seen him and his women in tabloids over the years.

Yes, this would no doubt end up being yet another one of her spectacular screw ups. Another case of Marissa trying to do the right thing and making matters worse. It wasn't supposed to go this way. Wasn't supposed to be a problem having a little fun with a hot rich man in a big city. Naomi had even told her as much.

She closed her eyes and let gravity pull her head back against the seat. The plane was taxiing and soon she'd be back home to her tiny little basement apartment, her normal class schedule, and her boring life. Because there was no way she'd be able to do something like this again. She'd take the money Vince had offered—mostly because she'd taken him seriously that her time was worth something and that she shouldn't be taken advantage of—pay off what debts she could, and would put an end to this relationship.

No, not a relationship. Arrangement.

Vince snapped his seatbelt together, before taking a sip of wine. "Do you have anything that you have to prepare for class tomorrow?"

Her courses had been the last thing on her mind, but like everything else that had happened, reality had a way of rearing its ugly head to demand her attention. "I have some readings. I put the files on my phone. I'll probably read them once we're in the air." Yes, she had them, but given how distracted she currently was, she doubted she'd get very far. "Do you have something you need to work on?"

Vince pulled out a tablet that had been tucked beside him in his seat. "I have some financials to review."

It was weird, no longer having the warmth coming from him. It was completely her fault, of course, seeing as every time he got too close to her, she did her best to move away. It was going to be hard enough to say goodbye to him without having the constant physical reminder of what she was going to miss. "That's good."

The plane came to a stop, before the pilot's voice filled the cabin. "We're taking off momentarily. Please ensure your seatbelts are on." The roar of engines blasted and within minutes they were in the air.

She carried with her such mixed feelings about her time in New York. Someday, she'd have to go back, see the rest on her own, with no worries of someone making her private adventures public.

"I'm sorry."

She looked up at him. "Pardon?"

He didn't meet her gaze, instead he continued to review whatever was on his tablet. "I'm sorry our weekend was ruined by one fool. But you don't have to worry about those pictures getting out."

"Why not?"

He reached beside him and pulled a phone from his pocket. He'd wrapped her panties around it. "I got his information from the hotel and had a friend track him down. I paid him enough money to make up for the lack of his prize, and so he could get himself a new phone." He held it out for her to take.

Marissa hesitated, but claimed the prize. Her panties were...well, she didn't exactly want them anymore, but she appreciated the sentiment. "That's, unexpected. Thank you."

"No part of the arrangement was for your privacy to be invaded. I wanted to make things right."

Relief rolled through her and she was finally able to relax. "I don't know why it should matter. All of my friends would kill to do even a fraction of what I'd done with you here. They'd be excited for me, but probably also jealous. And my mom...I don't know how she'd feel about everything. And... it's probably the second most terrifying thing I've ever had to deal with."

"It's knowing that the flow of information is out of your control. That they could spin it any way they wanted and you'd have no control over the narrative." He tapped the top of the tablet. "It comes along with the limo and private jet."

A world so far removed from her own, she couldn't imagine living in it permanently. "I don't think I could get used to it."

"You'd be surprised what you can accept as normal given enough time. Which reminds me." He made some movements on the tablet. "I'm transferring you what I owe you to your account. Plus, some extra for the disruption. Think of it as a thank you. The password will be panties."

And he winked at her.

Her unexpected laugh helped ease the tension between them. "Thanks. I won't forget that one." *Or you.* "I'm sorry the deal with Simon didn't work out."

"There was always a risk that things would fall through. I wasn't exactly keen on selling it to him in the first place."

It was strange that this little company seemed to mean so much to him. "Why sell it at all? I mean, there must be some way you can convince your dad to let you have it. I mean, he's your dad. He won't consider selling it to you?"

Vince shrugged, a far too casual move for him. "I'm not the majority owner. Dad wants to sell it to Simon, then that's what we'll do. If nothing else, I'll be done having to dance to his tune."

And with that their conversation ran dry.

Marissa leaned back and did her best to relax and look at her notes for class. As she'd suspected, her attention span didn't last more than a few minutes at a time, and she ended up re-reading the same paragraph multiple times. Sleep then won out, and she slept until the plane began its decent to Toronto.

* * * *

Marissa couldn't understand why she'd grown nervous on the drive back to her house. Maybe because she didn't want Vince to know exactly how horrid her living arrangements were, especially after where they'd stayed for the last two nights. Maybe she didn't want to run the risk of him coming back in at some point in the future to convince her to go out with him again.

Perhaps, she simply wasn't ready to say goodbye to him yet.

"I don't have your address. We'll need to let Jason know exactly which one is yours so he can help you with your bags." Vince had been quiet for most of the drive, and the sudden rumble of his voice startled her.

"It's fine. He knows basically where to drop me off." Yeah, it was mostly embarrassment. If he saw the house, he'd think it was cute. Then he'd offer to bring her bags inside for her, being a perfect gentleman, or some crap like that. Then, he'd step one foot inside the house, see the conditions and no doubt go on a tirade.

She most definitely didn't want to listen to that. Marissa knew he'd mean well, but she also knew their lives were never meant to intersect.

Vince's body tensed as his gaze snapped from her, to the privacy window, and then back to her. "You're being stubborn."

"No, you're trying to push me into revealing something that I want to keep private. You knowing my address wasn't part of our arrangement, and I would like to keep it that way." She took his growl as all the agreement she was likely to get.

The limo came to a lurching halt, and Marissa heard the driver get out and move to the trunk to retrieve her bags. That would only give them another few moments alone, a few more minutes for her to relish the elegance of the past few days. While she knew he was annoyed, she didn't want to part company with him even a little irate at her. For all she knew, this would be the last time they'd see one another.

Shifting in her seat, she got up onto her knees and cupped his face with her hands. "I will never forget this weekend. Every little thing we did was something I will always cherish. Thank you for this gift."

"That sounds like you're saying goodbye." The muscles in his jaw jumped.

Was she really doing this? Walking away from a man who'd been nothing but amazingly kind to her. She sighed. "I think...I am. I'm...it's weird, but the photographer made me realize that there are too many things outside of my control. That picture could have ended up in the press, and everyone who wants money from me would have come looking. God, Andrew could have seen it."

"I would have paid all of it."

She smiled, letting her thumb rub across his cheek. "I know. And I wouldn't have been able to live with myself. I never intended to take advantage of you, or your money. I...I like you too much for that."

Then, she leaned in and kissed him long and hard.

Her tongue flicked across his, teasing and taunting him until the ice that had encased his personality since they'd landed cracked beneath her ministrations. He deepened the kiss, and pulled her fully against him, forcing her to straddle his thigh.

God, she was going to miss this. Miss him.

But even now, her body on fire from the simplest of touches, she knew she could never do something like this again. Her soul would never make it out alive.

As the kiss reached its natural conclusion, Marissa slowly pulled back and opened her eyes. "You make sure to call Simon tomorrow. Tell him he's not your only option and if he wants a shot to get in on the ground floor, then he better get his ass in gear now."

Vince blinked at her several times before gracing her with a small smile. "Yes, ma'am."

She then disengaged from him, taking a moment to straighten her dress before opening the door herself. The driver quickly moved around to hold the door open and helped her out of the back seat. "Careful for the sidewalk. I parked a bit close."

"No problem. Thanks so much for getting me home safe."

He smiled at her, and blushed. "No problem at all."

Marissa turned as she heard Vince get out and come around to her side of the car. "Before you go, I have a small thank you gift."

After everything he'd done for her, the last thing she needed was another present. "You really don't have to."

He went around to the trunk of the limo and retrieved a small, perfectly wrapped present. The paper was silver with little purple stars on it. "I was planning on this being a thank you gift, not a goodbye present. Either way, don't open it until you're having a bad day and need a pick-me-up."

Tears pricked at her eyes and for a moment she thought she was going to lose her shit over a present. "I will."

Vince looked around as the street light clicked on above them. "At least let me help you with your bags."

I knew he'd try some chivalrous shit. "That's okay. They're not exactly heavy."

"It's dark out, and you're alone." Vince threw one look at the driver, which sent him scurrying away. "I promise I won't come inside. I'll bring them to your back door and leave them there."

Marissa looked around her little, boring neighborhood and there was no one in sight. She could only imagine what it looked like to him; rundown, perhaps even a bit dangerous. She'd walked these streets many times by herself. She knew the shadows and the places to avoid. And while she might get herself into more than a few messes, Marissa was nothing if not resourceful.

She reached out and took her suit case handle from him. "I really appreciate you wanting to look out for me. Honestly, I'm going to be fine."

Oh, she could tell from the look on his face that he wanted to argue with her. He wanted to throw his weight around, insist on *doing the right thing* and ignore her request. She could also tell the moment his brain chastised him for those thoughts. "Fine. Text me so I know that you made in it safe and sound."

"Absolutely." It was the least she could do, given everything he'd given her this weekend. "Take care."

Vince looked down at her bare arms. "You better get in before you freeze." He leaned in and kissed her cheek. "I had a good weekend, Ms. Roy."

"Me too, Mr. Taylor."

She waited for him to climb back into the limo, and for the car to pull slowly ahead before she yanked on her suitcase and trudged across the uneven sidewalk home. A lump built in her throat, squeezed at her chest until her emotions threatened to explode. She knew it was the right thing, to end this before it got too out of control.

Vince didn't want a relationship. He'd been clear about that from the start. She hadn't wanted one either, not really. Though, it had been wonderful having someone who genuinely seemed to like spending time with her. Andrew had been hard, untalkative, and not at all the man she'd fallen in love with. Vince, while a no-nonsense kind of man, had shown her more passion and caring than Andrew ever had.

Shit, she was really going to miss him.

Marissa waited for the limo to finally turn the corner of the street, before she picked up her pace and raced up the driveway as quickly as she could. It was freezing out, and all she wanted to do now was slip into her fuzzy pajamas, crawl into bed and go to sleep.

The house was dark, except for the outside light. Shelia knew she was coming home tonight and had left it on for her. As quietly as she could manage, Marissa opened the door and crept down the stairs to her apartment.

There, taped to the middle of her door was a collections notice.

She was too tired to be upset about it, and simply pulled the paper off as she unlocked it and went inside.

Chapter 17

An entire week had passed since New York, and Vince was no closer to accomplishing his task of getting Marissa out of his mind. Or selling GreenPro, for that matter. Both Caroline and Nate had given him a wide berth since his return, only coming into his office when they absolutely needed to. Even then, they had kept conversations short and to the point.

Possibly, *maybe* that might have something to do with his snapping at them.

But really, they were being a pain in his ass. What did they expect?

The financial report he'd been staring at finally snapped into focus for him, and he quickly noted the amendments he needed to address in their next board meeting. His fingers flew across the keyboard, making the necessary changes. The more engrossed he got, the more his body relaxed. It felt good to be doing something productive.

He wasn't exactly certain how much time had passed, when he heard someone clear their throat. Nate was standing in the doorway, looking pointedly at his phone. "It's nearly seven o'clock. Did you want to get out of here and get a beer?"

"Is it?" The ache in his back and neck confirmed he'd been at this a while now. "Yeah, let's go."

As they went, Nate waved and said goodnight to several staff who were getting packed up for the night. Vince tried to remember their names, but he had few dealings with them, preferring to let Nate handle the daily operations of the firm. "You going to say goodnight to the janitor too?"

"Yes, if I see her. She might be late coming in tonight. Her son had a school concert and he was lead sax for one of the pieces."

Vince stopped walking and stared at him.

"What? Candace's a great janitor." Nate shrugged. "I'm here late most nights when she comes in. After a few months, you tend to engage in conversations."

"I don't." Marissa did the same thing as Nate. No one was beneath her notice. "I should probably get better about engaging with people."

"Yes, you should." Nate shoved his hands in his pockets. "Come on. I need to get a few drinks into you so you'll finally tell me what the hell has climbed up your ass."

Vince groaned. "None of your goddamned business."

"I'm your PR guy. Everything you do is my business. The very definition of *in this together*." He came over to Vince and pulled him toward the elevator. "There's a great microbrewery that just opened up half a block from here. I've been wanting to try it."

"Fine." It wasn't *fine*. Very little had been since he'd received Marissa's text letting him know that she'd safely gotten inside. But as far as Nate and Caroline were concerned, his little adventure with her was over and done with, never to be repeated again.

He'd texted Marissa only once since their departure. It was Monday morning when he suspected she was heading out to class. Instead, she informed him that she'd been at work for two hours already and couldn't talk to him. Vince wasn't certain if she meant she couldn't talk to him then, or wasn't going to speak to him again.

The latter of those two options was what had bothered him most.

Nate wasn't much for small talk, but when he was out to get something, he could yammer away with the best of them. For the next hour, the two of them chatted about work, clients, the names of the employees Nate felt Vince should get to know, and exactly how hoppy a good IPA should be.

Nate took a long sip of his pint. "I want to be able to taste the bitterness from the moment the beer hits my tongue. But after a few seconds, it should dissipate. A good disappearing magic trick, that's how I want my hops."

"I prefer reds. I'm not big on hops." He was big on the truffle fries they'd ordered to go along with their drinks, and shoved another one into his mouth. "We need to order more of these."

"I was under the impression you preferred blondes." Nate leaned back in his seat, holding his glass to his chest. "At least, that's what Caroline said."

It took Vince's brain a moment to catch what he was implying. "We went to New York and had a good time. That was it."

"Yeah, I don't think so. You did this whole thing as a way of getting back at your dad. Don't bother denying it."

"I stepped in and saved her from Geoff. Plus, it made things easier for me, having someone sane with me while I tried to negotiate with that asshole Simon Berry." Vince still hadn't heard back from him on whether or not he was interested in GreenPro. With each day that passed, he was less certain he ever would. "It didn't matter in the end. Dad showed up in New York and made things worse by his presence. I doubt Simon will buy it now, and I know Dad will use this as an excuse to make life harder."

"You'll sell GreenPro, make your money, and finally be rid of your dad. Of that I have no doubt." He took another sip and cocked his head as though he was trying to look into Vince's brain. "Caroline said your girl was night and day from women you've dated in the past. I think she might have even liked her."

If Caroline liked Marissa, then perhaps the end of the world was coming. "Caroline thinks any woman who isn't Thea is awesome."

"Well, she's a practical sort." The smile slipped from Nate's face. "I heard she's dating one of the Matheson boys. Thea, not Caroline."

The Mathesons owned the second largest grocery store chain in Canada. The sons were all rich, good looking, and loved the spotlight. Exactly the type of man Thea would be drawn to. "Good for her. I hope she can finally find some happiness." More importantly, he hoped she'd finally stay away from him.

"I'm sure she'll find what she's looking for there. The two of you were never a good match. Now, this other girl...what's her name?"

"Marissa."

"Right, Marissa. She might be better suited for you."

God save him from matchmaking friends. "You do remember how we met, right? I was being serious when I said this was nothing more than a business arrangement. She lived up to her end of the bargain."

"Then you'll just have to make arrangements for her to attend another event with you." Nate shrugged and finished his beer. "I'm sure the reason for her signing up for the site hasn't changed. We have more than a few parties that need our presence. Give her a call. See if she'll come."

Vince hadn't considered that it would be as easy as how Nate was making it sound. While she hadn't come right out and said that she didn't want to see him again after New York, there'd been something in her demeanor when they'd said goodbye that had given him the impression that it was an ending and not a *see you soon.*

"I think her experience with my dad and Simon Berry was more than enough to put her off of lifestyles of the rich and obnoxious. Not to mention the asshole who took her picture. I've never seen someone that freaked out before."

"Please, I've seen you talk people into deals that they didn't even know they wanted. I have no doubt you could change her mind in a heartbeat."

"What kind of man does that make me? If she doesn't want to see me again, or go out again and I force her hand, then I'm no better than my father." Yes, he wanted to see Marissa again, but it had to be because she wanted to and not because she felt pressured.

"Call her." Nate flagged the waiter down and ordered them another round. "Worst case she tells you to fuck off. You won't know unless you give it a shot."

Vince touched his cell phone in his pocket before Nate had even finished speaking. He had her phone number, though to this point he'd only ever texted her. It really couldn't hurt. She was probably working or studying and he'd no doubt get her voice mail. He'd leave a message and then the ball would be in her court.

What harm could there be in trying?

He pointed at Nate as he pulled his phone out. "Do I need to go somewhere else?"

"Nope. I promise to be good." Though there was a look in his eyes that Vince didn't exactly trust.

"Fucker. I'll be back." Vince stood, snatching the last of the truffle fries before heading for the door.

The evening air had turned cold the last two nights, making the contrast between it and the warmth in the bar startling. He didn't plan to be out here long. Pressing Marissa's contact, he waited as several bar hoppers passed by, laughing and having fun. She could be out right now with her friends. What did he actually know about her life beyond the few bits and pieces she'd shared with him? Nothing.

The line kept ringing and for a moment, he braced for the inevitable message to pop up. He was mildly surprised when he heard the click and her voice echoed through to him. "Hello?"

Something was quite clearly wrong. "It's Vince."

"Who?"

His mouth fell open. She couldn't have forgotten who he was. Was he about to get the brush off? Shit, Nate would never let him live that down. But before he could answer, he heard her yelling at someone.

"What the hell are you doing? Leave that there and I'll pack it. Just... please stop."

That didn't sound right. "What's going on? Marissa?"

The pause on the other end was punctuated by the sound of her heavy breathing. "Vince?"

"Yes. What's happening and how can I help?"

"There was a flood…why are you calling me?"

He didn't know much about her living arrangements, but a flood was never good by anyone's standards. "I wanted to check in and make sure you were doing okay. Clearly you're not."

"I'm fine. No, please just leave the dresses. I'll go through those." She sounded as close to tears as he'd ever heard her.

"I'm coming over."

"What? No." He heard her thumping up some stairs and the noise in the background dying out. "No, please don't. I'm fine. My landlady had a burst pipe upstairs and neither of us were home. It's a…we're saving what we can so they can start the cleanup."

God, she sounded tired. Vince turned and marched back inside to the table, grabbing his jacket and waving Nate off as he stood. "Give me an address and I can be there in thirty minutes."

"Vince—"

He stopped dead in his tracks. There was nothing he could do if she refused his offer. This was a situation he couldn't buy his way out of. Closing his eyes for a moment, he took a breath. "You sound like you need help. You also sound like you could use a friend. I can be both of those things for you. No strings attached."

The seconds ticked by until finally, he heard a small sob. "I'll text you the address."

"Thirty minutes." He waited for her to hang up first, before jogging back to the office and his car.

* * * *

There was a cleaning service parked in the driveway when he finally arrived, forcing him to park on the street. He didn't see Marissa sitting on the steps, wrapped in a thick woolen sweater, until he was half-way around the van. Dried tear streaks shone on her face from the overhead light of the back porch. She looked small, tired, and scared.

He'd been working on a speech on his way over. It had been all noble sounding, putting him in the best light as well as his willingness to be her savior. The second he saw her there, he knew every syllable of it was stupid and selfish. Forgetting everything, he climbed up the stairs and sat down beside her.

Marissa didn't say anything. She took a deep breath that shuddered slightly on the exhale and rested her head against the side of his arm.

The voices of men were easily heard from inside. Vince couldn't imagine what the mess was like inside, but whenever water was involved, he knew it wouldn't be pleasant. If their tone of voice was anything to go by, it was even worse than what he'd initially assumed.

"I just got home an hour and a half ago." She sounded exhausted. "Shelia isn't even home. She's away on a business trip. I don't know what happened, but my apartment is soaked. The pipe above my living room exploded. It could have been going for hours."

"Shit." He wrapped his arm around her. "Shelia is your landlady?"

"Yup." Another sigh. "She's also a hoarder. The repair guys are freaking out because there's also water upstairs and everything is soaked. Lots of paper and boxes and—" she swallowed hard, "—and they don't have enough people to clear things out. They can't make the repairs until that's done. And there are some health concerns because of mold, so they won't actually touch anything because Shelia isn't here. They're in a holding pattern."

With each word she said, Vince's temper threatened to explode. He had to keep his emotions in check if he was going to be the help she needed. "Has Shelia been contacted?"

"Yes. She's out of the province, but she's booked a flight home first thing in the morning."

"Have they shut the water off?"

"Yup."

"Then there's nothing else you can do tonight." He got to his feet and started up the stairs. "I'll get your things and then you can come with me."

He knew it was more a comment on her current emotional condition than anything, when she didn't protest. "Thank you."

Vince had seen a wide variety of conditions over the years. His business would swoop in and save a failing company or business, fix it up financially and physically, before selling it and moving on. Nothing he'd ever seen in his life could have prepared him for what he saw the moment he stepped into the house.

At one point, it might have been considered quaint. The older home was stretched to bursting with garbage. Perhaps the contents meant something to the resident, but no one on the outside looking in would have any idea what any of this was. Vince had neither the time nor the patience to give the contents much thought. Instead, he found the crew supervisor and told them to come back in the morning. He then made his way to the basement apartment that Marissa called home.

How could she choose to live in this place? The must and mold was too strong for it to be the result of the water damage, meaning she'd been living in these horrendous conditions for a while. No wonder she'd refused to give him her address before now. She was no doubt scared he'd try and swoop in and fix everything.

Exactly as he was doing right now.

Pushing those thoughts away, he slogged through the water to her bedroom, grabbed a backpack that was on her bed and filled it with whatever clothing he could find. The dresses she'd worn to New York were laid out on the bed, the silk and sequins soaked in dank water.

The sight pushed him over the edge. He took what he'd gathered and marched up the stairs. He could barely look at her as he exploded from the porch. If she was upset by his mood, she didn't show it. Instead, she stood as he walked past, trailing behind him to his car. She didn't speak when she climbed into the passenger seat, nor when he tossed her backpack into the rear seat.

Vince slammed his door shut, forcing himself to relax before starting the car. He had too many thoughts and feelings racing around him to speak coherently. She didn't seem to be in any better condition. Looking over, he saw that she had his present, still wrapped, firmly in her grasp. At least that didn't get ruined, one bright spot to the evening. He took a breath, started the car and took her to the once place he knew she'd be safe.

His home.

Chapter 18

Marissa had heard about people being shell-shocked after a personal misfortune. Families being torn apart from floods, fires, and other disasters. She'd always assumed she'd be able to handle something like that if it crept up in her life. Maybe she would have been able to deal with a home flood if it wasn't one more in a string of disasters that had infected her life.

Lights and shadows passed over Vince's face as he drove. She wasn't exactly certain she knew where they were going—a hotel or something she assumed—but she knew wherever it was, he'd be sure she was good for the night. She wasn't even certain why he'd called her tonight. She didn't think she'd hear from him again, let alone see him walk up the broken driveway to come to her rescue.

"Why did you call me?" Her voice sounded rough, even to her own ears. "You normally text."

"I'm glad I didn't." His fingers flexed on the steering wheel. "I was checking to see if you wanted to go to another event with me." His tone was clipped, his annoyance clear.

Why would she think he'd be happy to be in this situation? He'd wanted to set up another date, such as they were. The last thing he'd want to involve himself in was in the disaster that was her life. He was rich and successful. She was a business arrangement. That's all they would ever be to one another.

"I promise I'll be out of your hair by morning. I would have called my mom tonight, but she usually turns into a pumpkin around nine thirty and she doesn't drive, so she'd only end up worrying about me until I showed up. I don't think I have that in me tonight."

"Marissa." He stopped at a red light, turned and looked at her. "Whatever you're thinking, stop. It's fine."

Her life was currently the furthest thing from *fine* that it could possibly be. Most of her meager possessions were now water damaged, and her apartment wasn't exactly livable. Despite her best efforts, she was going to have to move back in with her mom, which meant getting to and from school was going to be a nightmare. Not to mention needing to catch super early transit so she could make the open shift at the Pear Tree. Chances were, she would have to find a different job, one closer to her mom's.

Her brain screeched to a halt when Vince reached over and took her hand in his. He gave it a squeeze, causing her to look over at him. Rather than the annoyed look she'd expected, Vince appeared concerned. She squeezed back and swallowed down her unshed tears.

The light turned green, but he didn't immediately move the car. "I promise I'll help you." The car behind them honked, and Vince returned his attention to driving.

Marissa looked out the window, not focusing on any one thing as they drove past buildings, houses, and stores. It wasn't until they pulled into a gated driveway that she realized he hadn't brought her to a hotel. "Where are we?"

"My place." He turned the engine off, but didn't get out of the car. "I wanted to make sure that you were going to be okay tonight."

"I would have been fine at a hotel." She didn't exactly have spare money to cover the cost, but seeing as she wouldn't be paying rent for the foreseeable future, she could have managed something for a night or two.

Vince's face was half shrouded in a long, black shadow. Light wouldn't have helped her determine what he was thinking. The same cool mask he'd worn the first night they'd met on the yacht was firmly in place. "I'll take you to one if that's what you want."

The offer was made and the choice was hers.

She held his gaze, barely seeing him. Her mind tore through all the possibilities of what could happen if she got out of the car and went into his home. What would that mean for their strange and varied relationship, if anything? A room in a nice, basic hotel would be the smart decision, the move that would make the most sense given how she was going to need to move forward with her life.

Vince wouldn't give her any grief. He wouldn't even question her decision. He'd simply turn the car back on and take her to the nearest hotel.

Marissa reached for the handle and opened her door. "I hope you have a spare room, because I don't know if I could handle a couch tonight."

She heard him snort before the door shut behind her.

Vince didn't say much of anything as he got her bag and led her toward the back door. A few security-button presses later, and she walked into the most amazing kitchen she'd ever seen in her life. "Wow."

He set her bag down by the wall. "Make yourself at home. I have a well-stocked fridge and pantry. If there's something you want that I don't have, let me know and I'll have the service drop it off tomorrow."

"I won't be here any longer than tonight. I'll give my mom a call tomorrow and I'll head over there later." Which was a shame, because she really could have a lot of fun in this place. "Thanks though."

Vince had his back to her, so she couldn't tell what he was feeling. "Let me show you where the spare room is. You'll probably want a shower and to go to sleep."

Marissa did her best not to stare as he led her through the house, upstairs to a bedroom that was larger than her apartment living room. No wonder he stayed at penthouses when he traveled, if this was the standard of living he was used to. The bedroom had a full-sized bathroom attached, fresh towels folded and placed as though the room had been staged for a photoshoot.

"Do you live here alone?" It seemed strange that a bachelor would live in a huge house and not some upscale condo. "Don't you get lonely here?"

Vince hadn't followed her into the bedroom, but he loomed large in the doorway. "I have lots of things to keep me busy."

She didn't have a clue what any of those things would be, but no doubt they were important. "That's good."

"I'm going to leave you alone. Sleep and I'll see you when you wake up. Okay?"

"Yup."

He shut the door as he left, the click of the latch snicking into place echoed in the quite of the house.

Marissa stood in the middle of this beautiful room, everything she could possibly want at her fingertips and sighed. This past week, she'd dreamed about seeing Vince again. She'd woken up horny, her mind replaying every bit of pleasure he'd given her while they'd been away. In a short time, he'd obliterated all thoughts of Andrew, of what her life could have been with him, and replaced it with thoughts of what it could be with Vince.

Vince, the man who had no desire to have a relationship.

She looked over to the bed, knowing she should strip down and climb between those sheets. It was nearly midnight, and after the day she'd had, sleep was the perfect cure to help her. Vince would stay true to his word, letting her rest. That was the thing about him, not once had she ever doubted his word, doubted that he genuinely cared for her well-being. It wasn't the big things, like tonight, coming to get her. It was more the tiny gestures that had been seriously lacking in her relationship with Andrew in the past few years. The steadying hand to her back on the ship. The gentle teasing when he knew she needed cheering up. The unexpected gifts—their trip to The Met, the dinners, the clothing, the spa day, his present—that had nothing to do with their arrangement, and everything to do with him wanting to make her happy *just because.*

She'd rescued his present for her when she'd walked into her apartment and saw the disaster. It had been sitting on the dehumidifier, which was ironically the only thing that had remained dry in the place. The sparkling wrapping paper was damp, but undamaged, giving her no idea what was hidden inside. Marissa moved to the bed and sat down on the edge, knowing if there was ever a time she needed a pick-me-up, it was tonight.

Starting at the edge, she slowly picked at the paper, taking care not to rip even a corner as she pulled the tab free. Her heart began to race and her fingers shook—whether from excitement, or from the shock of the evening's events, she wasn't certain—as she peeled the paper back to see what was hidden beneath.

Darth Vader's face looked up at her, announcing that she was now the proud owner of a new *Star Wars* Blu-ray. A sob exploded from her loudly before both her hands could fly to her mouth to keep it from escaping. It was the exact version she'd had before, though there was no way Vince would have known that. She continued to stare at it, though it took a surprising amount of time for her to realize that there was a note card sticking out from beneath the case.

Marissa was less careful ripping into the envelope, and pulled the card free. She'd half expected feminine handwriting when she looking inside, but wasn't at all surprised when she saw typically masculine pen scratchings filling the white card.

> *Marissa.*
>
> *I get why these movies mean the world to you. But I'll be honest, had anyone but you told me to watch it, I probably wouldn't have given it the attention it deserved. The passion and joy you generated when you spoke about it ignited a curiosity in me that I hadn't felt in ages.*
>
> *You do that to me. Make me look at the little details.*
>
> *When you have the world at your feet, it's easy to forget about the small things. The kindness of speaking to a waiter. Of*

smiling to a coworker as you pass in the hallway. You made me
stop and look.

So thank you for reminding me. Maybe we can watch the
next one together?

V

Oh.

There was no stopping the tears now. No way to put a finger in the
bursting dam of emotions that now consumed her. She let them fall, let
them wash away every horrible thing that had happened to her. She'd given
him something that money couldn't buy, something she never would have
been able to plan for. Marissa needed him, needed to touch and feel the
warmth of his body.

Setting the movie and note on the bed, she got to her feet and wiped
away her tears. She turned and walked to the door, not exactly certain of
what she was going to do, but knowing she had to do something. The knob
was cold in her grasp, a last little jolt to try and shake her from her ill-
conceived plan. *Turn around, go to bed. You'll regret this in the morning.*

Fuck it.

The knob turned easily and the door slid open.

The hallway was long, but while the house was large, it wasn't exactly
difficult to know where Vince would have disappeared to. The only other
light in the house came from a room down the hall and on the right. She
could hear Vince move around inside, could picture him getting undressed
and ready for bed. Each step she took closer to him sent her heart pounding.
There was a chance that he wouldn't want her, that he'd send her back to
her room the moment his eyes landed on her. She'd have to respect his
desires as much as he'd respected hers.

She'd nearly made it to his room when the unmistakable sound of a
shower starting up reached her. That nearly made her turn around and race
back to her room. She didn't know what kind of day he'd had. Maybe her
little crisis was the final nail in the coffin of a day from hell. They hadn't
exactly spoken much since he'd showed up in her driveway. Instead of
listening to her better instincts, she took a breath before pushing open the
door to his bedroom and stepped inside.

The room suited him. It was large, with a large wooden bedframe along
the middle of the far wall. An electric fireplace filled most of the opposite
wall. The flames danced hypnotically as heat rolled off it in waves, warming
the space. Marissa stood in front of it for a moment, remembering their

night in New York, the warmth from a fire long extinguished and a passion she hoped to feel again.

The sound of water splashing in the shower jerked her back to the moment. Vince wouldn't be long in there. Her shirt came off easily, as did her jeans. Her bra and panties took a few seconds longer, as her fingers shook from the unexpected nerves that hit her. She left her clothing on the floor in a small pile, just in case she needed to grab them as she made a hasty escape.

Naked, she made her way to the bathroom and pushed the door open.

Vince had his hands leaning against the shower wall, the full spray of the water hitting his head and upper shoulders. The shower was stone, the floor slanted so no door was needed as the water made its way to the long drain along the side. There was nothing between them, not even their clothing, and yet she felt as though they were worlds apart.

They probably were.

The sight of him wet, his defenses down, had guilt run through her. She should leave, give him his privacy and let him rest. Marissa started to move, when he turned his head and looked at her. He didn't say a word, didn't move or give her any indication of what he wanted. His gaze had locked onto hers, and she couldn't tell what he was thinking, despite the torrent of emotions that flitted across his face.

She took a step back, suddenly very conscious of her nakedness. Vince straightened, water rolling down his body in small rivers, splashing across his thickening cock. With his gaze still on hers, he held out his hand. Relief so strong it nearly sent her into tears washed through her. Carefully, she walked into the shower and into his arms.

The water was too hot for her, and she gasped at the sting of it against her skin. He reached past her and turned it down. "Sorry."

She kissed the middle of his wet chest. "It's not like you knew I was coming."

The idea of having sex with him there and then was beyond tempting. It was what she'd intended to do the moment she'd heard the shower in the first place. She should have known Vince would have had other ideas. "Turn around."

He maneuvered her so she was looking up at him as he backed her into the water. Her hair was soaked in seconds, as her skin soaked up the moisture. The must and mold from her apartment was flushed away in moments, leaving her feeling clean. Vince reached over and took a squirt of shampoo from the bottle on the side, and proceeded to wash her hair.

Oh, what a glorious thing.

His fingers scratched circles against her scalp, sending shivers through her body as he scrubbed away the dirt. A moan slipped from her, earning a chuckle from him as he then backed her into the water once more.

She was treated to a second scalp massage when he repeated the motions with conditioner, leaving her body electrified. Her nipples had hardened from the contact, and her pussy heated from lack of attention. Forcing her eyes open, she looked up at him. "You're way too good at that."

"I'm better at this."

Bracing his hand on the wall behind her, he reached between her thighs with his free hand and pressed against her wet clit. Marissa moaned, her hands flying to his arms, seeking stability. "Shit."

"Relax."

No way in hell that was happening.

Her head fell forward against his chest, as he teased her clit with her fingers. She sucked in the smell of him and soap deep into her lungs as she panted, trying to hold back the orgasm she knew would be coming soon enough.

Vince leaned his mouth to her ear and sucked on the lobe. "I was thinking about you while I stood here. I was picturing you standing naked in your shower and wondered what you'd do if I came in. Then I opened my eyes and you were standing there." He pressed harder against her clit, the circles coming smaller and faster. "I keep remembering the sounds you made while I fucked you. I wanted to hear that moan again. Moan for me, Marissa."

She bit on her bottom lip, trying to keep the sounds he desperately wanted trapped inside. Then he slipped a finger into her pussy at the same time he pressed down on her clit with his thumb, and there was no way she could stop it. Digging her nails into his arms, she moaned and began to buck her hips in time to his fingers.

"Yes, just like that." He nipped at her earlobe again. "I want to feel you come on my hand. I want to hear and taste you. I want you to come so hard you scream my name."

She resigned herself to inevitability of her orgasm, and instead of trying to hold back, took what little remained of her ability to think and relaxed into the pleasure. The moment she did so, she became intensely aware of every ripple, every touch of his body against hers. She pressed her forehead to his chest, and breathed him in.

Her eyes squeezed shut and her body shook moments before her orgasm came. One moment there was everything, and in the next all she could focus on was the pleasure that whipped from her core. The scream dripped from her, low and slow, only to build to a crescendo that echoed loudly in the shower. Through it all, Vince held her up, kept her steady with a strong arm and firm body.

Once the onslaught of her pleasure subsided, all she was aware of was her own panting and the hardened cock jutting between them. She wanted nothing more than to reach down and stroke him, feel the veins and soft skin as she slid his hand up and down the length of him. Before she could put her plan into action, Vince reached past her and snapped off the water with a quick twist of the handle.

Without breaking contact, he reached around the corner and grabbed one of the thick, blue towels that had been hanging there. The soft cotton felt good against her skin as he wrapped it around her shoulders. He rubbed her skin gently, and even made a passing attempt to dry her hair.

She laughed as some of the strands fell into her face. "I must look like a banshee."

He smiled, his eyes sparkling. "You're gorgeous."

"And you're horny." She did reach down and ran her thumb across the head of his cock.

He groaned, but instead of letting her have her way with him, he reached down and scooped her into his arms. "Behave."

Marissa clung to him, the towel hanging precariously from her shoulder. "God, I'm heavy. Put me down."

Ignoring her protests and still dripping wet, he stepped out of the shower and carried her over to his bed. He somehow managed to hold her to his chest as he reached down and yanked the duvet cover back. "You're exhausted and need sleep."

Protesting seemed pointless as she yawned. Instead, she let him tuck her into his bed. "You're going to join me, right?"

She could tell he was debating doing that. No doubt, the chivalrous part of him had some noble plan to go off and sleep somewhere else. The last thing Marissa wanted was for that plan to become the winner. Reaching over she flicked the opposite side of the duvet down and patted the empty spot.

Vince swallowed as he stared down at her. "Just to sleep."

"Okay." That was all she really could manage. Considering everything that had happened and the amazing orgasm he'd just given her, sleep was a given.

He snatched the towel from the floor where it had fallen, and quickly dried himself off. She had to smile at how he avoided his erection, and spent extra time drying behind his knees. When he finally climbed onto the bed, she relished the way the mattress dipped under his weight.

She waited until he was settled, duvet over them both, facing inches apart. Only once he stopped moving, did she lean close enough to press a soft kiss to his lips. "I opened your present."

He stiffened for a moment. "Did I get the right one?"

"It's perfect. Thank you."

"You're welcome." He touched the side of her face. "Sleep."

As though her brain was programmed to accept his command, she closed her eyes and did exactly that.

Chapter 19

Vince had managed to stay in the same bed as Marissa for four hours, before he had to get up. His hard-on came and went over the course of that time, making it difficult for him to sleep. The sweet little noises she made weren't helping matters either. Marissa awake was all laughter and energy, her beauty generated from the force of her presence. Marissa asleep, at peace was a far more seductive image.

He'd been surprised when she'd come into the shower. Seeing her wet, emotional, was a sight that would never leave his memory for the remainder of his days. Knowing that it was his gift to her, his note that had propelled her to seek him out, brought his desire to make her happy to the forefront.

It also was the strongest turn-on he'd ever experienced in his life.

He got up as carefully as he could manage, and crept to the bathroom, his cock once again coming to life. There was no chance he'd get back to sleep now unless he took matters into hand, and got rid of this uncontrollable desire to wake her, to make love to her.

He closed the door, pressed his back to it, and took himself in hand. The strokes came fast as he fisted himself from sac to tip, teasing himself the way he knew Marissa would. The memory of her here, skin damp, the slickness of her pussy as he fucked her with his hand, was as vibrant as if he'd recorded it.

Marissa with her head thrown back, her lips parted. His desire to guide her to her knees and slide his cock into her mouth. To watch her with those beautifully large eyes staring up at him as he thrust past her full lips and against her tongue. He wanted to know what it was like to make love to her in his bed, to know that her unique scent would forever cling to his sheets, replacing the generic scent of fabric softener. He wanted to wake her up with kisses, wanted to put her to bed with orgasms.

He simply wanted her.

Fisting his cock, the first tingles of orgasm heated his cock, his very core. Within a minute, his balls tightened and he felt the first splash of his release cover his hand and belly. His legs shook from the force of his orgasm, and he fought hard to keep his cries bottled up, scared his moans would wake her.

His thick cum stuck to his fingers, and clumped in the sink as he washed it away. It took him longer than normal to clean away the evidence, as he did his best to do what he needed to in the dark.

Once he'd finished, he crept back over to the bed, hoping that now perhaps he'd be able to get some rest. Marissa had shifted in his absence and now took up the middle portion of the mattress, cuddled around the duvet as though she were holding a person.

Great.

He could move her over, but then he'd risk waking her. Given the type of day she was going to have ahead of her, that was the last thing he'd wanted to do. The even air was cool and he was still naked, making his decision one of importance. Instead of risking waking her, he grabbed his gym bag and left the room. It would be quiet out on the streets, which meant it was the perfect time of day to go for his run.

Vince changed, grabbed his water, and headed out into the cool morning.

* * * *

Marissa sighed as she rolled over, letting her arm flop out across the mattress as she stretched. Warmth held her brain in a cocoon that prevented her from forming thoughts. It was nice to not have to worry about thinking. There was always too much on her mind, too many details to work out and worry about. This emptiness was heaven she hadn't experienced in forever.

Wait, why was she alone?

Sitting up, she looked around the room for Vince. It was nearly eight o'clock, and he was not in the room. "Shit."

Her clothing was back in her room, but the damp towel she'd used last night was still on the floor where they'd left it. She shivered as she crawled out of the warmth of his bed and wrapped herself up, before racing to the door. Peeking out, she saw that the pile of clothing she'd left on her little failed trip to seduce Vince, was gone. He must have collected them when he'd gotten up this morning. No one else was around, so she scurried to the spare room, to find her things on the bed.

She got dressed and pulled her hair into a ponytail at the back of her neck, before heading downstairs. "Vince?"

"In the kitchen."

Oh, thank God. If he'd actually left her for the day, she didn't know what she would do with herself. While she appreciated him putting her up for the night, there was no way she'd be able to stay here long-term. She had too many issues that she didn't want causing problems in his life. Better to cut her losses now and move on.

Even if the only thing she truly wanted to do was to take him by the hand and pull him back to bed.

The smell of coffee hit her before she made it to the kitchen. God, that smelled even better than what they made down at the Pear Tree. The moment she crossed the threshold and entered the kitchen, he'd poured her a cup and set it on the counter. "There's cream in the fridge and sugar on the counter."

"You're a prince."

One thing she'd come to appreciate about Vince, was the fact he didn't say an awful lot early in the day. Her mom was a chatterbox from morning to night, and Marissa had always found it difficult to deal with her before her brain had kicked in. She dressed her coffee and took several long, savoring sips before she turned to talk to him.

Vince looked awful. "Did I kick you out of bed? I'm so sorry if I did. I sometimes will get these really vivid dreams and then I get talking in my sleep. I even punched Andrew once right in the spine, but I haven't done that sort of thing in months."

With each word she said, his eyebrows rose higher. It was only once she stopped did he smile at her. "I couldn't sleep, so I went for a run. Nothing to do with you." He looked away as he said that, so she didn't exactly believe him.

"How far do you run? I tried to do that for a few weeks last year. I had this dream that I'd start training for a marathon or something. I ended up doing the zoo run and walked most of the five kilometers. Naomi laughed at me."

Vince turned and pressed his back to the counter. The shift showed off the muscles in his forearms and biceps. "I normally do ten K, three times a week. Helps with the stress and it helps with all the eating out I normally do."

Ten kilometers? Three times a week? *Dear God.* "I think I'd die."

"You get used to it. Like anything else."

"I've personally gotten used to sleeping in and drinking coffee. But if you want to get up before daylight and run around in the dark, go for it. You do you, crazy-head."

When he smiled, the last remnants of the previous night's darkness were chased away from her mind. There was something wonderful about seeing him having fun. Now that she'd read his note to her, knowing that despite everything that he had available to him, that he didn't enjoy things as perhaps he should, was more than a little heartbreaking.

She was about to say something else, when there was a knock on the back door. Vince's head shot up and his entire body went rigid. "The fuck?"

"You're not expecting anyone?" The hackles on the back of her neck went up, and she clung to the coffee mug a bit harder than necessary.

"No, I'm not." He strode to the door, his large body blocking her from being able to see who was standing on the other side. "How did you get into my yard?"

"Hey. I'm looking for Marissa Roy."

"This is private property. Get the fuck out or I'll call the cops."

Blood pooled in her stomach, making her nauseous. How the hell did a creditor follow her here? Before she could say anything, Vince stepped out the door, forcing the creditor to back up. He then shut the door.

Yeah, that wasn't going to happen.

She put the mug down and followed them both out. Vince had his finger in the guy's face, his body appearing a hulking mass next to the smaller man. "...see you here again I'm going to kick your ass."

If the creditor was concerned, he didn't show it. His gaze snapped to Marissa's the moment she'd come outside. "You owe us money."

"I don't owe anything. That's my ex. Go collect it from him"

"You co-signed the papers. That means it's you too." He then turned to Vince.

"How did you find me?" She'd been so careful the past few weeks, especially since Vince had come into her life. She couldn't imagine how they would have known where she'd disappeared to.

"I showed up last night as you got into his car. I followed you here and waited until one of you came out." He looked at Vince. "You need to be smarter about locking your gate door when you come back from your run."

The growl that came from Vince sent a shiver through her. He got right into the man's face and shoved him hard.

"I'm doing my job. She's the one who's been an asshole by not paying what she's owed. But since you're Big Shot Mr. Rich guy, you can grab a cheque book and pay off what she owes too."

"Fuck off!" And before Marissa knew what he was doing, Vince punched the guy—hard.

The man stumbled backward, blood trickling down from his split lip. "You're going to regret that." He then turned tail and ran.

Vince stared after him, shaking his hand out as he did. The guy opened the door next to the driveway gate and disappeared. Marissa's heart pounded hard enough she was terrified it was going to stop. Everything she'd hoped to prevent had come to pass, all because she'd given in to the temptation of his comfort. Just like she'd done to her mom when she was younger, Marissa had brought him unwanted attention and pain.

"I'm sorry." She'd said it so softly, she wasn't sure he'd heard her. She cleared her throat and tried again. "Sorry."

Vince turned slowly, his gaze morphing from annoyed to confused. "For what? I'm the one who didn't lock my own security gate. I should be apologizing to you." He gave his hand another shake. "No doubt I'll be getting a visit from the cops later. Assholes like that will press charges every time. They love nothing better than being able to take down a celebrity." Vince spun in a tight circle, before throwing his head back. "Fuck!"

Marissa might be many things, but she was not normally one to cry. And yet, here she stood for the third time in less than twenty-four hours with tears streaming down her face. "I can't seem to do anything right. Andrew thought I was cheating on him when all I was trying to do was set up a surprise party, and then I can't get out from under all these bills. And now I'm dragging you down into a bunch of shit that you'd done your best to keep out of."

She didn't see him cross the distance, but suddenly his arms were wrapped around her and her face was pressed to his chest. "You've done nothing wrong. Do you hear me? This wasn't your fault."

God, it would be so easy to believe him, to let Vince simply make everything all right in her world. But what kind of person would that make her? She'd never become the woman she'd always wanted to be if she continued to let everyone fix her problems for her. "I should go."

He reached down and tilted her head back, until she had no choice but to look him in the eyes. "You go if that's what you really want. If you need to leave to sort some things out, then I'll drive you to where you need to be myself. But if you're leaving because you think I don't want you around, then that's not acceptable."

She couldn't believe after everything that had happened, that he wasn't ready to toss her to the curb. "How can you say that?"

"Because everything that's happened hasn't exactly been under your control. Including that asshole finding us." He brushed her hair from her face. "If you let me help, then I can fix this for you."

"Then I'll owe you. I don't know if I can handle that."

Vince shook his head. "Then we'll see if there's another option. But you're not in this alone. Understand?"

The ache in her chest lessened slightly. "Okay."

"Good. Now, why don't we go back in, eat and get dressed. I can then take you to your mom's if that's where you'd want to go."

She didn't deserve this, or him for that matter. "Thanks. I'd like that." No matter how screwed up her life got, or how badly she wanted to keep her mom from getting involved, Marissa would always need her.

"Food first, then we'll go."

Carefully, she lifted his hand, surprised that it was already bruising. "We need to get some ice on this too. It's going to hurt later."

"Hurts like a bitch now." Still, he casually looped his arm across her shoulders. "Let's get that ice."

The weight of his touch on her should be reassuring, as should his words. And yet, Marissa couldn't help but worry that as hard as he'd tried to make things better, they were only going to get worse.

Chapter 20

Vince had barely made it into his office when Caroline and Nate barged in. Caroline's hair, normally neat and contained was wild. If she'd slept the night before, then it had been restless. Her gaze snapped to his and the next thing he knew, she was in his face. "What the actual fuck did you do?"

Whoa. In the five years that she'd been a part of the firm, he'd never heard her swear. "What do you mean?"

"She means we've both been inundated with calls for the past thirty minutes." Nate crossed his arms and glared down at him. "You punched a dude?"

Vine groaned. He'd hoped he was going to have longer than that to give everyone a heads up. "He was trespassing and insulted my guest."

"That wouldn't be your little sugar girl, would it?" Caroline ran her hands across her hair, smoothing it back. "Because the media has caught wind that there's something going on at your place and that it had to do with a girl."

"Media?" There'd been no one at his house when they'd left that morning, but that didn't mean his privacy would stay that way. "I'm not going to be able to go home now."

"I've already called the cleaners to come in and open up the condo. It will be ready for you when you want to head over." Caroline rolled her eyes. "And I've already had a heads up call that Simon Berry wants to talk to you this morning."

Acid in his stomach churned as Vince leaned back in his chair. "Great. If he's finally swinging over to my side of things and wants to buy GreenPro, a scandal is the last thing I need."

Nate and Caroline shared a look, before Nate moved and leaned his arms on the back of Caroline's chair. "We're here to help you with whatever you need. But I think, and I'm sure Caroline will agree, that you need to cut ties with Marissa."

Logically, it made sense that they'd make that suggestion. While his initial dealings with Marissa had to do with ensuring he had a cleaner image for the New York trip, having their relationship around long-term would no doubt eventually be discovered by Simon and potentially ruin his business.

Logically, he should cut ties, give her some money for her debts so she's not struggling. She'd be able to pay off her debts, get a better place to live, and move on with her education and her life.

But he'd be fucking damned if he'd let that happen.

"No." Vince turned to the computer and logged into his e-mail. "You can leave."

He didn't need to be looking at them to know they were both shocked.

Caroline laughed, but it sounded sadder than anything. "You know what, I've put up with your moods and bullshit for years now. Even when you decided to intervene with your dad and take his place with Marissa, I went above and beyond to make sure she was happy. I didn't agree with it, and I was all for her being in your life if she made you happy. But this is interfering with our company now and—"

"My company." He looked at her then. "My company and my decisions."

Caroline stood, her face flushed and hesitated in front of his desk. "Of course, sir." She shook her head. "I'll be at my desk when you need me." She then turned and strode from the office.

Shit, he'd never intended to hurt her. Caroline had always been there for him, gave him the reality check he always seemed to need. He'd have to apologize to her later, but for the moment, he needed time to figure out how to make everything work. Nate was still there, and that was also a conversation he didn't want to have. "I'm serious, Nate. You need to leave."

"I know last night I was encouraging you to reach out to her, but I now think that it was a mistake."

Vince was on his feet and around the desk before his brain registered what he was doing. "Marissa is many things, but she's not a mistake."

"I've never seen you be rude to Caroline before. You're an asshole all the time to me, but not to her. She doesn't deserve it, especially when she's right."

The anger that had been propelling him for the last few minutes fizzled. "I'll make it up to her. But I'm not giving up on Marissa, not when she has no one else to help her."

"Are you prepared to lose out on this deal? Because if Simon hasn't heard about your little run-in and the media attention by now, he will soon. And once that happens, it will prove to him that you're no better than your dad, and he'll bail."

"Then I lose the sale." He never wanted to sell to Simon in the first place. "I'll find a way to talk Dad into going down another path, to sell the company to someone better suited. Sooner or later he'll realize it's the best option."

"You've been saying that for years. If you haven't managed to convince your dad by now, it's not going to happen. ETS is the best and currently only option to take GreenPro off our books."

Nate wasn't normally one to care about Vince's little side projects. "What aren't you telling me?"

Nate shoved his hands into his pockets. "I was having lunch with a friend, who has a business partner who was speaking with Peter."

Vince couldn't unclench his teeth to say anything.

"He told me that there's another company, a start-up who have a similar product. They've been in talks with several cities to launch a pilot project to prove their facilities can convert pet waste into energy. I've heard that Simon has sent out feelers to them. If you don't lock him down now, not only will you not sell GreenPro, you'll lose the edge on the industry. Simon will take that company public and you'll get left behind."

All of the potential he saw for GreenPro to make an impact would be lost.

"Shit." Vince was never one to succumb to the pressure of a deal gone wrong. He'd learned to fight his way through the problems, and more often than not, he'd come out on top. But time was against him, as was Simon Berry. If he didn't move quickly, then everything he'd put into GreenPro would be lost. "I need to get him on the phone."

"I agree. But you also need to deal with Marissa."

"She's at her mom's place. I'm sure she'll be fine there and no one will bug her."

Nate shook his head. "Fine. I'll leave you to it."

But as he left, Vince got the impression that Nate didn't believe him. Well, fuck him. Marissa had problems, but together they'd work it out. He'd help her as soon as he dealt with Simon.

He took a breath, picked up the phone and prayed he'd be able to pull this off.

* * * *

The coffee mug was warm between Marissa's hands. Unlike the sinfully amazing coffee she'd had at Vince's this morning, she was currently drinking the hours-old, grocery store brand coffee her mom favored. There was something disconcerting about sitting at the kitchen table while her mom hummed as she made cookies. Sure, she was at a safe place, and she loved her mom more than anything, but this small apartment wasn't home.

Her mom had sold the house she'd grown up in a few years back, when it was clear Marissa had finally moved out for good, and moved here. It was perfect for her, close to work and transit, and small enough for her to manage on her own.

Marissa would love to have a place like this, but it was becoming more and more unlikely the longer her financial troubles continued. Maybe she could convince Vince to let her move in with him. It wasn't as though he didn't have the room. *Yeah right.* Despite what had passed between them last night, she knew that the disparity in their background would make any sort of real relationship difficult at best.

No, she'd have to be prepared to walk away from Vince. Even if she was now beginning to think it would break her heart.

"That's some serious thinking you're doing over there." Her mom came over to the table with a plate full of still-warm chocolate chip cookies. "These will help."

"Thanks."

"So, what's going on? And don't say nothing because you don't show up here on a Tuesday morning. Ever."

Shit, she was going to have to ask Naomi for today's notes. "I didn't want to bother you with everything."

Her mom shook her head as she reached out and covered Marissa's hand with hers. "Baby, I've tried to tell you this before. You're never a bother. I know you've had problems in the past, but we worked through them together. Whatever is going on, we'll get through this too."

It was strange how a few choice words from someone who loved her could slip silently through all the emotional barriers that Marissa had erected. Tears blurred her vision, before the sob popped from her. She couldn't hold the tide back, and instead let it slam into her. Marissa put her head on the table and cried.

"Oh baby. Oh my God, what's wrong?" Her mom stroked the back of her head and pressed kisses to her hair. "It's going to be okay."

"No, I don't think it will be Mom."

"Look at me." She waited until Marissa complied before reaching over to wipe at her tears. "You can't take the weight of the world on by yourself. No one can. You need to share the burden, even if I can't do much to help practically, I can at least be here for you."

For the past three years Marissa had done her best to keep her problems from her mom. Not because she thought her mom wouldn't be supportive, but because she'd wanted so desperately to prove to herself that she could handle everything herself. The pain had grown hard, like a ball of lead that lived in a corner of her chest. The more she'd avoided talking to her mom, the more that weight had grown.

Marissa sat up, wiped her face, and took a cookie from the plate. "I'm in financial trouble."

"You mentioned that you needed money for your meal card. I was wondering what was going on."

"Andrew. Andrew is what was going on." She took a deep breath and let the words she'd been holding back come spilling forward.

The look of concern on her mom's face morphed to horror, then fury by the time Marissa had told her everything that had been going on for the last six months. "I spoke with Shelia on my way over here. She's getting everything cleaned up, but because of the sheer number of things she has in her house, the process is going to take far longer than normal. I'm going to have to find a place to live in the meantime."

"Why the hell didn't you tell me what he'd done? I could have helped you. God, Marissa, I gave him your new phone number."

"I know. But I also know that you don't have extra money yourself. And don't try and tell me that you do. You work hard enough to pay for your own things. I know you don't have extra for me."

"That's my decision to make. Not yours."

"Mom—"

"Don't *mom* me. You made assumptions about me. You're my daughter, my only one. Knowing that you were hurting, struggling and you didn't feel you could come to me for help…" It was now her mom's turn to wipe tears from her face. "That kills me, baby."

Marissa moved her chair across the floor so she now sat beside her mom. "I'm so sorry. But I didn't want to be a burden to you anymore. I was so much trouble to you when I was younger, and you never really liked Andrew to begin with. I didn't want my bad judgment to cause you problems."

"Your problems will always be my problems. That's probably not the healthiest mentality for me to have, but that's how I'm built."

"Well, I thought I'd come up with a solution and that I wouldn't have to tell you any of this." She shoved the last of her cookie into her mouth, immediately regretting what she'd said. Because there was only one logical response to what she'd said.

Her mom frowned. "What did you do?"

Yup. And now, Marissa was going to have to tell her. She shifted, wanting to move away, but knowing there was no point. The truth would have to come out one way or the other. "So, there's this website."

"Marissa, what did you do?"

She closed her eyes. "I signed up for a sugar daddy site. But only millionaires. Though Vince is a multimillionaire, practically a billionaire, and he gets all particular when I don't say that correctly. My friend Naomi was the one who got me on it because she's there too and it's not even all about sex. So yeah."

When she opened her eyes, her heart sank at the look of horror on her mom's face. "You're prostituting yourself."

"No. Vince in fact didn't want anything from me other than to go on some work dates with him. He didn't want a relationship, but he needed some arm candy." She shrugged. "He bought me some dresses. And what's wrong with that? We're both consenting adults who negotiated exactly what we wanted from the arrangement before we did anything."

Well, mostly. Things hadn't exactly gone according to plan since they'd come back from New York.

Her mom stood up. "I need to go for a walk."

The little flicker of hope that she'd accept what Marissa had chosen to do was snuffed out. "I'm sorry."

"Don't be. I just…" She grabbed her sweater. "I'll be back."

Marissa sat alone in her mom's apartment, staring after the closed door. Her mom hadn't taken her purse, which meant she wouldn't be gone for long. Marissa had always known she was a crap daughter, but this certainly confirmed things. In the span of half an hour, she'd made her mom cry, feel as though she wasn't wanted, and be horrified by her actions. Wonderful.

The kitchen counters were covered with the dirty bowls her mom had used for baking. It would give her something to do while she waited for her mom to come back. She filled the sink with hot water and soap, enjoying the way the bubbles filled the sink and scent of fake lemon filled the space around her. She'd gotten through most of the bowls when there was a knock on the door.

Marissa wiped her hands on the dish towel and went over to the door. She opened it without looking through the peep hole, or else she wouldn't have gone near it.

There, standing as smugly handsome as ever, was Andrew.

"Hey, baby. I think we need to talk."

Chapter 21

Marissa wanted to puke. "What the hell are you doing here?"

"I missed you." He shifted his foot so it was now against the doorjamb, preventing her from closing it. She tried anyway, slamming it as hard as she could. "Shit, stop that. I'm serious, I just want to talk."

"Fuck you. You've ruined my life."

"What? I've done nothing."

"That's exactly the point, Andrew. You haven't paid any of your bills. I have debt collectors chasing me down at home and where I work. I've had to change my phone number because they won't leave me alone." She tried to close the door again, but this time he caught it with his hand. "Get out."

"I promise I will as soon as we talk." His brown hair had been cut recently, giving him a GQ look. His day-old scruff looked as though he'd simply forgotten to shave, but she knew the effort he put into his appearance. She should have been prepared for the pleading look he'd perfected, but it caught her off guard. "Please."

This was a horrible idea. But then, she seemed to be full of those these days. "Five minutes. Mom will be back soon and if she finds you here she'll call the cops."

"I'll be long gone before that happens."

Marissa didn't immediately move. *Stupid, horrible idea. He's fucked you over and now he's going to try and talk himself out of it.* She backed up, letting him into the apartment, at the same time she grabbed the baking timer from the counter and turned the dial. "I'm serious. Five minutes. Starting now."

If Andrew felt the time pressure, he certainly didn't show it. He came into the apartment, and made a beeline for the cookie plate. "God, I have to say I've missed your mom's baking since we've broken up. My mom doesn't cook and the store-bought stuff isn't anywhere near as good."

"Four minutes, twenty seconds."

"I've been thinking a lot about you since we parted ways. I mean, we were together for five years. That's not exactly an insignificant period of time. I'll be doing something and think, hey, Marissa would love this. And then I remember that we're not together and get sad."

Coming from anyone else, the words might have come across as sincere. But it was hard to buy what he was selling when he was eating a cookie and smirking at her. "You're the one who left me, even though I told you I wasn't cheating on you. You didn't believe me. That's not my fault. It's yours, and I'm not going to accept even the suggestion of blame from you."

"You're right, I didn't believe you. Not at first. And for that I'm sorry." Andrew had an annoying habit of saying the right words, without appearing to mean them.

"You're sorry?" She got to her feet as she threw the dishcloth at him. "You're fucking *sorry*? You've ruined my credit. I can't afford to cover all these debts that you racked up with your business. I never even wanted to co-sign those papers, but I thought we were going to be together forever and that this was an investment in our future." She didn't want to cry in front of him, but she couldn't stop the angry tears from falling. "Three minutes."

"You have a student loan and your mom won't let you starve. I knew you'd be okay." Andrew also got to his feet, taking another cookie. "I especially know you'll be okay now that you're fucking that rich asshole."

Marissa's world bottomed out on her. "What are you talking about?"

"Don't play coy. I heard all about your rich boyfriend who took you home and punched my friend."

She wanted to throw up. She'd worked so hard to move on from him, and her relationship with Vince—while not exactly what she'd initially set out to achieve—had been a wonderful bonus, a positive change she'd needed more than anything. That Andrew knew she was now spending time with Vince somehow tainted what she'd hoped to build with him.

Doing her best to relax and stay calm, Marissa cleared her throat. "How did you find out?"

"It was the strangest thing. Some guy called me out of the blue a few weeks back. Don't even know where he got my number." Andrew's smirk had her skin crawling. "He told me you were banging some sugar daddy, getting all sorts of cash from him."

"Oh God." There was only one person she suspected would throw both her and Vince under the proverbial bus that way—Geoff. "What I do with my life now is none of your business."

"I wouldn't dream of stepping on your new man's toes." His lips pursed and eyes narrowed. "Who you fuck is up to you now."

"Then why are you here?" When he didn't say anything else, Marissa shifted impatiently. "Andrew?"

"I couldn't figure out why he looked so familiar when I saw a picture of him. Then it hit me. I had the DVR and checked and I was right. He's that prick from the show you never let me delete. You must have shit yourself when you saw the chance to screw him. And it turns out that the paparazzi are really interested in this guy when I called them."

Marissa swallowed hard. Why would Geoff do this to them? Vince had done everything to make him happy, to sell his company to the person Geoff wanted. None of this made sense. "One minute."

"Then I'll make this quick." He got right in her face and for a moment she thought he was going to touch her. "You were mine. You like to play all innocent that you hadn't done anything wrong, but that's a lie too. Five years we were together and you just moved on. Naw, you're out for his money."

"I'm not—"

"I want his money too." His leaned in so close she thought he might kiss her. "If you don't get me fifty thousand dollars from your boyfriend, then I'm going to go to the media with all the juicy details of who you are, and what you've been doing. I know about your sugar daddy thing. And so will the rest of the world." He then stepped back and gave her a little wave. "I'll be in touch."

Marissa froze, could do nothing by watch Andrew leave. The door *snicked* shut as the baking timer rang.

* * * *

Vince's head throbbed and his back ached, but there was no way he was going to move now that he'd finally gotten Simon on the phone. "I understand your concerns, Simon. But GreenPro is far more established than other companies. Not to mention I have connections here in Toronto. If you're looking to start with a pilot program, what better place than here?"

"The Canadian market is not exactly my area of expertise. If I'm doing this, I want to be sure everything is going to be transportable to the States."

It was an excuse, and a flimsy one at that. Vince could spend hours beating around the bush on this, but he was tired and wanted nothing more than to wrap this up so he could call Marissa and make sure she was okay. "Let's cut to the chase. I know you've been looking at other prospects. What's it going to take for you to buy GreenPro?"

The silence on the other end of the line wasn't exactly reassuring.

"Simon?"

"Did you know that I went in on a deal with your father, oh, it must be about fifteen years ago now. Did you know that?"

"I did." The fact Simon was bringing up his father was unsettling. "What does this have to do with my proposal?"

"It had been not long after your mother had walked out on the two of you. Geoff had been drinking and started carrying on…well, you know. He never came out and said it was because he wanted to get back at your mother, but it was obvious."

Vince knew exactly the time period Simon was referring to. He was in high school, nursing his own shattered heart because his mom had simply gotten up and left them, with little explanation. She'd left him a letter, one that did nothing to ease the pain that encompassed him. He'd tried to connect with his dad, to offer solace and hoped to receive some in return. Instead, his father had gone out, dating and chasing every woman who looked at him. Vince had never felt so alone.

Vince cleared his throat. "Her leaving us broke him."

Simon ignored him. "He too came to me with some amazing opportunity. We'd been acquaintances for a few years at that point, and I was willing to take a chance. He too, came to New York in the hopes of wooing my wallet. He did. He also slept with my wife."

Shit. "I'm not my father."

"It's been my experience that the apple doesn't fall too far from the tree."

"They why speak with me at all? If you hate my family, why continue to do business with us? I haven't hid the fact that Geoff is a partner in this, nor have I hidden what we hope to get out of it. I've done my best to keep him as far away from this deal, from you, as I could."

Simon said nothing for a long moment. "The business your father got me to invest in made me close to half a billion once I eventually sold it. And he showed me that my first wife was a cheat, which helped me get rid of her. Because of our prenuptial agreement, it didn't even cost me anything, so it worked out. But I never trusted him again. But as you said, you are not your father."

He couldn't imagine what things would have been like had he gone to New York alone to meet with Simon. Marissa's presence had saved him in more ways than one. "If that's settled, then what's the problem? Why can't we move forward with this?"

"Because as much as you're not like Geoff, I don't trust that you won't become him. Your reputation as a womanizer didn't surprise me when I'd heard it. Your sins are yours to bear, but I want nothing to do with them. Even that...woman you brought, there's something about her."

"Marissa is sweet and kind and has nothing to do with this." He had to force himself to relax his grip on the phone receiver. "Leave her out of this."

"Perhaps Natalie is incorrect, then."

"What did she say?"

"She suspected your lady friend wasn't exactly who you were presenting her to be."

Vince didn't know if Natalie had actually said that, or if Simon was simply fishing, trying to get Vince to slip up and say something. Either way, he wasn't going to play this game. "She's my girlfriend." That wasn't exactly right, but it was the easiest thing he could manage. "And my personal life shouldn't have an impact on this deal."

"It shouldn't. But I'm the one who gets to decide where my money gets to go. If I want to be sure the recipient is of a certain character, then that's my prerogative." Simon went silent for a moment, the faint sound of a keyboard clacked away in the background. "I do have another prospect, but they're not as advanced as GreenPro. It would be much easier to go to market with your company than theirs."

His unspoken warning came across loud and clear—Simon would work with Vince on this deal, but he'd be willing to switch teams if he didn't like what Vince had to say. "Then let's work together to make this happen."

"Send me a complete company profile, market projections, and growth forecasts. I'll have my lawyers look everything over and then we'll talk. If I like what I see, and if everything remains unchanged, then I'll seriously consider the purchase."

Vince would need to keep his head down and his nose clean, at least until this deal went through. "You'll have the documents first thing in the morning."

"Wonderful. A pleasure speaking to you as always." And then the line went dead.

He put the receiver back down and closed his eyes. Okay, Simon was on board and if everything went his way, Vince would be able to broker the deal within the next three to six months. Then he'd be free of Simon and his history and would be able to get back to his normal life. He'd be free to have whatever relationship he wanted with Marissa, and anyone who had any issues with it could bugger off.

He needed to hold on to this just a little bit longer and GreenPro would be gone, he'd have his money back and his father wouldn't have an excuse to try and control Vince's life.

How had things gone so wrong between them? Vince had given up years ago trying to change his father's erratic behavior. Then *Bull Rush* had come along, and it was easy to throw himself into the intense filming schedule and ignore the growing mess that his father's life had become. Regardless of what Geoff had done, he was still Vince's father. They had no one else, no other close family. And despite the anger, the wall that had formed between them, there would always be a part of Vince who loved and missed the man his father had once been.

His hand was still on the phone, the temptation to call his dad strong, but he knew he wouldn't. While he was willing to try again, to move beyond past hurts, he knew Geoff wasn't there. Maybe he never would.

The loneliness Vince had felt since his mom had left them had never quite gone away. It was only in those moments he'd spent with Marissa that everything felt a bit easier, the world seemed to be a bit brighter. Releasing the receiver, he instead reached for his cell phone.

As though she'd read his mind, there waiting for him was a message from Marissa. *We need to talk.*

He hit the call button and even waited for her to answer before he spoke. "I'll pick you up. We can't go back to my place."

"I'm going to stay at my mom's."

While he was certain that the woman who raised Marissa was no doubt an amazing woman in her own regard, he had no intention of letting her stay anywhere but with him. "I'll be there soon. We'll head to my condo."

"Didn't you hear me? I can't stay with you."

"Did I do something wrong? Something that has made you uncomfortable?" He'd gone an entire goddamned night without touching her. In his mind, he was up for saint status. "Because if this is you worried about taking advantage of me because of my money, that's not an issue."

"It's not that."

"Then get what you need from your mom's and be ready to leave." For the second time in an hour, the silence on the other end of a phone call made his chest tighten. When she let out a little sigh, he got to his feet and grabbed his jacket. "I'll see you soon."

This was going to work out. He'd sell GreenPro to Simon, even if that wasn't what he wanted. His father would have whatever he'd hoped to get out of the deal, and Vince would be able to move forward with Marissa.

He'd make this work, no matter what.

Chapter 22

Marissa followed Vince into the lobby of the luxury condo high-rise, not knowing how the hell she was going to get out of this. She'd been unable to talk to her mom once she'd returned to the apartment. Her mom was still upset, which was probably the only reason why she hadn't picked up on Marissa's panic. It wasn't as though she'd be able to help with this, and given her earlier reaction to Marissa's status as a sugar baby, she doubted her mom would care too much about Vince's reputation.

The last thing Marissa wanted to do was hurt Vince. Andrew was a bastard, and she knew him well enough to realize that he wasn't going to let this go until he got his money. She'd never known him to be violent, but Andrew was smart and clearly more devious than she'd ever given him credit for. She needed to warn Vince about what was going on so he could cut ties and stay as far away from her as possible.

He'd clearly had a far better day than she had. He'd been relaxed and smiling from the moment she'd slid into the passenger seat of his car. Not that she'd ever tell him, but she loved that he'd been picking her up himself, rather than sending the limo. While he was used to that level of wealth, it wasn't exactly something she'd gotten comfortable with.

"I'm in the penthouse. It's actually owned by the firm, though none of us really use it. Caroline had the cleaners in so we wouldn't have to worry about anything."

Caroline was a saint as far as Marissa was concerned. "I'll need to say thank you the next time I see her."

"I've already sent her a thank you gift." Vince looked up toward the elevator ceiling. "A nice one."

"Pissed her off again, did you?" Marissa couldn't even pretend to be surprised. "She's going to leave if you're not careful."

"I know." The elevator doors dinged open to reveal a small hallway. "We're down here."

The contrast of this hallway to the one leading to her mom's apartment was staggering. There were no random smells of cigarettes and spices spilling from the other doors as they walked past. In fact, there were no other doors on this side, which spoke to the opulence she had no doubt she'd find on the other side. Even the exterior door shouted *a wealthy person lives here*, as the wood grains were natural and not the thin press wood, painted gray.

Vince pressed a code that unlocked the door, the deadbolt whirring and clicking as it opened. "I'm not sure if there's much food here, but we can always order in. Probably the best idea given the paparazzi are on the lookout for us."

The condo was stunning. The far wall was composed of floor-to-ceiling windows that looked out over Lake Ontario. There was a balcony that had lounge chairs and lush potted plants that would never survive the cold winter if left outside. The living room was open, with a white couch that looked simple, but no doubt cost more than a year's worth of her rent. The kitchen was open, with marble and wood that made the hotel in New York look like a cheap reno.

"It's a bit cold. Let me know if you need a sweater. I'll turn up the heat." Vince turned on the fireplace as she continued to explore.

"I can't believe you have two amazing homes." She didn't even have her little basement apartment. "How do you choose where to stay?"

"The house is mine. I bought it from my dad years ago, when he was more interested in traveling than staying in Toronto. This place is mostly a tax write-off, but Nate uses it more than me. We have it when we're working late, or if we have a client we want to impress from out of town."

"So, I'm the one you're trying to impress?" She couldn't imagine he'd think too highly of her once she told him about Andrew's demands. "I'm flattered."

"Our friend from this morning reached out to the press. We have a bunch of photographers buzzing around the house trying to get a glimpse of who you are." He took off his jacket and tie, and rolled up his sleeves. "I figured this would be better than fighting the crowds."

Marissa sat down on the couch—God, this was as comfortable as it looked—and tried to relax. "I don't think I should stay here."

Vince held up his hand before she said anything else. He then grabbed a bottle of wine and two glasses. "I know something's wrong. I can tell from the look on your face that this is even bigger than the flood."

"It is. I need you to know—"

He flopped onto the couch beside her and handed her a glass. "In a minute."

"You're being stubborn."

"I'm being practical." He filled her glass, then his own, before putting the glass down. "Whatever you're about to tell me is probably serious. I've had one hell of a day and for a little while, I need something not serious."

She could only watch as he clinked their glasses together. "Like wine?"

"Like a glass of wine with a beautiful woman who makes me smile." He took a sip, his eyes locked onto hers. "Is that so wrong?"

Marissa shivered from the intensity he was shooting at her. "No. I guess not."

Liar! Everything about this was incredibly wrong. Andrew was blackmailing her and threatening him. If things were to come out about their relationship, she had no doubt it would put his deal with GreenPro at risk. She put her glass down on the table and turned once more to him.

Vince downed the rest of his wine in several gulps, set his glass on the floor, and took her face in his hands. "I'm going to kiss you now. I've wanted to kiss you since this morning when you got out of my car. I've had business calls, been dealing with pompous jackasses all day, and all I've been able to think about was getting back to you."

His breath came out in soft puffs across her face. They were so close, she could feel the heat from him, smell his arousal through his aftershave. Her gaze flicked to his lips. "I thought you didn't want a relationship?"

"I was wrong. I'm tired of being alone. Of having no one to come home to. No one to listen to, to hear what kind of day they'd had. I miss having a warm body in my bed. Not sex, but having another person there to hold on to, to listen to them breathe. I missed you."

Vince leaned in and pressed his lips to hers in the softest kiss she'd ever shared. She sighed, couldn't help it, and deepened the contact. His fingers flexed against her skin in a caress that had become familiar to her as only a lover's could. Sliding her hands up his chest, she ignored the voice in the back of her head screaming that this was a horrible idea.

Despite everything that had happened in the past few days, she needed this. It wasn't until she'd heard him express his needs that she realized she'd been craving that sort of contact herself. She wanted him, wanted to feel his body against hers. She wanted to relish the press of his cock inside her until she screamed from release.

When he slid a hand from her face to the side of her neck, Marissa reached up and encouraged him lower. Only once his fingers encased her breast did she give in completely. Her nipple was hard, rubbing mercilessly against the inside of her cotton bra. Pleasure sparked through her, as her skin became hypersensitive to every caress against it.

"Bedroom." She spoke the words against his mouth, loathing to break even that little contact. "Please."

Vince stood and somehow took her along with him. She'd long given up being surprised by what he could do. This was the man who'd swooped in and helped her in her moment of crisis, and yet hardly asked for anything in return. Even the meager barrier he'd put between them, the no-relationship rule, seemed to be little more than paper thin. Letting her head rest on his shoulder, Marissa followed his lead and ignored Andrew, her finances, and every other problem in her life.

As Vince carried her into the bedroom, she opened her eyes enough to take in her surroundings. The wall of windows continued here, presenting her with the most amazing view she was likely to ever wake up to. Vince must have noticed where her attention had gone, and set her down so she could have a better look.

"I don't think I could ever get used to something like this." She shifted back as he came up behind her, his hands falling to her waist. "It's amazing."

"Yes, you are." He pulled her hair to the side and began to kiss her neck. His mouth worked the skin, nipping gently as his fingers began to work on the buttons of her shirt.

They were going to do this, have sex in this place where she didn't belong. Marissa would take every last bit of pleasure she could from him, and then when they were done, she'd tell him about Andrew and the blackmail and await the inevitable dismissal from his life.

Marissa placed her hands on the window and arched her back like a cat. Her ass connected perfectly with his groin, and there was no mistaking the pressure of his cock against her. She wanted to turn around, drop to her knees and pull out his shaft. She wanted to lick up the length, from his balls to his tip, taste the bitter fluid that would have escaped from the slit. Instead, she bucked her hips back and prayed he wouldn't leave her hanging for long.

Vince was an intuitive lover. He'd managed to undo the buttons on her shirt, her bra-covered breasts now readily available to him. She held her breath as he slid his hands beneath the wire and up to fully cup their weight. He leaned against her, his forehead to the back of her shoulders as he teased her nipples.

Marissa moaned, not caring how she looked or sounded. She wanted to be wild, primal. Wanted to shed her clothing so she could enjoy the scratch of his clothing against her nakedness. She wanted to soak in his heat, taste his sweat, all while memorizing each sound that came from him.

Vince moved his hands up, taking her bra with him, and leaving her breasts exposed to the world below. A shiver passed through her at the unexpected exhibitionism, a thrill that she was bared to all of Toronto to see, and knowing no one could. He continued to move his hands up, capturing her shirt to pull it down her arms.

He caught her gaze in the reflection of the window as he looked at her from over her shoulder. "I want to see you naked."

"Yes."

They worked together to shed her bra, her jeans. He hesitated when it came to her panties, taking time to tease the sensitive skin of the crease of her leg with his fingers, before slowly dropping to his knees as he slid the silk down her thigs. "I've always contended that a woman undressing is the sexiest thing in the world. It's something special. Being the one chosen to see."

As she stepped out of her panties, now completely naked before him, Marissa leaned back against the cold glass of the window and spread her thighs. "And you like to watch."

God, she had this crazy powerful, rich man on his knees in front of her, horny. His shirt was half opened, though she didn't know when he'd done that. His blue eyes were hooded, heavy, as though the very act of looking at her was too much for him to handle.

She was a fucking goddess and he would do anything in the world for her.

Marissa spread her legs wider. "Lick me."

His gaze traveled lazily down her body until it reached her pussy. He rose to his knees, and shuffled close enough to do exactly what she wanted. His hot breath on her front was a stark contrast to the cold on her ass. Instead of reaching forward, to brace her hands on his shoulders, she flattened them even more against the window. "Do it. Please."

The growl that came from Vince sounded as primal as Marissa felt. When his hands found her thighs, he squeezed the fleshy muscles, kneading them as he drew closer. Marissa wanted to look, wanted to watch the expressions on his face. She was able to keep her eyes open long enough to see him smile before he pressed his nose to her pubic mound and breathed her in.

"You're so fucking wet." He moved his hands higher, until he parted her labia, exposing her clit. Marissa held her breath as she felt his hot breath kiss her wet skin a moment before his mouth engulfed her.

Unlike before, he teased her with small flick of his tongue. She bucked her hips forward, encouraging him to increase the pressure, to force the pleasure on her until she came. Vince wasn't having any of it. He held her still, held her open, and continued to tease.

"I hate you." Her voice cracked as a shiver ripped through her. Goosebumps crept across her skin, the combined sensations of cold and pleasure getting confused inside her.

Vince shifted down and ran his tongue from her wet pussy, up across her clit, and back down again. "I love how wet you are. How you taste." He pushed a finger into her, and pressed against the top of her passage.

She gasped at the unfamiliar pressure. He leaned in and sucked on her clit as he fucked her with his hand, milking her juices from her body. As her pleasure rose and her release threatened to breach, Marissa banged her head back hard against the glass. "Vince."

Before she could come, he slowed down and pulled his hand from her. "Not like this."

"Yes, like this." She cried when he pulled away completely. "Asshole."

He stood, pressing his body hard against her. His zipper rubbed against her hip, scratching her skin. The buttons of his shirt, the rub of the cotton against her chest gave her the feeling of the forbidden.

Well, he was her sugar daddy, after all.

Marissa looked up at him, at his wide pupils and his wet lips. She reached up, cupped the back of his head and pulled him down for a kiss. The taste of herself on his lips was uniquely wonderful, arousing. He stuck his thigh between her legs, forcing contact with her pussy.

Breaking the kiss, he moved to suck on her earlobe. "Like this." He lifted his leg slightly, increasing the pressure. "I want you to come on my leg."

Jesus.

Rolling her hips, she tentatively tried what he'd asked, not sure if the contact would be enough for her. She was wet and the cotton was dry, creating a friction that was different from anything she'd done to herself in the past. His hand found her nipple once again, this time he squeezed it gently, matching the rhythm of her hips.

Oh.

Her eyes closed and the only thing she could focus on was the pressure of his thigh on her pussy and the invisible line of pleasure that was connected between there and her nipple. His mouth on her neck licked the same spot, teasing the skin as he allowed himself to be used. The occasional word would escape him, an intimate look into his brain.

"Yes. That's it. Fuck. So wet. Feel you on my skin." He pinched her nipple harder. "Faster. Yeah. I can smell you. So fucking beautiful."

It became harder to breathe, and Marissa had to force herself to do so. Everything became amplified in her mind as she pushed harder down on his thigh. She was almost there, so close to the release she so desperately needed.

"Yeah, baby. Harder. You're almost there. Come for me. Come for me hard, love."

Something snapped and in an instant her orgasm ripped through her body. She slammed down hard against him, thankful when he braced himself, holding still so she could continue to grind against him. She cried out, wishing there was someone there to hear her, to hear what he'd given her. Her world shrunk to the two of them, to the sensations of his body and her pleasure. As the last wave of her orgasm washed away, Vince peeled himself from her.

They both looked down, and she wanted to laugh at the large wet spot that now covered his pants. "I made a mess."

"We're not done yet." He took her by the hand and dragged her to the bed. With a flourish, he spun her around and with a little push, sent her flying to the mattress. "I want to hear you come again."

He disappeared into the bathroom for a moment, reemerging with a cloth. She accepted the warmth, pressing it to her pussy as he dug into the night stand for condoms and lube. "I thought you said you had this place for clients?"

"And we like to make sure they have everything they could possibly need when they're here." He tossed them beside her on the bed.

"How considerate." She dropped the facecloth on the floor.

If there wasn't porn that consisted of men in suits getting undressed, then there damn well should be. She watched enthralled as he slowly undid each of the remaining buttons on his dress shirt. The sight of her cum on his dress pants drew her attention briefly, before he pulled off his shirt and dropped it to the floor, leaving him naked from the waist up.

"You're too handsome to be a millionaire."

He cocked an eyebrow. "Multimillionaire. And why's that?"

"It's just not fair. You've got looks, intelligence, and money."

"My personality more than acts as a counter weight."

She watched as he opened the fly of his pants and pushed them down. "You keep saying that, but I've never seen you be anything but kind to people."

"Did you forget my behavior on the yacht?"

"You were being cautious." She had forgotten the yacht. The Vince she'd grown to know might be abrupt and single minded, but he was also sexy, kind, and willing to do whatever he needed to for someone he cared for. He then pushed his briefs down, and all other thoughts flew from Marissa's mind.

When he reached for the condom, she snatched it from the mattress. "Let me." She carefully tore the packet and retrieved the slippery rubber from its home.

Before she slipped it into place, she leaned forward and sucked the head of his cock into her mouth. Vince shuddered, his muscles twitching as his cock pulsed in her mouth. He was as far gone as she'd been earlier, and no doubt this wouldn't last as long as she would like. She pulled back and slipped the condom on.

"I don't think you need to worry about the lube." Leaning back, she spread her legs. She reached down and spread her lips, rubbing the moisture across her thick hair.

Vince stared down at her, watching her as she teased her body. He knelt on the edge of the bed, as something in his expression changed. She almost asked him what was wrong, but as quickly as it appeared, it was gone.

"Think you can come again?" He moved between her thighs, his cock poised to enter her. "Let's see."

The full weight of his body pressed down on her, as he thrust fully inside her pussy. Her clit was still swollen from her earlier orgasm and sensitive from the friction. When he pressed against her, an overriding feeling of too-powerful pleasure came over her. It was gone as soon as he pulled back, only to come again on the next thrust. Her pussy grew damper, and holy shit, she was absolutely going to come again.

She shifted forward and wrapped her legs around his hips, encouraging him deeper. Vince thrust into her hard, fast, with an intent she'd never felt with another man. His body was slick from sweat, but unlike their previous times together, his body was familiar, a welcomed presence that was becoming precious to her.

"Fuck me." She ran her fingers through his hair, listening as his breath hitched. "You're so big. You're going to make me come again."

It must have been the right thing to say, because he rose up on his forearms, changing the angle. On their next connection, Marissa gasped as her clit rubbed perfectly against his mound. "Shit. Right there. Oh fuck."

Thank God, he listened, didn't change a thing. She held on, chased her release, knowing she'd have to work for this one. On the next thrust she bucked up to meet him, and that was all it took to push her over the edge once again. Every muscle in her body tensed so hard, she couldn't even cry out. Vince didn't stop, didn't slow down until she finally sucked in a giant breath and relaxed into the mattress.

He continued to pound into her for a moment longer, before coming himself. His cries were swallowed up by the mattress, but she heard them echo around and through her. Vince strained against her before coming to a stuttering halt, his body weight resting on her and his arms.

She didn't want him to move away, didn't want to break the contact. Everything that was going to come from this point on would be horrible, she just knew it. Andrew and the media, her own desires and his relationship issues—everything seemed too big to handle.

The tears came, slipping down her temple, through her hairline to her ears. Dread was such a horrible emotion, one that she'd gotten so comfortable with, it seemed to be her default setting most days. Vince pulled back, frowning. He didn't say anything, and instead wiped the tears from her face.

"We should get cleaned up." Her voice was small, so unlike her, that Marissa hardly recognized herself.

He didn't move, instead kissed her forehead. "Did I hurt you?"

"No. Not even a little."

"Did I do something wrong?"

"No."

"Then why are you crying?"

"If we're going to have this conversation, then I need to get up." She gave him a little shove, and this time Vince moved.

Not that he went far, to the edge of the bed. He stood and removed the condom, tossing it in the wastebasket in the corner. "Can I get you something?"

"Let me pee, then we can talk."

She couldn't look at him as she padded naked to the bathroom. Shutting the door only gave her a brief respite from the pain of what she knew she was going to have to do.

I fucking hate you, Andrew.

Who was she kidding? Vince hadn't wanted a relationship because he'd been worried about being taken advantage of. Here she was about to lay their worst nightmares and all she was worried about was being left alone.

Marissa peed and got herself cleaned up. She paused briefly to look herself over in the mirror, before taking a deep breath, and opened the door. Time to face the music.

Chapter 23

The moment Marissa came out of the bathroom, Vince knew he didn't want to hear what she had to say. His body still buzzed from the amazing orgasm he'd just had, his emotions charged from the unexpected closeness he'd felt. Never before, not even with Thea, had he wanted to lose himself with a woman the way he did with Marissa. She made him smile, had him appreciate the little things around him. It was strange, wonderful, and if he was being honest with himself, terrifying.

He watched her get dressed, missing the openness that she'd shared with him minutes earlier. She pulled her hair into a ponytail, and with a simple flick of her wrist, she was back to being the woman who'd found herself in a jam and decided to do something about it.

"You should get dressed." She looked him up and down, though she didn't smile in that coy way of hers that he loved so much. "It will be weird having a conversation with you looking like that."

There was no way he could put his dress pants back on and not get hard. The smell of her cum on the cloth would be too much. "I have a spare outfit somewhere. Why don't you get something to drink and I'll join you in a minute?"

"Sure." She couldn't look him in the eye, and bolted from the bedroom.

Shit. Marissa was no coward, which meant this conversation was going to be as bad as he assumed. Grabbing a clean T-shirt and a pair of jeans he'd stashed here months ago, Vince took his time getting dressed. With each passing moment, he rearranged his thoughts, mentally steeling himself against whatever she was about to throw his way.

He finally emerged from the bedroom to find Marissa sitting on the edge of the couch. She looked so small and more than a little tired. He'd taken a step toward her, instinctively wanting to go to her, to help her figure out whatever the problem was. He caught himself and changed direction to stand on the far side of the room. "What's up?"

"I need fifty thousand dollars." Each word that came from her seemed painful, which told him there was more to the request than that.

"Why?" His heart pounded in his chest, as though he knew her answer was going to ruin something he hadn't even realized that he'd wanted. Their relationship wasn't exactly traditional, or if he could even refer to it as one. But he'd grown comfortable with her, loved what they did in bed, wanted to see where they could take things.

She looked in the direction of where he stood, but her gaze didn't go higher than his chest. Opening her mouth, she tried to say something, but nothing came out. It was strange knowing her as well as he did, knowing she wanted to say something that he wouldn't want to hear, but stopping herself. "Think of it like a bandage. Rip it off."

She took a deep breath, and sighed. "Andrew came to see me at Mom's today. He'd found out about us and sent a buddy of his to follow me. That was the guy who came to your house looking for money. Andrew said if I don't pay him, then he'll go public with everything. About us. About me being your sugar baby."

He knew it.

It should have hit him harder than it did. Maybe he'd always been prepared for this moment—or something similar to happen—since he'd first laid eyes on her walking up to join him on the yacht. They'd brokered a deal, one that was mutually beneficial, but now the deal was done and it was time for him to move on.

No matter how well his relationship was going, things always came down to money. This time, he couldn't even fully blame her. He should have known better.

Marissa cleared her throat as she rubbed her hands on her thighs. "It if means anything, I'm sorry."

"Accepted. But I won't be paying a penny to your ex."

Her head snapped up and her eyes widened as she finally looked at him. "You're not?"

"Men like your ex are never satisfied. He'll take the money and go, for a while. Then he'll be back looking for more. It won't stop. And when I put my foot down, he'll go to the media anyway."

His father had fallen prey to someone like that back when his mom had first left them. Vince had watched him cut checks to men who his mother had slept with, while they were still married. All in a vain attempt at keeping the family name clean.

Marissa frowned, and got to her feet. "You don't know Andrew. He's… bitter, I guess is the best word. He still thinks I did something to screw him over when we were together. When he found out about us, it just confirmed his worst opinion of me. If you don't pay him, it won't just be the media. He'll find a way to screw you over that you never saw coming. I wouldn't be surprised if he went to see Simon."

"I'm tired of my personal life being an issue with that man." He turned his back and stared into the black night. He needed that sale to go through. Without the specter of GreenPro languishing between them, he'd never be able to get out from under his father's thumb. Simon was still the best way for that to happen. "I'll find a way to deal with Simon if your ex goes public."

"Okay." He heard her moving around, but he couldn't look back. The last thing he could handle was seeing the look of betrayal he knew was on her face.

"I'm sorry that Andrew is doing this."

He was sorry too. Sorry that the inevitable shit show had finally come around, that everything he'd feared would happen did. "I was prepared for something like this. It's part of my world."

"Blackmail is something you deal with all the time?" She'd moved beside him, the scent of her perfume and shampoo hitting him a moment before her hand caressed his back.

"Not all the time. But enough that Nate has a protocol setup to handle it."

"That's…horrible."

"It's business. It's why I'd agreed to our arrangement in the first place. I'd hoped to avoid something like this happening. I should have known better."

"Vince—"

"I should have realized that while you're not after my money, your friends and family probably would be. It's hard not to want to reach out and take what's never been available to you, when it's sitting there right in front of you."

Her gasp echoed in his ears. "My friends and family don't know a damn thing about you. Or your money. And even if they did, they'd never take advantage."

"Except for Andrew."

"Who got the call from…do you know what, it doesn't matter." She stepped back from him.

She couldn't see it, but it was clear to him. He'd been down this road with Thea, with other women as well. "And the next thing will be your mom. Or your cousin, or your best friend who will just need a bit of help. Thea promised me it wouldn't change things, but it does."

Marissa's breathing was ragged. "You're so wrapped up in your past, you can't seem to see that we're not all like Thea. I'm not like her. I don't care about your money. Yes, when we first met, that was what I needed, but it wasn't as though I was hiding that. If I never took another penny from you, if all I had was my paycheck from the Pear Tree and my student loans, it would be enough for me. I don't need yachts, or fancy dinners at restaurants. I need someone who will watch sci-fi movies and eat pizza. I want someone who doesn't mind me being silly. Who wants to have sex in the kitchen because they're turned on."

Vince looked up and met her gaze in the reflection of the window. "I want those things too."

"You could have had them, if you'd let your ego drop. If you took the time to see that not everyone is out to get you."

"History has taught me otherwise."

"Then there's nothing more I can say to you. While I like to think of myself as strong, I can't fight ghosts." She wiped at her cheek. "I think I should go."

"Probably for the best." He didn't even know why he was mad at her. Yes, it was her ex-boyfriend trying to do the blackmailing, but Marissa was going to be as hurt by all of this coming out as he would be. Hell, maybe he wasn't mad at her at all. Everything was so screwed up, he didn't have a fucking clue what he thought.

But this was the exact scenario he'd been trying to avoid since she'd walked into his life. When his fight with Thea exploded across social media, Vince had lost a part of his soul. Every aspect of his life had fallen under the social microscope, every relationship, every deal he'd made on *Bull Rush*. He'd never wanted to live through that again, to have his world dissected and judged by strangers who didn't care about him.

Marissa said nothing else, and quietly collected her things. Vince watched her reflection in the window as she went. When she finally started toward the door, he finally turned. "Do you want me to call the limo? I can have it take you to your mom's or anywhere else you'd like to go."

She shook her head, and it was only then that he noticed the tears on her face. "That's fine. I'll call an Uber."

"Where are you going?" He shouldn't have asked, but he still wanted to make sure that she was okay. That she'd be safe from the oncoming storm. "Your mom's?"

Her small smile broke his heart. "It's probably best if I don't tell you that. Easier for both of us if I just disappear. But thanks for everything. It was good while it lasted."

She took another step, which had him move closer to her. There was no reason why he should let her go. She was hurting and it was his fault. Vince could easily pull her into his arms, beg for forgiveness, and promise that they'd work it out.

Catching himself, he shoved his hands into his pockets. "Do you need more money? For school, I mean."

"No. I want nothing...I'm good." She opened the door. "Bye, Vince."

The silence once she'd closed the door behind her was deafening. He looked around the condo, his gaze landing on each place Marissa had touched in her short time here. The emptiness was oppressive, though it was the normal state of being for Vince. With the exception of Caroline and Nate, Vince had no friends. Plenty of acquaintances, of people who drifted in and out of his life. But no one he could call up, to come over and commiserate with him.

For a short time, Marissa had filled that void in his life. Had brought warmth and smiles. Forced him into conversations about things that weren't business. To speak to waiters and drivers, those people who intersected his life. She'd cracked open the wall he'd built to keep himself safe from the world, and invited him to look out.

The strength in his legs threatened to give out, forcing him to sit on the couch. The scent of Marissa was strong here, filling his head. While there was a part of him that wanted her in his life, he knew it was best for both of them if they went their separate ways. Even if it felt like he was making a terrible mistake.

Closing his eyes, he leaned his head back against the couch, and did his best to keep everything together.

Because despite everything, he missed her already.

* * * *

Marissa thanked the Uber driver, and climbed out of the car. Naomi was waiting on the steps of her apartment building, and came running down the second she saw Marissa. "Okay, I was worried before, but now I'm scared. What's going on? You look horrid."

"Once we get into your place. I…I can keep it together until then."

Naomi wrapped her arm around her and led her inside. "My roommate is out, but I gave her a heads up that you're staying over. She said she's fine with you staying with us as long as you need."

"Thanks."

The apartment building was a new construction and had a number of perks that Naomi said were well worth the extra money she paid for rent. Marissa had been here a number of times in the past, had been jealous of the large laundry room, the brightly painted walls, and the common room that ended up being a social area where most of the residents could gather.

But after just having been at Vince's condo, the entire place came off as small and more than a little basic. She squashed those thoughts as quickly as they came to mind. That was a world that she no longer had access to. And while she'd had a glimpse of what might have been, it was best not to dwell.

Naomi shut the door behind them and immediately grabbed the bottle of vodka from the cupboard above her stove. "We're going to have a few drinks, and then you're going to tell me exactly what the hell happened."

Marissa should really be able to hold her shit together. She'd never set out to have a relationship with Vince, certainly not anything romantic. This was supposed to be a means to an end, a way to help pay off the bills that had piled up around her, so she could concentrate on the important stuff. But ever since New York, her attention on school had been unfocused at best. Assignments had piled up as she'd continued to work extra shifts.

The good news was she'd been able to get several of the creditors off her back with the money Vince had given her. Valuable breathing room that should have been enough to get her on track.

The only problem was she wanted her old life, but she also wanted Vince.

"Hon, are you okay?" Naomi put two glasses and the bottle down on the table and came over to hug her.

She wasn't going to cry, she'd done enough of that over the past few days. She'd exhausted the deep well of tears, and all she had left was disappointment and anger. Hugging Naomi back, she let out a sad chuckle. "Let's get that drink and I'll let you know what's been going on."

It took over an hour, and at least three screwdrivers, for her to tell Naomi everything. With each word she said—what Andrew had done, her time with Vince, Andrew's blackmail—the pressure that had weighed her down began to lift. Seeing Naomi's face morph from shock, to adoration, to rage hadn't hurt.

"So, I left the condo and came here. I don't blame Vince for freaking out. I mean, he went through that whole thing with his ex a few years ago. He doesn't want to do that again. We were never supposed to be anything more than friends. I helped him with some events. He helped me with the money."

Naomi finished her drink, poured another few inches of vodka into her glass, and began to drink it straight. "Darling, I know you want to defend Vince, but he fucking kicked you to the curb when you needed him most."

"Actually, he picked me up from my apartment, took me to his house and looked after me when I needed him most. Then Andrew came along and fucked things up. The worst thing about this is that I couldn't even tell him that it was his father who'd put Andrew on our trail in the first place."

"I don't get that. If this guy is as big an asshole as you say he is, why not let Vince know? He's going to have to deal with him sooner or later."

"I don't know." In the moment, she didn't want it to seem as though she was deflecting the blame away from her and Andrew and over to Geoff. "I was hurt. He looked hurt as well. I guess I didn't want to make things worse."

"You need to call him and let him know." Naomi shook her head. "This wasn't supposed to turn into a big deal. I figured you might have to sleep with some guy, it might suck, but you'd get some cash to help out. I never dreamed this shit would happen."

Marissa laughed again, the absurdity of the situation finally hitting her. "Hey, at least he bought me a new copy of *Star Wars.*"

It was too bad they'd never get to watch it together.

Marissa was about to say something else, when a yawn stopped her. "I'm dead. Mind if I crash on your couch?"

"It's all yours." Naomi got her a pillow and some blankets. "We'll figure something out in the morning."

"Thanks."

Tomorrow. That seemed to be where she lived her life these days. Today was far too horrible to deal with, but tomorrow there was at least the hope things would get better. Maybe a good night's sleep would be all she'd need to figure out how to make things work.

Maybe.

Chapter 24

Vince sat at his desk and let the calm of the early evening wash over him. He'd been in meetings all day and his brain was full of *Bull Rush* shooting schedules, finance report numbers, and promises to look into a new company. He'd barely had time to catch his breath, let alone ponder what had become of his life in the last little while.

But every time there was a lull, his mind would flick to Marissa and the devastated look on her face when she left the condo. It had been over a week and with no new stories in the papers about him and his mystery woman, he had to assume they'd dodged a bullet with Marissa's ex. The separation worked as he'd hoped it would. There's no story if they're not together.

Even if he missed her more than he cared to admit.

Banging outside his office pulled his attention back to the present. The cleaning woman was making her rounds, emptying garbage cans and wiping down desks. Vince got to his feet, needing to stretch his legs, and went to watch. She wasn't old, maybe mid-twenties, and was bobbing her head in time with the music that was playing in her ear buds. When she caught Vince watching, her eyes grew wide and she pulled the buds from her ears.

"Hi, sir. Is there something I can do for you?" There was a slight quiver in her voice, as though she were scared of him.

Nate said he had a reputation of being an asshole in the office, but Vince hadn't fully believed him. "Nothing at all. I needed to stretch my legs."

"Oh. Okay." She looked around, unsure what to do. "I'm just going to keep going then."

"Sure." Marissa would have known what to say to her. She would have had the woman talking within seconds. Vince cleared his throat, suddenly feeling awkward. "Have you worked for us long?"

She blinked at him and squeezed the cloth in her hand. "About two years now."

"Do you like it?"

"I guess. I mean, yeah, it's a great job." She blushed and fumbled with the cloth.

He was totally screwing this up. He chuckled and shook his head. "Honest to God, I can talk to a boardroom full of people without a second thought. But the moment I try to have a conversation with someone one-on-one, I screw it up. I'm freaking you out, aren't I?"

"I bit." She finally laughed as well. "Absolutely."

"I promised a friend that I'd try harder at being more social. Clearly, I suck at it." He held out his hand. "Hi. I'm Vince."

"Candace." She hesitated for a moment before finally shaking it. "Nice to meet you."

"Same." He looked around the empty office, surprised at how strange it looked empty. "You have a big job."

"I don't mind. I work nights so I can go to class in the day. It's not going to be here forever and you guys pay well." Candace went back to wiping down the work station. "Besides, your job's a bit more important that mine."

This was the sort of thing Marissa was doing, the hard task of juggling school and making a living. She was doing the best she could, just as Candace was. "Never say that. Never thing that someone is better than you simply because their position is more visible. Or they make more money. Our entire office would fall apart without you."

Her blush deepened. "Thanks."

"You're welcome." The phone in his office began to ring. "Shit, I have to get that. It was nice talking to you, Candace."

"You too, Vince."

Striding across the office, he barely made it to his desk on the fifth ring. "This is Taylor."

"Hey Vince. It's Kyle Adamson from the *Toronto Gleaner*. How's the world of reality television, eh?"

Vince sank slowly into his seat. He'd known Kyle since the early days of *Bull Rush*, had done a number of interviews with the *Gleaner*. In all the years they'd known one another, Kyle had never reached out to Vince directly. "Good. We start shooting season six in a month."

"Awesome. Hey, I wanted to give you a heads up. We have a story that's going to run tomorrow. I wanted to vet it first, you know, make sure we weren't printing a bunch of gossip. Mind answering a few questions?"

With his heart pounding, Vince closed his eyes and did his best to keep calm. "Of course. Fire away."

"Great. I received some information from a source that you've signed up for a sugar daddy site. I mean, I'm on it now and wow. I don't have the bank account to even talk to any of these women. But to clarify. Is the profile yours?"

His mind raced through the site. It had been Geoff who'd registered for it, had used his information. Vince never had his name anywhere on it. "Not mine."

"Well, no. I mean it's technically your father's. He confirmed that to me when we spoke earlier. He said you'd been the one to actually go on the date with the woman. Ah…Marissa Roy, he said. That's correct, yes?"

Vince's hands shook, and his throat tightened as he squeezed the phone. "My *father* gave you that information?"

"He confirmed it. My source gave it to me initially, though there's some question about whether or not that might have been your father as well."

Geoff had been behind everything. Vince hadn't been able to figure out how Andrew would have heard about their relationship in the first place. Geoff disclosing it to him was the only thing that made sense. No doubt, Simon would also learn about their relationship, effectively killing the deal for GreenPro.

He'd deal with his father later. Right now, he had to contain this. "Your source is her ex and he's out to make her life a living hell." And if Andrew had gone to the *Gleaner*, then the chances were great that he'd have gone to a number of other outlets as well.

Everything he'd said to Marissa, to push her away in the hopes of sparing her from this nightmare, had all been for nothing. She would be hounded until she gave her side of the story, increasing her visibility, and making her more of a target for creditors. And he'd pushed her away, forcing her to deal with everything on her own.

He was becoming everything he hated in his father.

There was only one way Vince could think of to make this right. "Kyle, I appreciate you coming to me with this. Can you squash the story?"

"I mean, no. This is too big a scoop. My source said it would be exclusive and is looking for payment. I wanted to verify truth, which is why I called."

"What if I can offer you something better, and it won't cost you a dime?"

There was a pause on the other end of the phone, as Kyle shuffled some papers. "It would have to be quite the counter to top this."

"An interview. With me. For print and for online."

"Exclusive?" He hadn't heard Kyle that excited in ages. "If you're willing to do that, I'll kill the story for the paper tomorrow."

"Deal. I'll have Nate reach out to you, but we can do something on camera tomorrow morning."

"I appreciate that."

"I appreciate you not paying that asshole a single penny of what he wanted. He already tried to extort me and I'll be damned if I let him benefit from this."

"Lucky me. I'll wait for Nate's call."

By the time Vince hung up, he'd managed to get his temper under control. His father, the man who was supposed to love him unconditionally had not only betrayed him in the worst possible way, but clearly had intended to do so for quite some time. Since the day his mom had left them, Geoff had these moments of anger that inevitably ended up directed toward Vince. But dealing harshly with a confused and rebellious teen was light years away from this.

Vince knew they were growing past the point of him being able to salvage what little relationship they had. If Geoff was bound to make Vince's life a living hell, then he was just as likely to sabotage the sale of GreenPro to Simon. If he even wanted to sell it in the first place. Vince needed to cut ties, but needed to do things on his own terms.

He needed to do right by Marissa.

Picking up the phone, he made the call that in the back of his mind, he knew he'd always have to make. "Peter. Vince. We need to talk."

* * * *

Nate strode around the office, ensuring that the *Gleaner* had lived up to everything they'd promised to do. He'd been equal parts furious and relieved when Vince called him last night and filled him in on everything that had happened.

"Jesus, thanks for giving me next to no time to pull this off."

"You're a magician. Besides, Kyle is going to be tripping over himself to make sure this goes off without a hitch."

"It's a good scoop. Not to mention getting it for print and online. Far more generous than I would have been."

The fact of the matter was Vince wanted to make sure Marissa had the opportunity to see him. Not simply read his words, which could be misconstrued and lacking tone. He wanted her to see his face, to hear his voice. He wanted, no, he needed her to know that he was sorry.

Reaching up, he adjusted the tiny pin he'd placed on his lapel. He wasn't even certain she was going to see the video, let alone the pin. But if she did, he knew she'd appreciate the significance.

"Okay, Vince." Kyle marched over to where he was sitting, Nate half a step behind. "I think we've worked everything out. Are you good to go?"

He gave Nate a look, cocking his eyebrow.

"I looked over the questions." He clapped Kyle on the back. "He's sworn up and down that there will be no surprises for you once we're live."

Kyle held up his hand. "Scout's honor."

Nate nodded, which was all the reassurance Vince needed. "Let's do this."

The next few minutes were consumed with hair and makeup, and technical setup. Vince sat as calm as he could manage, all the while battling the war of emotions that had consumed him for most of the night. Nate waited for the makeup artist to leave before coming over. "You sure you want to do this? We can simply make a statement and leave it at that."

"I need to have this online."

"You mean you want her to see it." Nate sighed as he rubbed the back of his neck. "Why don't you just pick up the phone and call her? You've done that before."

"Before I hadn't been a complete asshole to her. Before I hadn't made her feel like shit because I was trying to protect myself. I owe her a public *mea culpa* at least."

"Okay. It's your call. I've let Caroline know what's going on and to be ready to forward all media calls to my cell." Nate shook his head. "Thanks for blowing up the rest of my week."

"You're welcome."

Kyle came over and took the seat opposite Vince. "Are you all set?"

No, this was the last thing he wanted to be doing. "Ready."

The final preparations came and went. Vince adjusted in the chair, getting as comfortable as he could. The lights lowered, Kyle gave him a nod and they were off.

"Kyle Adamson here from the *Toronto Gleaner*, and this is a *Gleaner* online exclusive. Today I'm here with *Bull Rush* star and celebrity investor, Vince Taylor. Vince, thank you so much for coming today."

The easy smile slipped into place like a reflex. "Great to be here."

"First, let's start off by saying the upcoming season of *Bull Rush* is shaping up to be the best yet. Want to give the viewers a preview of what we're going to see?"

He'd been thankful that Nate had negotiated some softball questions to help ease him into the interview. Vince rattled off the previously established sound bites and laughed at Kyle's lame joke. It was all part of the setup. When Kyle's face drew serious, Vince knew everything was about to change. He took a breath and got ready. *Please, let her see this. Let her know.*

"I have to say, this next bit caught me off guard when I learned about it. I'm hoping you'll be able to shed some light. There's a rumor out there that you participated, had an account even, on a sugar daddy site. Is that true?"

Vince leaned forward in his chair. He leveled his gaze on Kyle, giving him the look he'd fired off at so many *Bull Rush* contestants. "Partially. It was my father who'd initially made the account on the site, but I was the one who eventually met the woman and engaged in a relationship."

The words came out smoothly, but inside Vince's heart pounded. In so many ways, this was worse than the video of his fight with Thea. That had been a private moment caught without permission. This was deliberately exposing his underbelly to the world for everyone to take a swing at. He'd never felt this vulnerable in his life. *I'm so sorry, Marissa.*

Kyle tapped the top of his notebook. "Sugar daddy sites. Aren't they nothing more than a form of prostitution?"

"If they were about sex, you might be able to argue that. But they're not. Our arrangement was based on companionship. She attended a business function, she was my date. In turn, I financially assisted her. It was a win-win arrangement."

Kyle's frown deepened. "Why on earth would a multimillionaire television personality need to date someone like this? It's not as though you're hurting for women."

"Come on, Kyle. This isn't about dating. Though my relationship with… my companion turned into friendship. In my world, it's not always an easy thing to find the right someone. While this isn't a path I set out to follow on my own, when the situation changed and I had the opportunity to partner up with this woman, I knew it was the right thing to do." Leaning back, he reached up and casually brushed the pin he'd worn specifically for her.

Marissa had quietly worked her way into his heart, so much so that he'd been blind to how much he'd grown to care. She didn't need protecting from the world. She was strong, caring, intelligent, and more than capable of dealing with whatever the world threw her way. He missed her smile, her laugh, and wanted nothing more than to wrap himself in her arms.

Kyle cleared his throat. "If she were sitting here right now, what would you want her to know?"

"I'm sorry for what I said. She was right, I was scared. I was doing what I thought was best, instead of listening to what she was trying to tell me. I was slipping back into old habits. I know she'll probably not forgive me for what I'd done, and that's no less than I deserve. But I am so sorry and I wanted her to know that."

The ache in his chest grew to epic proportions. Marissa might never see this, or even if she did, she might ignore him. It would be his fault if that was the case, something he'd have to live with.

"I take it from the lack of a name, your friend would like to keep her identity private?"

"Yes. And while I know the speculation will run rampant, it's important to respect that. She never wanted the attention, and I'd appreciate everyone to please keep that in mind when speaking about her."

"You know the speculation will be there. Any chance we'll be able to meet the young lady in question ourselves? Perhaps another interview?" Kyle laughed, making the entire confession seem trivial, almost normal.

Vince relaxed back into his chair, glanced toward the camera and smiled. It wasn't his practiced one that he'd haul out at parties and events. This was the private one that he'd shared with her when they were in bed, or in the limo. When it was just the two of them and for once he could be himself. "That will be her decision."

Kyle shifted papers. "I've also been told that you're launching a new company. This isn't in the vein of your *Bull Rush* investments. Can you tell us a bit about GreenPro?"

"I'd love to. While the company has been around for a while mostly doing research and development, we are finally ready to take this exciting idea to production in the world of alternative fuel sources." It was easy to get excited about GreenPro, especially since he had his plan already set into motion. Kyle clearly could care less about poop power, but it was a great way to bookend the interview.

He wrapped up the explanation within a minute, and was finally able to relax. "I'm proud to be the owner and excited to see how far we can grow our idea." He was also braced for the phone call he knew he'd receive from Geoff the moment this interview went live. "I also want to let everyone know that as a way of giving back to the community, I've also established a bursary for women who are pursuing business as a post-secondary degree at local colleges. There are a lot of people out there struggling to make ends meet, while trying to improve their future. I wanted to do something to help."

"You can find the link to the program below in the video description." Kyle smiled at the camera. "Thank you, Vince, for your time today. We hope you'll check out our other videos in the stream below."

"And cut!"

They shook hands and Kyle grinned at him. "That was fantastic. It should help get you out ahead of that asshole, and it's going to be killer for our site hits."

"I owe you one for this."

"I just hope she forgives you for whatever it was you've done." Kyle got up from his seat. "Which reminds me, I need to give my husband a call. I'll let Nate know the moment this is live."

"Thanks."

And that was it. Vince knew the ball was now in Marissa's court. She might never forgive him. Or worse, not care about his apology. All he could do was sit, wait, and hope for the best. In the meantime, he had to get across the city to his lawyer's office. He jumped up from the chair and waived at Nate. "I'll see you soon."

It was time to remove the axe hanging over his head, once and for all.

Chapter 25

"I want her to know that I'm sorry for what I said. She was right, I was scared." Marissa paused the video and stared at Vince's face on her computer screen.

The video had been posted yesterday afternoon. Naomi had been the one to show it to her, going so far as to script how Marissa should tell Vince to go to hell, and exactly how to get there. They'd had a good laugh at that, even though Marissa wanted nothing more than to fall to her knees and cry.

He'd been wearing a *Star Wars* Rebel Alliance pin.

It had taken her watching the video three times before she'd picked up on it. He'd gone so far as to reach up and touch it at one point. There on the lapel of his suit jacket was the tiny gold insignia, clearly meant only for her.

She didn't know if she should be excited, or annoyed.

"Do you want to know what I think?" Naomi had picked up a pizza on her way home from class. While Marissa hadn't been publicly outed, the idea of going to class had been too much for her today. So, Naomi had grabbed her notes and food, both of which she set down on the table beside Marissa's laptop. "I think you should sell your story to the media. You'd make a small fortune and he'd get what's coming to him. Men suck."

"Not all men." Naomi was right that she would make money if she were to sell her side of the story to the media. It would probably even be enough to pay off the remainder of her debts. But despite everything he'd said to her, she couldn't do that to him.

Plus, he'd been wearing the pin.

"Oh, come on. Yes, he's rich and famous and really good looking, but there's more to life that wealth, security, and a hot guy." Naomi frowned as she flicked open her text book. "Actually, scrap that. You should totally hunt him down and make him beg for forgiveness. That'd be hot."

"You're a jerk." Marissa flopped back against her chair. "Seriously, I don't know what to do."

"What do you want to do? What's that first terrible instinct that you've had to squash down more than once? The thing you know if you told your mom you were about to do it, she'd be all, that's a terrible idea?" Naomi smiled, licked her finger and flicked the pages in the book. "Because that's probably the thing you should do."

She rolled her eyes. What she wanted to do was to go down to Vince's office, ask Caroline to hold all his calls and have a serious face-to-face conversation about how much he'd been an idiot. She was no more like his ex than he was like hers. Tell him that despite their differences in financial status, she'd come to love him for who he was, not what he could do for her.

And she couldn't help but wonder if he loved her as well.

Because if he didn't love her back, she didn't know how the hell she was going to move forward.

"I need to go for a walk." She snapped her laptop closed and got to her feet. "I'll be back."

"Don't do anything I wouldn't do!"

Marissa rolled her eyes. "You'll do anything."

"It's great, isn't it?" Naomi waved, before turning her attention to her reading.

Marissa slipped on her sneakers, grabbed her purse, and headed out. She didn't have a destination in mind, but in her heart, she knew there were a few things that needed to be done before she could face Vince. The first thing was the most painful of all.

She waited until she was a good half a block away from Naomi's apartment before she pulled out her phone and dialed the number that her heart had known well. The phone rang three times before he picked up.

"What do you want?" Andrew was clearly angry that he'd missed out on his opportunity to make an easy buck.

"I wanted to let you know that everything between us is over. I reached out to a lawyer yesterday about the debts, something I probably should have done when this first started. I'm working things out. If you thought this was going to break me, was going to ruin my life, or force me to come running back to you, you're wrong. I'm going to be fine."

"Nothing your rich boyfriend can't handle." His hate was so strong, she could almost feel it like a physical blow.

"Actually, he had nothing to do with this. I solved the problem. I made things right. As far as he knows, I've gone far away and am living my life without him. So, whatever you'd hoped to get from this is gone."

She stopped walking and waited for him to say something. After a long pause, he took a deep breath. "I only wanted you. I wanted you to need me."

"I did need you."

"But not for everything. You were going to college and wanted to start your own business. You were being selfish when I needed you more than anything. You were my rock. What am I supposed to do without you?"

She'd heard this before, his plea for her to be there for him. But unlike the first few times she'd heard him speak these exact same words, this time she heard the manipulation. "Andrew, I was there for you. But I have my own dreams. I'm more than some supporting act in your life. And if you can't see that, then we were never going to work."

"Things were good."

"For a while, yeah. But it wasn't going to last. We're too different."

"I'm not rich, is what you're saying."

"This has nothing to do with money, and you know it." He wasn't going to understand, to see her side of things, no matter how hard she tried. Andrew had his version of events cemented in his mind, forever making her the villain. "I'm sorry things didn't work out, but I'm going to hang up now. We're not going to speak again. You're not going to see my mom again. If you contact me or her, I'll be in touch with the police. Do you understand?"

His sob came through loud and clear. "Don't do this. I love you."

"I'm sorry. I don't love you. Goodbye, Andrew. I hope you figure out what you want from life." Marissa hung up and blocked his number.

She immediately texted her mom, and quickly explained the situation. *Don't talk to Andrew if he calls.*

O.K. baby. I love you.

Love u 2

While she was worried things with Andrew weren't over, for the first time since everything had started to fall apart, Marissa felt she'd wrestled control of the situation from him. She was the one in charge of how things would play out, and moving forward with her eyes wide open.

The next thing she needed to figure out was what to do with a particularly frustrating multimillionaire. Searching through her contacts, she found the number she'd never thought she'd have to call. "Hi, Caroline? It's Marissa. I was wondering if you'd help me with something?"

* * * *

Vince checked his watch for the third time in the past hour. Caroline had assured him that his father had confirmed and said that he'd be here. The other men in the room were looking more than a little annoyed at having to continue to wait, but Vince knew they wouldn't say a thing. They wanted this deal as badly as he did.

He got to his feet, pulling his phone out as he went. "Please excuse me for a moment." He pressed his father's number before he'd made it out of the room. "Where are you?"

"I'm in the lobby, coming up." The chatter of voices in the background only served to confirm his story. "What's got you all riled up?"

"I'll see you in a minute." He was standing beside Caroline's desk when he hung up. "He's going to kill me."

She looked up at him with that intensity that made her the perfect assistant. "Need me to protect you?"

"No, I need him to agree to sell this company."

"He will."

Looking down at his assistant, his friend, Vince knew he needed to do right by her. "Stand up for a second, please."

She frowned, but did as he asked. "Okay. I didn't think you actually wanted me to protect you, but I will if you—"

He pulled her into a fierce hug, cutting off the rest of what she was going to say. "Thank you. I don't say that enough. You're more than an assistant to me. You're my friend, and I need you to know that I care for you. And I'm sorry for being an asshole."

When he let her go, he couldn't quite place the expression on her face. She was blushing, but looked as though she might cry. "Ah…thank you. I…" She reached out and gave his hand a squeeze. "You're forgiven."

"I'm glad." He needed things to be right between them. "And you have my permission to kick my ass if I ever do something that stupid again."

"Deal." She sank back down to her seat as the elevator dinged in the distance. The elevator doors slid open, revealing Geoff. Caroline picked up her headset and slipped it on. "Oh gee, I have a call I have to take. I'll leave you to him."

"Coward." Not that he blamed her in the least.

"I'm here if you need me." A call came in, and she smiled up at him. "Mr. Taylor's office. This is Caroline Macy. How may I help you?"

Geoff grinned at Caroline as he got close. "I'm here. What's so important that I had to come across town?"

Vince mentally braced himself. "In my office."

Thankfully, his father didn't balk as they entered and he saw the trio waiting for them. "Dad, this is Stu Masters and his lawyers. Stu and I have been in touch about him taking over GreenPro."

Geoff didn't make a move to indicate he was angry or thrown off by the unexpected meeting. "Nice to meet you, Stu. Could you excuse my son and I for a moment?"

Geoff looked between them and nodded. "Certainly."

Geoff took Vince by the arm and led him back out of the office. "What the fuck is this?"

Vince took a breath. He needed to say exactly the right things if this was going to work. "This is our only shot at selling GreenPro."

"I told you I would only sell to Simon. No one else." Geoff's face had grown red and his body shook.

"I'm aware. But Simon is stringing us along. He's never going to buy. He's never going to give you the satisfaction of…whatever little game the two of you are playing. Never."

Geoff's eyes narrowed. "You don't know that."

"Yes. I do." Vince knew he had one shot at this. "I spoke to Simon. I made him aware of my confession. He knows everything about my relationship with Marissa, knows that you were the one to get the media involved."

If his father was angry about losing whatever edge he'd perceived he'd had, he didn't show it. "What did he say?"

"Nothing. I didn't give him a chance. I told him that I was out ahead of this thing. If anything, my interview was going to give me and my company better visibility. My fans are eating up my confession, my begging for my secret love to forgive me." He hadn't talked to Nate yet, so he didn't have a clue what people were saying about him. Nor did he actually care.

All he needed was for his father to give a shit long enough for this to work.

"I can just imagine what he said." Geoff's face had returned to its normal color.

"He wants GreenPro. Badly." Vince, lowered his voice. "But we're not going to sell it to him."

Geoff narrowed his gaze. "That's what I want."

"Here's the thing. It's not what *I* want." Vince stepped into his father's space, well aware that they were drawing attention from the people around them. "I wanted to do this my way. I'd worked hard for years to bring this business to a place where it was going to do good. You didn't care about it. Didn't care about what I wanted. Your goal was to what? Screw Simon over? Give him a company that he wouldn't know what to do with and then watch him fail?"

"Something like that." Geoff pulled back slightly. "Step back, Son."

"No." Vince sucked in a breath. "I'm done with this. With your games. Ever since Mom left us—"

"I told you never to mention her—"

"—you've been a hateful sonofabitch. I'm your *son*. I was there picking you up when you were too drunk to drive home. Running interference at the company when you were too depressed to come in. I've done everything for you, and all you've done in return is try and make my life miserable."

"That girl was after your money. You're a fool if you think otherwise."

"That's my mistake to make. I'm not some child who can't figure out my own life. I haven't been since I had to learn to look after you." The more Vince spoke, the lower his voice got, the angrier he was. "My relationship with Marissa has nothing to do with you."

"You're a bigger fool than I thought."

"Maybe. Or maybe it took me this long to realize that I was becoming just like you."

He'd been terrified of having a relationship, a real one, for years. Even his time with Thea hadn't been without him putting up barriers, keeping her at arm's length to ensure he wouldn't experience what his father had.

The muscle in Geoff's jaw jumped, but he said nothing.

"When Thea left me, I thought you were right, that we weren't meant for a real relationship. But you're wrong. I had that with Marissa. And while I don't know if she'll take me back, I'm going to do whatever I can to make sure I don't become the bitter, angry man you are."

"She was using you."

"No, she wasn't. She was showing me that even if life throws you for a loop, that doesn't mean you have to give in to the hate. Her life had been turned upside down by someone she loved, and she didn't let it destroy her. She was still kind to strangers, stood up for herself and others. Marissa is amazing and I'm lucky to have had her in my life."

Vince stepped back. He needed to end this once and for all, so he could finally move on. "You tried to take that from me. I know it was you who called her ex, who tried to ruin everything."

Geoff's shoulder dropped. "I was doing it for your own good."

"No, you were doing it for yours. So now, you're going to come into the office and you're going to sign the papers. We're selling GreenPro, and we're ending all business ties with one another."

"It sounds like you're getting rid of me for good." It was strange, but Geoff sounded scared.

Vince shook his head. "I'm separating myself. Only time will tell if we can fix this, but I'm not going to allow myself to be held hostage any longer."

"And if I refuse?"

"I'll sue." Vince had hoped it wouldn't come to that, but he was prepared to go the distance if need be. "It's your choice."

Geoff stared at him for a moment, before pushing past him and striding into the office. "Fine. Let's do this."

Stu was on his feet, throwing Vince a look before sitting back down. "Do you want to see the terms Vince and I discussed?"

"I assume my son is competent enough to sell off a single company." He pulled the papers from Stu's lawyer and began signing and initialing the pages. When he was done, he tossed the pen onto the desk.

Vince leaned in and reviewed the papers. Everything, Geoff had done everything he'd needed and Vince was now free. "Thank you."

His father didn't move, but Vince could tell he was overwhelmed. "We have nothing tying us together."

"Financially, no we don't." He couldn't speculate what would happen to their relationship going forward.

Geoff gave him another look before leaving. Relief washed over Vince and for the first time in weeks, he felt as though things were finally going to settle. "Sorry about that."

Stu shrugged. "We all have some sort of family drama. I'm just happy to be benefiting from yours." He then pulled out a second set of papers.

This had been what he'd been after. A chance to do what he wanted with the company. "This outlines everything?"

"It does. You'll be a mostly silent partner, equal shares with myself. I'll run the day to day stuff, and you can help keep things in the media when we need it to be. The money from your part of the sale to us will be put into the company."

"Perfect." Vince turned and signed the papers. "This means a lot to me, Stu."

"It's a brilliant idea. I hope we'll be able to roll it out to cities around the country starting by the end of this year."

They shook hands and Vince waited for them to pack up and leave before letting himself finally relax. "Excellent. Keep me in the loop and let me know what I can do to help."

Caroline stepped into the office once everyone had left. "Did it work?"

"All done." He wasn't sure how is father would react when he learned the truth, but at this point, Vince didn't care.

She smiled. "Good. Because you have another appointment to get to."

"What? Where?"

"I've called the car. They'll be able to get you there in time if you leave right now." She was trying to contain her excitement about something, which wasn't a good sign for him. "Go."

"Dare I ask what's going on?"

"Nope. Have fun."

Vince had long ago learned not to argue with Caroline. Instead, he grabbed his jacket and did as he was told.

Chapter 26

Marissa sat in the middle of the empty movie theatre with a gigantic bag of popcorn in her lap and listened to the sound of footsteps approaching. She knew it was Vince without looking. Not only could she tell from the sound of his confident stride making its way toward her, but besides her and the projectionist, no one else knew the theatre was open.

She didn't look over when he made his way down the aisle and sat beside her. Instead, she held out her popcorn. "Want some?"

"Is it fresh?" He took a handful before she answered.

"Yup, I made it myself." She snuck a glance at him, and her heart raced. He looked relaxed, happy. Not stressed in the way he had back at the condo.

"You work here?" He tossed a piece into his mouth. "I thought you were a waitress?"

"I am. And no, I don't work here. But they'd left everything I needed to make the popcorn out for me. The rest I figured out."

The theatre was old, and normally used for special screenings of older movies. She'd come here a number of times over the years, normally with friends late on a Friday or Saturday night. The seats were old, wider than their modern counterparts, and there was more than ample leg room between the rows. But despite that, she held herself still, contained. Vince had come, but she wasn't sure exactly how to move forward from here.

So, they ate popcorn in the dim light.

Vince reached over for another handful, clearing his throat softly. "Did you see my interview?"

"I did." She placed the bag on the chair arm between them, making it easier to share. "I was curious about the bursary."

He nodded. "I've setup three different ones, at three of the colleges. You're not the only person out there who was trying to live and go to school. One is at your college."

Her face heated. "I saw that."

"Don't think that you'll be the first recipient. It's up to the college selection committee to choose who gets it."

"So, you're not trying to bribe me. That's good."

"Marissa…no. I never want you to feel that you owe me. Never that."

"I don't." She cocked her head slightly. "I saw your pin."

"I was hoping you might notice that." He shifted, turned more toward her. "I know I said it on tape, but I wanted to say it again. I'm sorry for what I'd said to you. You didn't deserve being pushed aside. You didn't deserve me not listening to what you were trying to say to me. You didn't deserve being used as a pawn in any of this."

When she reached over for another handful of popcorn, he placed his hand on hers. Marissa finally looked up at him, her breath catching in her throat when she saw unshed tears in his eyes.

He swallowed, before dipping his head. "Everything about us, about our relationship has been unconventional. That scared me for a long time. I'd promised myself that I would never become a man like my father. Seeing him devolve from a family man who worked hard, to an angry, resentful man who wanted others to be as miserable as him, broke my heart. It also pissed me off, because he was making excuses for unacceptable behavior."

"I know it's nothing to do with me, but I am sorry you both had to go through that. It's hard to hold yourself together when someone you loved has betrayed you that way."

"You did." He reached over and cupped her face. "Not only did you not allow yourself to become broken, you took charge and figured out a way to make your life better."

"I joined a sugar daddy site."

"And I'll be forever grateful that you did." He let his hand slip from her cheek and she instantly missed the contact. "I'm sorry for how I treated you. It won't happen again."

They were only words, and Marissa knew that despite his sincerity, it would take time to rebuild the trust they'd created. But she knew he would. Because despite their differences, the complete opposite ends of the social spectrum that they came from, when they were together, they were simply Marissa and Vince, strange friends and lovers.

She picked up the popcorn and placed it on the floor as she stood. "I wasn't sure if you were going to come, but I had the projectionist get ready just in case."

"I think Caroline would have killed me if I'd refused. Not that I would have if I'd realized I was meeting you."

"A girl has to have some fun." She got a wave from the booth, and the lights in the theater were lowered. "Ah, there we go." Before she took her seat again, she flicked up the arm rest between their seats and leaned up against him.

"Dare I ask what we're watching?"

"*Empire Strikes Back*. These guys have it set up so we can show DVDs on the big screen. The owner is a regular at the Pear Tree, so I was able to pull some strings." She snuggled in as he wrapped his arm around her. "I'm so excited to see your reaction."

The fanfare blared through the speakers so loud, Marissa almost missed the soft kiss and words Vince spoke against her head. "I love you."

She almost, *almost*, said "I know."

Instead she looked up at him and smiled. "I love you too. Now shut up and watch this."

"Yes, ma'am."

* * * *

Vince hadn't been this excited in a long while. Marissa was draped on his arm as they walked down the street. After the movie had ended, neither of them had wanted the evening to end, and he'd suggested getting dinner. Marissa was still talking about the movie and with each passing moment he fell more in love.

"And I nearly said 'I know' when you told me you loved me, but then I realized that you wouldn't have gotten the reference. Which would have totally sucked." She laughed and her entire being appeared to glow.

"You can tell me *I know*, all you want now."

She laughed. "Naw, it's a bit corny. Though I might start calling you a scoundrel."

He leaned in and kissed her temple. "I like the sound of that."

It had taken him a surprisingly short amount of time to realize that's what he'd been feeling for quite some time. It wasn't until he saw her sitting in the theatre with her crazy-large bag of popcorn that he knew it was love. Marissa was unstoppable, unbreakable, and far too good for him.

"What are you in the mood for?" He pulled her a bit closer to him. "I know a great sushi place around here."

"Oh, I love sushi. Yes please."

He was about to lead her to the crosswalk, when a group of five approached them. One was already pointing, which meant he'd been recognized. "We're about to be accosted."

She frowned, until she caught sight of the group. "Oh. This happens a lot?"

"I don't normally walk down the street with my girlfriend. This is a new one for me." Normally, he'd do whatever was in his power to avoid something like this. "Do you want to avoid them?"

Marissa looked up at him, her eyes sparkling with mischief. "Not unless you do."

"Well then, get ready to be introduced to the world, because you're about to go viral."

A woman who didn't appear to be much older than Marissa was the first to approach. "I'm sorry, are you Vince Taylor?"

Vince nodded and gave Marissa's arm a little squeeze. "I am."

The girl's eyes widened as her gaze slipped to Marissa. "So, that means you're the woman?"

Marissa blushed and chuckled. "I guess I am."

"Oh wow." She turned and beckoned the group over. "Can we get our picture taken with you? Because no one will believe us if we don't."

Marissa shrugged. "Sure. I'm not someone famous though."

"Dude, everyone wants to know who you are. Actually," she turned around and held up her camera. "Guess what people. She forgave him!"

Marissa laughed and turned her face into his chest. "He was really sweet and yeah."

The group cheered and the girl turned off her camera. "Awesome. I hope you guys are happy."

Vince pulled Marissa closer, and kissed the top of her head once again. "She's made me happier than anything in the world."

The group waved as they parted and Vince led them toward the restaurant. Marissa had shifted so she was now holding his hand. "Do I really?"

"What?"

"Make you happier than anything in the world?" She flexed her fingers against his. "You have boats—"

"Yachts."

"—and planes, and you're a millionaire—"

"Multimillionaire."

"—who can have anything in the world. Honestly, I'm the one thing that makes you happy."

"Yes."

"Why?"

He stopped walking and turned her so she was looking right at him. "Because you're the first person to see me as Vince. Not the man on television. Not the guy in the gossip pages. Not the asshole business man. You see me as me. And I love that about you. I love you."

Marissa hesitated for a moment, before throwing her arms around his neck, and kissed him. "I love you too. So much."

Wrapping his arm around her, they started walking once more. "Why don't we eat and talk about what you need so you can concentrate on your courses. Then we'll go back to my place and we can figure out the rest of the important stuff."

"Like what?"

"Like can I make you come more than twice in an evening."

Marissa burst out laughing. "I don't know if even the great Vince Taylor can do that."

"Challenge accepted."

It was going to be sweet living his life with her.

Epilogue

"Did you deactivate the account?" Vince's voice echoed from the kitchen, along with the scent of pizza.

Marissa had a craving, but things were still too hot for the two of them to be seen in public as a couple, so delivery pizza had been their best option. The buzz around Toronto had been crazy when the video of the two of them together had gone viral two weeks before. She'd had to quit her job at the Pear Tree because her presence was way too much of a distraction.

"Working on it." She'd just managed to log in when her cell phone rang. "Hello?"

"Hi, baby."

"Mom. What's going on? Did another reporter call you again?"

The sigh that came through the receiver was overly dramatic. "Oh, you know these reporters. They want nothing more than to sweet talk me into telling them all about how cute you were as a kid."

Marissa groaned. "God, please don't show them the red rubber boot picture."

Her mom laughed. "Never. Though I should probably show Vince when you bring him over for dinner."

The words Marissa had been planning to say died in her mouth. She'd talked to her mom over the past few weeks since everything happened, and they'd come to an understanding. Her mom promised to give Vince a chance, to do her best to ignore how they'd met, and to treat this the same as any other relationship. But dinner? "I wasn't sure you'd want to meet him yet."

"The girls and I down at the church watched that video of his. The one where he's begging for forgiveness."

"Well, he wasn't exactly begging—"

"Darling, that was some high-class groveling. But that wasn't what changed my mind about him."

"It wasn't?" She couldn't imagine what her mom saw that she hadn't. "What did?"

"His smile." There was a wistfulness in her voice. "Your father used to look at me like that all the time."

Marissa hadn't heard her mom speak of her father since she was a child. His death had hit her particularly hard, and Marissa had learned early on not to talk about him if she didn't want to see her mom cry. Marissa had to swallow past the growing lump in her throat. "He did?"

"I know I don't talk about him. It…still hurts. Even after all these years. But he did, look at me that way. It was one of love. Deep, messy, hurtful, all-consuming love. If your Vince looks at you that way, then yes, I want to meet him."

Marissa didn't bother to stop the tears from coming as she looked up at Vince who was now standing in the doorway, a pizza in one hand and a look of concern on his face. "How about we come by for dinner Friday night."

"You don't have homework?"

"Nope. Midterms will be done by then, so I should be fine."

"Good. Because I don't care how rich this man is, you make sure you finish your degree. A woman needs her education as much as she needs a man."

"Yes, Mom." She laughed and wiped the tears away. "I love you."

"I love you too. Okay, I'll expect to see the two of you Friday at six."

"We'll be there."

Vince had placed the pizza on the floor beside where she was sitting and didn't say a word until she hung up. "Are you okay?"

"Yeah. Just Mom, catching me off-guard."

"Ah." He reached over and flipped the pizza box open. "So, I'm going to get to meet your mom?"

"You are." The thought of the two people she loved more than anything in the world meeting, made her heart sing. "Though I'll have to warn you, her place isn't very big."

"It won't matter. She's your mom, and I have no doubt I'll love it, and love her."

Marissa dropped her head to his shoulder. "Thank you."

"Now, can you please deactivate your account so we can watch this. I want to know how they rescue Han."

Marissa laughed as she sat back up and grabbed her laptop. Her account for *millionairesugardaddies.com* filled the screen. There were a number of unread messages sitting there, waiting for her response. So many men she could have responded to, and somehow, she'd gotten lucky and met Vince.

Without a second thought, she moved the mouse over to the *deactivate* button and clicked it. For good measure, she deleted her account. "There we go."

The tension bled out from Vince. "Thank you."

"For what?" She closed her laptop and set it aside. "It wasn't like I needed it any longer."

Vince wrapped his arm around her and pulled her to his side. "No, you don't." He placed a kiss on her head. "So, we're going to do this?"

"Eat pizza on the floor while we watch a movie? Hell yes." She grabbed the remote and pressed play, getting a little thrill at the sound of fanfare echoing through the surround sound. "This is much better than the movie theatre."

"Hang on." Vince spread his legs wide, and pulled her over so she now sat between them and could rest her back to his chest. "That's better."

Yes, everything about this was better. For the first time in months, Marissa knew everything was going to be okay. Looking up at him, she smiled. "I love you."

"I love you, too. But you need to be quiet now because droids."

She burst out laughing, turned back around and snuggled down against him. Yes, everything was going to be just fine.

Keep reading for a sneak peek at

the next in the Sugar Series!

Coming soon from

Christine d'Abo

And

Lyrical Caress

SUGAR AND SPICE

"Oh my God, I just found the perfect thing for you!"

Kayla Arnold looked up from the menu she'd been vacantly staring at as her best friend Simone fell into the chair opposite her. She'd been twenty minutes late for their weekly lunch date, which meant Simone had become fascinated by something. And given Simone's entrance, that meant Kayla was about to be in trouble.

Closing the menu, Kayla took a steadying breath before she folded her hands, looked at her friend and smiled. "Hi."

Simone frantically arranged herself and her belongings, before she finally settled, resting her elbows on the table and her chin on her clasped hands. "Hello my wonderful friend. And you won't distract me from my good mood with that brooding look of yours."

Kayla had to fight a smile. "But brooding is my best skill."

"It's not fair to the men of the world if you steal all their good moves." Simone squirmed in her chair as she released her hands and picked up the water glass. "Aren't you going to ask me what I found?"

"I'm more than a little terrified to do that." Still, Kayla knew there was no point in delaying the inevitable any longer. "What did you find for me?"

"The very best website in the world." Simone's blond ponytail swung as she pulled out her phone and began to type. "I was conducting an interview this morning when I found out about this."

Simone's fingers flew across the keys and within a moment, she held out her phone. Kayla snorted as she took the phone, and leaned back in her chair. "A sugar daddy site? Aren't I a bit rich for that?"

"Not to *be* a sugar baby, silly." Simone pushed up her glasses and grinned. "You should be a sugar mamma."

Kayla stared at the screen, blinking away the first three responses that had popped into her head. Simone was her dearest friend, and one of the few who'd known her before her business *Fashion Finds* hit big and made Kayla a multimillionaire. She'd been with Kayla through her rise to fame, her whirlwind marriage, and subsequent divorce. She knew most, if not all of Kayla's deep, dark secrets.

"I have no intention of being anyone's Mamma. Or anything else." Simone always meant well when she'd show up with one of her crazy schemes, but Kayla knew better than to give in to them. "Feel free to sign up yourself though. It might be fun picking out some young stud for you to ride."

Simone's giggle-snort blew an errant strand of hair that now flitted around her face. "I'm not rich enough to even be looking at this one. It's millionaires only. That's so not even close to my bank account."

"If you came to work for me in PR, rather than be a journalist, you might inch a bit closer to that goal."

"Oh please. Toronto needs me. I'm an intrepid reporter, digging up dirt on…well, whatever the *Toronto Record* wants me to dig up."

"Wasn't your last article on the best places to get sushi?"

Simone sighed. "So much sushi. So freaking good."

"You're too much of a cinnamon roll to exist in this world. And I'm not signing up for a site like this."

She could only image what would happen if someone on the board of directors found out about a stunt like that. The watercooler gossip would be impressive. "Where did you find out about this?"

Simone looked around the restaurant, before she leaned in. "Do you remember a few months ago, Vince Taylor and all the noise around him and a mystery woman?"

Kayla had crossed paths with Vince over the years. Toronto might be large, but certain social circles were far smaller than most would assume. "I remember. He went online with a *mea culpa* if I remember correctly."

"What you might not know is how they met." Simone lowered her voice, her brown eyes sparkling. "Guess."

Kayla leaned a bit closer as well, enjoying the unexpected silliness of the moment. "They met on the sugar daddy site?"

"They met on the sugar daddy site!" Simone cringed as the couple at the table beside them looked over. She waved briefly before turning back to Kayla. "And they looked so happy when I interviewed them. Marissa is so sweet—that's her name, Marissa—and smart. She's a student and we got talking and she told me all about it, even though Vince was giving me that brooding look. But you really do it way better than he does." She snorted again and pushed her glasses up with her finger. "You should sign up too."

"I have an idea." Kayla stood and brushed the wrinkles from her linen pants. "Why don't I take you out to lunch early?"

Simone stopped moving and looked at her for a moment, before the smile slipped from her face. "You're not going to do it."

"Darling, you know I'm not into relationships."

"But this isn't about that."

"What's it about then?"

Simone stilled and the energy around her changed as she grew serious. "If you must know, I think you're lonely. And it's killing me to see you like this."

Was she?

Stuck in a rut—yes. Heartbroken—for sure. But lonely?

She happened to like her life.

Kayla's day always started the exact same way. She'd wake up alone by four am to get to the gym on time to meet her personal trainer for her session. Ali pushed her as far as she'd let him, then a bit more until she could no longer think. She always had time to shower and dress impeccably before making it to the office by seven. Her day would inevitably be filled with meetings, until it was finally time for her to go home. She'd end her day with a single glass of red wine and a soak in her tub.

Every day, with the exception of needing to attend the occasional birthday party, holiday event or corporate all-hands meeting. The routine had become a boon, a salve to her wounded soul after her husband had walked out on her five years ago.

Kayla needed the familiar, even craved it. She'd promised herself that she wouldn't let anything send her down the emotional rabbit hole of despair that she'd fallen into when Christoph had so politely ended their marriage and broken her heart.

Her throat tightened, forcing Kayla to swallow more than once. "I appreciate this. I know I haven't been the best friend you deserve. Not recently. But signing up for a sugar daddy site isn't the answer."

"You don't know that." Simone began to play with her napkin. "According to Marissa, and Vince too, it wasn't what either of them had expected. It worked out to be so much more."

Kayla reached across the table and gave Simone's hand a squeeze. "Thank you."

"For what?"

"For caring so much about me."

Simone squeezed back. "Always."

When Kayla finally pulled back, she made a point of putting on her best smile. No sense in making matters any more uncomfortable. "How about this? Let's order the most expensive thing on this menu and talk about your idea. My treat. After, we can stop for pedicures at that spa you like so much. And if after that I'm still not convinced that this is the right idea for me, you'll promise to let it drop. Deal?"

Not that she had any intention of seeing the idea through, but it was better for both of them if she humored Simone. She knew by the time their toes would be dry, the idea of Kayla being a sugar mamma would be off the table.

Simone cocked her head, and after a moment, grinned. "Deal. I'm not worried though. I know you'll agree to it."

"We'll see. For now, let's find our server."

"And wine. I'd love some wine." Simone looked around until she frowned at the clock. "Is eleven thirty too early for wine?"

"Never." Kayla caught her waiter's eye, which got him moving.

If she was very lucky, Simone would soon forget about this website and Kayla would be able to get back to her normal—lonely—routine.

* * * *

Devin was ninety percent certain he was hungover. He cracked open his eyes and tried to lift his head from the couch pillow, before a bolt of pain lanced through his skull.

A hundred percent certain. What the hell did I drink?

"Ray?" He barely managed to get his roommate's name out, and had to swallow a few times before trying again. "Ray?"

"Hmm?"

Devin opened his eyes for real this time, and saw Ray facedown on the floor, the Xbox controller still in his hand. "You alive?"

"Hmm."

"Hungover?"

"Ummhmm."

"Pancakes?"

"Nah na."

"Can you form words?"

Ray lifted his head and looked around the room. "Words are hard."

"Food?"

Ray opened his mouth to say something, before rolling onto his hands and knees. Devin didn't need his Ph.D. to know what was coming next. Thankfully, Ray made it to the bathroom this time before he got sick. "Bacon and eggs it is."

Rolling to his feet, Devin had to give himself a moment to ensure he wouldn't be joining Ray, before carefully padding to the kitchen. He pulled out the bacon and eggs without being fully aware of what he was doing. He was trying to remember exactly what had happened last night.

They'd had an Xbox LAN party, joining up with a bunch of people from their ethics class. There was some sort of bragging that had needed to be addressed when it came to who was better in Overwatch. Cassie had kicked all their asses, as was right and good in the world.

Cracking six eggs into a bowl, Devin's mind tried to pull out the remaining details that had been dampened by the alcohol. They'd been teasing someone about being single. Cassie, maybe? And then there was something about online dating…an account?

He tossed the shells and picked up a fork as Ray came out of the bathroom. "That's better."

"You managed words." Devin beat the eggs as he turned to Ray. "Hey, did we setup a profile for Cassie on a website? Or something like that?"

Ray frowned. "Don't know. Sounds like something we'd do."

"She'll kick our asses if we did."

"I'll text her." Ray pushed papers from the counter and retrieved his phone. "She'll laugh at us for being hungover."

"I told you not to bother going shot for shot with her. East coast girls can hold their liquor." Devin knew better than partying like this. He rarely drank to excess, but last night had been special.

Yesterday he'd defended his Ph.D. And it hadn't sucked.

Yay him!

Unfortunately, that meant he really didn't know what to do with his life now. Well, not beyond drinking too much and playing Overwatch.

"Ah shit." Ray was staring down at his phone, a hand pressed to the side of his head.

"What? Is Cassie threatening to come over and kick your ass?" He looked back over at Ray when he didn't immediately respond. "What's up?"

"Well, apparently, I told Cassie she should get a sugar daddy."

Devin snorted. "So she'll be over in five minutes to kick your ass, or—"

"Naw, we're cool. She said she'd do it if one of us signed up for it first."

"None of us are gay, so that won't work."

"Apparently, there are women on the site too. Not many." Ray started scrolling through the site. "I guess I agreed to do it."

Devin tried to laugh, but it hurt his head too much. "That's fucking hilarious."

Ray flipped him off. "You did too, asshole."

He set the frying pan down on the stove a bit too hard, and the resulting *bang* sent a wave of pain through his head. "What do you mean 'I did too'?"

"We both did. Cassie didn't." Ray held out his phone for Devin to see. "Millionaire chicks."

For half a minute, Devin had been freaking he'd done something stupid. But the quick look through the site showed him he didn't have much to worry about. "It's mostly dudes on here. And I hate to tell you, we're not exactly material for rich women to be chasing after."

Ray scratched his fingers through his hair. "Speak for yourself. I'm prime meat, baby." Devin watched as Ray's face drained of color, before he turned and bolted back to the bathroom.

Turning back to his breakfast task, Devin continued to look through the few profiles of the rich and famous on the site. It was more than a little strange seeing all of the men looking for younger women to pamper. Devin couldn't imagine what those women would have to provide in return for the money, and it was probably for the best if he didn't. Faces of women, some of whom could be his classmates, smiled at him from the computer screen. Their profiles highlighting their likes, interests, and desires.

Curious, Devin moved the mouse to select the profile they'd created for him in their drunken stupor. The picture had obviously been taken with the laptop camera, its slightly fuzzy image in stark contrast to the other pictures he'd seen. He wore a sloppy grin, one that shouted he was more than a little intoxicated.

His profile was filled with enough pretentious answers and cocky innuendo to ensure no woman with even the slightest blush of common sense would want to have anything to do with him. It was basically a giant waste of time.

He should delete this crap.

"Dude!" Ray's voice echoed from the toilet. "Help."

Devin slammed the laptop cover closed and went to help his friend. He'd worry about dating millionaires another day.

"Sexy, fun and deeply
emotional. Bravo!"
—J. Kenner, *New York
Times* bestselling author

christine
d'Abo

*What a difference
a month makes...*

30
days

30 nights

Love is the ultimate hands-on experiment...

christine d'Abo

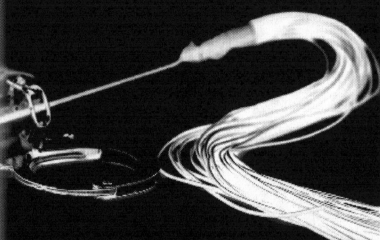

SUBMISSIVE
SEDUCTIONS

christine d'abo

About the Author

Christine d'Abo is hooked on romance. As a novelist and short story writer with over thirty publications to her name, including the immensely popular Long Shots series, the imagination is always flowing. She loves to exercise and stops writing just long enough to keep her body in motion too. When she's not pretending to be a ninja in her basement, she's most likely spending time with her family and two dogs.

Printed in the United States
by Baker & Taylor Publisher Services